Summer's Sins

EVANNA RHOSWEN

Dedication

For everyone who has been there, knows the feeling, remembers that kind of pain. This is for you. I see you.

Reader Warnings

Dear Reader,

As you start this story be aware this story deals with a taboo step-relationship that turns exploitatively romantic. There are themes of abuse and racism as well, wrapped up in a secret-child second chance romance.

The love scenes are explicit, the situation is morally grey at best.

Enjoy! Or, please do enjoy the next book you find to your tastes.
Xo

Vibes Playlist

1. BABYDOLL – Ari Abdul
2. Still Into You - Paramore
3. Pretty Girl (Cheat Codes x CADE remix) Maggie Lindermann, CADE, Cheat Codes
4. Shut up - Lauren Sanderson
5. Sinners (ft. Thomas LaRosa) - Ari Abdul
6. Untouched - The Veronicas
7. Not Going Home - Beautiful Disaster
8. Wish you Stayed - The Haunt
9. Dirty Little Secret - The All-American Rejects
10. Don't Kill My Vibe (Griffin Remix) - Sigrid, Griffin
11. Boys - Charli XCX
12. Easier than Lying - Halsey
13. I Writes Sins Not Tragedies - Panic! at The Disco
14. good 4 u - Olivia Rodrigo
15. Pretty Girls - Britney Spears, Iggy Azalea
16. Break the Rules - Charli XCX
17. Control - Halsey
18. Cravin' - Stileto, Kendyle Paige
19. Promiscuous - Nelly Furtado, Timbaland
20. Devils Is A Woman - Cloudy June
21. Colors - Halsey
22. More than friends - Isabel LaRosa
23. We Go Down Together (with Khalid) - Dove Cameron, Khalid

Table of Contents

Part I. THEN 1

Sweetest Ruination 3

The Realities of Daylight 23

Shifting Emotions*(ish) 38

Never Want to See You Again 48

Yours. Baby, I'm Yours..69

Good Intentions Can be Wrong 85

Part II. NOW 99

When You're a Bastard and You Love Her.....................101

The Problem with Family 106

Reunions..122

The Problem with Christmas 131

Like Calls to Like 148

I Can't Walk Away 158

Checking Out to Check...166

Lofty Memories...171

Connection, Collision...185

Epilogue 207

Part I.
THEN

Sweetest Ruination

Theodore

14 May

"Well, well," I drawled with a smile on my lips. "Hello, Eva."

I didn't yell over the music. I'd been looking for her on the dance floor. However, from the back, I discounted her appearance. My dear younger cousin wasn't allowed to dress provocatively, after all. So it was a shock to realize this girl was 'my' Evanna. As she turned, her eyes widened into saucers. I loved seeing her eyes do that. The way they'd brighten with fear before dulling with resignation; all of it highlighted by the tight pinch of her mouth.

If I were to have believed her grandparents-turned-parents, Eva could do no wrong. She was a good girl. It was the line that the whole family parrots. For some reason, from the time Uncle Jake and Aunt Clara signed the adoption papers to take Evanna from Jasmine, they'd made it their duty to distance the pair. Jasmine was the outcast, the failure. Evanna was the golden girl.

Yet, ever since Evanna'd gotten her license, I'd seen her more often. Half of those instances, of course, were at work, but the rest? The rest were thanks to my asshole cadre of friends who enabled me. Whenever one spotted her, they called me. I got a front-row seat to Evanna's rebellion. They got a front-row seat to the melodrama of it all.

When you took the teacher's pet and gave her a free pass to freedom; she'd get a little wild. She'd save up, she'd keep wearing her mask of perfection, and then she'd make her own hours. Clearly having hidden more colorful aspects of herself.

"Theodore," Evanna's lips wrapped around my name in a way so familiar it slid over me like a caress. When Evanna used my name, or even a diminutive, she may as well have wrapped her hand around my throat. She had the uncanniest ability to fuck with me. She didn't need to put effort into it, but she was especially effective when it was clear she wasn't making an attempt. A look or murmur of my name while she was angry or distraught made me falter. A sarcastic comment at my expense destroyed the calm I'd carefully erected in a blink.

There was no way she'd expected or planned on seeing me that night, and I wasn't surprised. Hopping the border on a Friday was the most obvious option to stay hidden in plain sight. Our friends and family wouldn't have looked for Evanna here.

And given the fact I'd left my teens behind six years ago, and my sister, Andi left hers seven–it wasn't like we'd've been great sentinels. We didn't have time to go off clubbing and shit. Our focus was on keeping our respective bills paid. Richard, an old high school friend, had called me, tipped me off that Evanna was here. He'd seen her walk in with her friends. I was positive that Rich called me in order to drum up a little excitement. Either to have gotten to view the dramatic scene of me cutting into Evanna before having dragged her out, or having gotten to hear about it after. He lived for the drama more than anyone else I knew. Still, the point stood. He'd told me she was there. Now I'd arrived and I owed him.

Even shocked, Eva looked like she'd stepped out of a wet dream. She'd chosen a denim skirt that was beyond inappropriate by her mother's standards. But I definitely didn't hate it, not the way it stretched across her hips. Her abdomen was bare, thanks to the absolute lack of length on her top.

Aunt Clara would've never allowed Eva to even try on an outfit like that. The idea of Clara allowing Eva to buy it or even let it into her house is preposterous. Eva standing in front of me in it would give Clara a heart attack. That, or Eva'd be sent to the nearest and strictest finishing school Clara could find. Looking at her, it seems impossible for her to have a bra under the cropped polo.

The club lights dimmed, and I dragged my eyes away from Evanna's body. I was fully aware of being a sick fuck, but broadcasting it in a five mile radius for everyone to know wasn't on my to do list. As the music faded out, someone approached Evanna from behind and slung their arm over her shoulders. I didn't pay attention to who it was. My attention was on her face. I wanted to see just how worried Eva was that I was there with the new development.

It was my self-appointed duty to make Eva as uncomfortable or more so than she'd ever made me.

Her eyes widened as her head swiveled to look at her-friend? Date? Designated Driver? I didn't know or care.

"Oh. Hey, man! Damn, it's been forever, Theo."

Correction, I *hadn't* given a damn. When I looked over at the voice's owner, only to find 'Thorn', the asshole that should've graduated with me, yet only managed it the year before Eva, made me care. His arm laid so casually over Evanna's shoulders that it made my blood thunder. For a few moments that was all I could hear. There were many reasons to dislike Thorn. Mainly because of his stupid ass nickname, but his hard-on for Eva was in the top five for me. He'd thought Evanna was hot before she was remotely legal, and when I found out, I wanted to dismember him for thinking about her. Fuck, I wanted to dismember him for daring to touch her at that moment.

"Thorn," I said, finally. "It's weird to see you and Evanna together. Let me guess, date night?" I pasted a smile on my mouth, one aimed for an unnerving but cordial look. I doubt he missed the dig at him, but one never knew. A single glance thrown Eva's way let me know my smile distinctly lacked any kind of friendly vibe. I just wanted that fucker's hands off her, so it didn't matter anyway.

"Oh, Nah." He laughed while his arm pulled Eva closer. "You know Eva doesn't date."

The smile on his face was more akin to a leer, and it sent my blood pressure skyrocketing. Eva looked horrified. She looked a little green at the implications he'd laid out too, which was all the information I needed.

"Eva," I called, pitching my voice so she heard it over the music, "come here."

It might have be fucked, but I knew what tone to use with her. The same tone that my dad or Uncle Jake used to get her attention while on a build site. Authority and immovability. Fucked as it was, I took advantage of over a decade of conditioning that way. It worked.

Evanna's eyes settled on mine while she ducked from under Thorn's hold on her. She moved to stand beside me, body tense, shoulders hiked defensively. It wasn't entirely clear at that moment if Eva moved because of the tone I used, or because she feared I'd rat her out. Or maybe, just maybe, she was taking the out she'd been presented with. Thorn wasn't Evanna's type, friend or otherwise.

I wrapped my arm around Eva's waist, tucking her in against my side while I watched my former year-mate process what had happened. I took way too much joy in how I'd upended Thorn's plan.

"You're not wrong," I said with a smirk. "Eva doesn't date, and she may be easy, but not easy enough to fuck with you."

"Theo," Eva hissed my name, drawing my attention down to her. "Don't."

"It's real cute that you think I give a shit, princess. We're leaving," declaration made, I turned, steering her with me. My fingers dug punishingly into her hip when she tried to resist. The pained hiss made me smile as I dragged her out of the club. In the clear summer air, she smelled like sugar. No. She smelled like a goddamn cupcake, one that took a healthy dip in some vodka before getting decorated.

I got her in my truck long before I decided to say anything. I kept it simple, since I didn't know where to start.

"Passport."

I only glanced at her as I made the request. We had a while before we hit the border. Given Evanna wasn't so secure to think, she could hop into the first club five miles from the border. Still, I wanted to be ready. No one wanted to get pulled over. Especially because the scantily clad young woman in your car took too long to get her identification out.

"Here," she said and thrust the little booklet into my reach. Her tone was somewhere between terse and petulant. I had to wonder where the hell Eva kept that.

"What do I have to do for you to keep this little adventure to yourself, Theo?"

A pleased feeling coiled in my gut. Evanna was clearly attempting to head this off at the pass. She had good instincts; I had often tried to get Clara to bitch at Evanna. My word against hers. The sheer number of times that the scale had come down on my side was still flabbergasting.

"Who said I would tell anyone?" I asked as I looked at her properly. Immediately, I noted her shoes on the floor, feet propped against my dash silver painted toes caught the light and only distracted me for all of point five seconds. Her skirt was too fucking short for that. Truly, her skirt was too short to stand in, never mind dance or walk. But I didn't say shit about it. Why? Ultimately, I was the sick fuck who'd fantasied about her since I figured out what sex was.

"Won't you?" she said with no small amount of irritation. "It's the perfect way to ruin my life. An opportunity for Clara to confirm that I'm *exactly* like Jasmine. Somehow another rebellious, slutty daughter has come out of her pristine, proper house."

"Whoa," I exhaled, frowning as I looked at her for a moment. This was new. Evanna had never, to my knowledge, said a cross word about Clara.

"You've gone off the rails. I mean, look at you? But comparing yourself to Jasmine … That's a stretch."

"Fuck off," she snapped. "It's apparently a crime to want to look hot, feel pretty, and go have fun. You know, like anyone else my age?"

"Right, because traveling through Wercen over the border into Canada with a group of equally aged friends to drink and shake your ass is fun," I remarked, highly amused. I'd found Evanna's apparent form of rebellion. One that'd likely been in place for ages. I was almost sad I never went to one of those irritating school dances. Had I gone, I bet I could have traced her behavioral evolution.

"Well, it's better than messing with the guys from my class." Evanna shrugged carelessly while she answered. I was struck, like a powerful static shock, that little Miss Oh-So-Perfect-Bishop was just tipsy enough to be frank with me. She would never have given me this much ammunition against her otherwise.

I huffed a laugh, "Well, well, well. Someone seems to have grown up."

That's the best I had. It was a lot – processing little Eva had been learning about what kind of sex she liked. Or at the very least, learning what she didn't. The lights of the border lit up the black sky as Eva's feet came off the dash. She was quiet, only answering when spoken to when we approached and stopped at the border crossing. Notably, Eva was equally quiet when I made the turn to take her in the opposite direction of her house.

"So," I broke the silence ten minutes in. "Who's your cover tonight?"

"Dawn. Mom trusts us when we're together and obviously vice versa, so we've worked out a system. No need to field calls or any of that shit," Eva said after a moment. I heard her shift around but didn't take my eyes off the road.

On the cusp of summer and at that time of night? I didn't want a ticket because there were more troopers out there. Even getting pulled over would've spell disaster for both of us. Small towns, man. Small fucking towns.

"I'm really surprised that you didn't just take me home as loudly as fucking possible." Eva was suspicious. It dripped from her tone, voice a little too sharp, a little too high. I understood, though. If I were her, I would've been cautious, too.

"What, you want me to give up perfectly good blackmail material? Do you know me at all, cousin?" I smirked at her, not really worried if it increased or decreased the stress she felt.

She was quiet for a bit. Then, I heard the sound of denim against leather, and I flicked a look her way. Eva had moved, so she was mostly facing me. It was odd to have so much of her attention on me in an environment where I didn't necessarily have to restrain myself.

"Oh, I know you, Theo." She leaned against the seat, eyes lidded, but I couldn't tell if she was tired, being unknowingly seductive, or suspicious as hell. "Which is why I'm wondering what the angle is."

"That's fair," I replied slowly, trying to shake that first curl of arousal that hit me. Eva's eyes were always what got to me first. Dark brown and lined in kohl. The rest of Evanna was hot as hell, but her eyes conveyed everything. Even when I didn't translate quite right. Her eyes always broadcasted her emotions. From the fascination she thought hidden when interesting gossip or people came around, to her unrelenting anger at me.

"I don't have an angle tonight. Not outside of keeping you from fucking Thorn." I shrugged, and endeavored to keep my voice casual, normal.

"I wouldn't fuck Thorn with someone else's borrowed vagina," Evanna drawled, a derisive snort followed. "That he thought I would, or hoped, I don't know. It's gross."

"Ageism, Eva, really?" I took an innocent enough poke at her.

"No, this is purely a personality and lack of attraction speaking. He's not my type, an asshole without the desire to own it. You should be unrepentant if you are going to be a dick. He tries to frame himself as a sweetheart boy next door. It's gross." Her head leaned against the seat back while I quietly goggled at the fact, we were having a conversation with no animosity or hostility. Sure, she was wary, but she wasn't antagonizing me anymore than I was her.

"Does he know that?" I asked it automatically, even though I remembered how out of sorts she'd been in the club.

"Doubt it," she sighed, "but he knows you're a possessive bastard now."

Laughter bubbled out of me. She wasn't wrong. I was possessive, obsessive, and selfish as hell with my toys, my things, my people. Eva fell firmly under that umbrella. She just wasn't aware of it, or maybe Eva knew. I wondered if I'd find out.

"If he didn't know before, then he never paid attention."

"I dunno about that, Theo." Her voice dropped out of her 'for public' range. There was a slight difference that wasn't there when we were kids but had developed over the course of her middle and high school career. I much preferred her sounding this way. Her voice wasn't deep, per say, but certainly not the typical straddle of high and melodic. "I paid attention, and I missed exactly how possessive you are."

"That is hardly my fault, Eva," I replied quickly with another laugh leaving me. "You being blind is a whole you issue."

"Not blind," Eva mused while the city popped up around us. "I just didn't quite put together what I was seeing."

Another curl of arousal hit me square in the cut. If I felt shame over how I wanted Evanna, I'd worry that she'd figured it out.

"And what, little cousin, is it you failed to put together?" The last series of turns before my apartment started up as I heard the click of her belt.

~

All at once, that vodka-cupcake scent washed over my senses. Her chin was set on my shoulder. Her body warmed my side.

"I failed to put together that no one may have me or my attention when you're around but you. Glares, cutting remarks, or the sad attempts at them at least. You hate when I don't pay attention to you."

"That was hardly a secret," I replied, flicking the indicator before I turned. "You're *mine* to upset, hurt, and make cry. I won't tolerate someone else trying it."

I also wouldn't tolerate someone trying to seduce her in front of me. Nor those who implied that was their aim, which didn't need to be said, considering how the night progressed.

"Mm, but you don't like people looking, either. I know you look, I know you're the king of assholes and the worst thing that's happened to me half the time. D'you know what's hilarious about that?" The combination of Evanna's pitch, proximity, and utter knowledge of what Evanna wasn't wearing made those few sentences torture. A new, wonderful sort.

"What, exactly, is so funny?" I asked while I pulled into my parking spot.

My belt clicked before I even turned the truck off. She'd been docile to that point. So when she planted herself in my lap, I got the hell shocked out of me. A good sort of shock, too. The sort that came with a hit of warmth. It was the first twitch of serious interest, heralding a yawning hunger would soon follow.

"What's funny is I know all that. Yet, I *still* want you." Her arms draped around my shoulders and behind my neck as she spoke. I'm not short. When Eva sat herself on me, she needn't have been so close. There was hardly a breath of room between us.

The entire situation was sexier than I wanted it to be, and damn if my dick didn't whole-heartedly agree. But a brief flicker of anger made itself known, too. I was angry because it felt as if she thought she'd figured out a way to get what she wanted from me.

"What made you think I want someone who plays whore?" I asked roughly. Following the urge to make Evanna retreat was not the smartest thing I'd done during a civil conversation with her. But old habits died very hard with me. I'd lived to do anything to make Evanna as mad or pained as I was. A sober Evanna would've shown her claws viciously, backing me into a corner at the same time. But, tipsy Evanna, she was much harder to aggravate.

"Obviously because you want to put me in my place," Eva replied, tone patient, like I wouldn't have realized part of my obsession with her. It made me hold on to her hips tighter, which got her to shift on my lap while she just kept talking.

"I bet you want to make me cry, to ruin my long-term plans or something, right? You want to remind me of where I belong." Something edged into her tone then, an assertion I wouldn't lay claim to. "Silly little Evanna, she thinks that she's going to get out of this shit-ass series of little towns."

I made a note to explore *that* later.

"But, you can't, can you, Theodore? You're stuck here," she shifted into a bright, almost sweet cadence. It would've startled me had her eyes not been trying to poison me. Even with the projection in the middle, I deserved this attack. From the first time I met her after my mother left, I'd made it my mission to fuck up Evanna's life. From shoving her and calling her names, to feeding racist rumors into the ears of gossips, I'd made life here awful. It was unclear if Evanna knew the extent of it, or how I'd backed off as a sad form of repentance.

Eva's declaration barely stung. I knew I was fucked. A farm boy through and through with a community college degree? Oh yeah, I wasn't going any-damn-where. I'd end up as fuck all to boot. But, Eva. Clara'd been crowing *nonstop* since the middle of her junior year that Evanna'd been awarded *every* scholarship she'd set her eyes on. From small scholarships to a few that were frankly obscene. Eva, apparently, just had to make her choice.

"Maybe I should be more creative then," I said thoughtfully. "I could always make sure you leave with a permanent part of me; a stain you'll never shake." While I intended to shock her, I hadn't meant to let that cat out of the bag. I'd had this fantasy, it approached a fetish in its fucking intensity, for years. Ruining, claiming Evanna in an unforgettable, undeniable fashion, appealed to me in dangerous ways. I wanted my hold on her to be absolute. A claim so deep and sure it became a defining feature of her. The mere thought was delicious. Almost as good as knowing that claim would leave her reputation shredded.

Given the suggestive threat I'd made, I wasn't expecting much in the way of a response from Eva. Yet, even in the crap lighting of the cab, courtesy of the streetlights, I watched her eyes dilate. Not fear. That was what I would expect, along with a healthy slap or punch. Her eyes showed arousal, though, not fear. I couldn't muster even an ounce of shame upon recognizing it. My dick, though, that took over. It twitched and swelled, fast enough I wasn't able to hide my interest from her. Certainly not while she'd sat on my damn lap.

"So, what?" Evanna licked her lips while starting the question, "you want to give me some weird version of a tattoo?" Eva played at being coy in the way she leaned in after a beat. Her lips were glossed in deep plum, and she spoke slowly so I could watch her form the words. "Or do you want to bite me until I bleed, leave a scar on me, something I have to explain? Share with the class, Theo. I'm curious."

It didn't take a genius to spot that Eva was taunting me. All that sugary sweetness was a mockery of her actual intent and feelings. And I gave exactly zero fucks. She wanted me to share, so I shared.

"*Oh*, I want to 'mark' you, princess. I want to leave a mark on you so fucking bold and permanent that you're not just ruined. No. What I want to do to you will make people disgusted. No one will ever touch you after you admit who did it to you." The words flowed with an ease I hadn't imagined. It was remarkably easy to use the hold I had on her hips to push her down while I lifted mine up. Just enough so she felt the rise of my cock against her.

"Teddy," she sighed out my name, shook her head as her cheeks turned a more pronounced pink. "You want to fuck me? No, no. You want to knock me up? Really? I'm your *cousin*."

I laughed, a harsh sound in the cab's quiet. "Sweetheart, you won't bait me with the cousin line, Miss I-still-want-you. It's the perfect ploy, princess. I get inside that hot pussy and fuck it until you're round with my child. Not only that, I'll make it my business to ruin you for anyone else. Plus, I get to sit back and watch your world fall apart. And maybe I'll do it again afterward. After all, one time is a mistake. Twice is a pattern."

"God, you're such a dick," Eva said while shaking her head at me. "If you want me so bad, Teddy, I'm *right* here."

To me, that was a pretty damn clear challenge. She thought I wouldn't do it. Too bad for Eva that that was basically Christmas come early. I didn't need to be told twice. My hands dragged her flush against me as I smirked at her.

"You really want to try this, Eva?" I was a bastard, but I wouldn't take what she didn't give me. Even though her body told me yes, I needed to hear the words.

"Do your worst, Teddy."

Her permission was what I needed to cover her mouth with mine. From there, it was a blurred chain reaction of events that led to Eva topless on my lap. I'd bunched her skirt up around her waist, one of my hands held her ass. The plot may have been mine, but fuck, Eva was completely on board. She was absolutely shameless the way she rode the rise of my dick and ground her clit against me. Eva gave me every feverish moan I could've wanted.

"Fuck, Eva. Your tits are amazing." I groaned, not sounding like myself. "So soft. With these big, sensitive nipples that are perfect for my mouth."

I wasn't a fan of talking during sexually charged situations. However, I was bound and determined to make sure Evanna remembered this. I needed her to remember tonight, regardless of how often it was repeated. To recall how she whimpered when I gently bit her, or roughly pinched. She had to remember every word of praise shared. I wanted Eva to think about this and squirm in shame, so aroused she couldn't stand it.

"Do you like that, Eva? Do you like me playing with these gorgeous tits?" I asked while I pulled back to relinquish the nipple I'd taken hold of.

It should've been illegal how pleased I was with how flushed I made Eva, how she squirmed when I asked her that. Her pearly teeth dug into her bruised bottom lip. I particularly enjoyed the coral against golden brown of her complexion.

"Yes. Don't stop, Teddy, keep going." Even in this compromising position, she was still bossy as hell. But if the bossy girl wanted her breasts played with, who was I to deny her? With a smirk, I ducked down my head to return to nibbling and sucking at her nipples. Eva's hands ran over my shoulders, down my chest as she kept on riding my erection. In turn, I simply traded between breasts, so she kept moaning.

"Teddy. Oh, my god. Feels wonderful." The little cries and whimpers Eva made were better than any porn I'd heard. With a grunt against the tit in my mouth, I rolled the nipple between my teeth. The other cupped in my hand received a similar treatment. Eva responded gorgeously, she arched up against my mouth, hands buried in my hair. A wordless cry filled the cab, one I wouldn't ever forget.

It also snapped my tenuous hold on restraint. I was done. That wasn't enough. I couldn't sit there with her soaking my zipper anymore. I wanted to fuck her, wanted to make her scream for me. And I couldn't accomplish that properly in the damn truck.

"Upstairs, now."

We had to wrestle with her clothes but got them back in place and soon after we were in the muggy May air. As we climbed the stairs, I all but dragged Eva behind me. My key protested dangerously in my door's lock, and I practically threw her onto the couch. I didn't move from the door, I focused on throwing the deadbolt, locking the door handle, and slapping the chair into place. After I flicked on one of the lights. I wanted to remember this, every moment of it. With all that done, I turned to face her. Even that much of a delay hadn't calmed me down.

A glance over at her while I tossed off my shirt and shoes, showed me it hadn't calmed her down either. Disheveled, her outfit was more enticing. Perhaps because it'd been me who had left her wrinkled and ruffled.

"You want me to play with you some more, Evi? Need me to touch you?" I asked while I tugged my belt free of my jeans. The way things had progressed, I hoped I wouldn't need it or my jeans soon.

It was one thing to hear Eva respond to me. It was another entirely to see it without having her wrapped around me. Her legs looked a mile long as she rubbed them together while she moaned softly. Without an answer, she sat up from where she'd landed, and started undressing. First her shoes slipped off before she dropped her shirt on top, the skirt followed right behind it.

"Yes," she whispered, her fingers fidgeted with the strings that hugged her hips while she spoke. "I want more, Teddy. I want you to make me feel good."

Her cheeks were still bright with color as she told me she wanted me. I strode across the room, more than happy to fulfill the request as I shoved her none too gently down onto the couch. It didn't need to be said I was eager to get my mouth on her. I was so wound up, I latched onto a nipple through the lace of her bra. Impatiently, the cup that covered her opposite breast was tugged down. My fingers then took hold of her nipple, plucked and pinched lightly to tease her.

Eva, blessed horny little thing that she was, made room for me to lie between her legs while her fingers sank into my hair. Her nails rasped over my scalp as she kept me close to her body. I lifted away to trade side, moving the remaining cup away from her breast. With them bunched beneath, it made for a hell of a picture. One I stored away while Eva did her level damn best to chase away my coherency.

Her hips kept moving against mine. Eva gave me encouragement with these soft, breathless moans. It was torture. Beautiful torture. My mouth kept at her until I felt like I might lose my mind.

"Teddy," she whined so sweetly. "Hurry."

"Damn, princess, spoiled much?" I ripped at the buttons of my jeans with one hand, the other laid on her mound, where my thumb rubbed lightly over her clit.

"Teddy!"

"Eva," I laughed as I finally got my dick free of all the cloth barriers. Settled on my knees, I unintentionally pulled too hard at her thong, so the seams gave way. While I tossed it aside, I nearly missed her shocked gasp. Pleased, I smirked while I positioned my cock against her lips. "Goddamn, Evi. You're soaked."

I thrust lightly before I looked up at her. "Are you feeling needy? Do you want me to make you come, baby?"

"Yes, Theo, please. I want you to make me come." Her ragged consent was like ambrosia. This? This was so much *better* than her rage.

I considered warming her up with my fingers, but I didn't actually care if I hurt her. So, I lined up and rubbed my crown along her lips until she flowered open for me. I was torn, as I rubbed against her hole. I wanted to listen to her whimpers and whines. But I also wanted to watch how her eyes glittered and lips shimmered in the light. In the end. I did some of each. I stayed pressed against her without breaching longer than I'd have liked.

When I pushed against her, she clung to me, her legs shook against my hips. It made me resolve to take it slow. There was, however, a single mishap. I pushed and she lifted, which made me slip against her opening. I took hold of her hips, swearing a blue streak as she bucked with a yelp. We tried again.

"Teddy." There was a thread of pain in her tone. She was so small. Soaked, but tense and obviously nervous. I could just barely work my head inside her.

I found her eyes wide when I looked at her. Her body was taut beneath me. She was barely fucking breathing, so I stopped. Worried, I moved a hand between us, and set my thumb against her clit. I tried swiping side to side before I landed on circles that got her to relax. "You all right?"

"Uh huh," she sighed out while I kept up the attention. Her hair was a river of black silk against the blue of my couch. As sexy as it was, I hated that Clara kept relaxing Evanna's hair. It should have been a wild riot of curls, as wild as she was.

"Mm." Her eyes fluttered shut, and I smirked. I rolled my hips a bit while I continued with the circles.

"How's this, Evanna? Do you like my cock in your little cunt? Do you want me to give you more? Get that little hole nice and stretched to take me?" I kept a careful gaze on her while I asked to move in the lewdest way I possibly could.

"Jesus, Theo." Her soft exhalation made me grin. "I— Maybe?"

"I'll keep playing with your clit. Does that sound better?" I was desperate to move but unwilling to force her. This only worked if she wanted it, her eventual humiliation only counted if she admits she wanted it— wanted *me*.

"Try," she whispered. I kept stroking over her clit as I nodded and began working more of my cock into her pussy. The whole of my head slipped inside. However, Eva clamped down like a vice as I tried more. I swore I saw stars. I redoubled my efforts on her clit to get her relaxed while I pulled back and took a ragged breath. Once the pressure let up, I tried pressing inside quickly.

Her hips came up off the couch as she cried out and became tense. I'd gotten maybe two inches into her. My hips pressed forward, and she tossed her heads, legs clamped against my hips to stall me.

"Hurts, Theo." Her chest heaved as her hands settled on my stomach.

"Sorry, baby." I wasn't not; not at all. "Let me just stay like this. I'll use my head to get off. If I can't feed you my entire cock, I can at least get off and make you come." Maybe.

"Yes," she nodded, her cheeks vibrant and eyes glassy - I hoped with how badly she wanted this. "It's like you're…"

I thrust as she spoke; her moan cut off her sentence. But I filled in the blanks of what she meant. As I loomed over her, a smirk curled my lips. "I'm just jacking off with your pussy, right Eva? It's not sex, right? I'm just using this hot as fuck hole to get off with. Gonna fill it with cum and keep right on playing with my new toy, if that's the case."

I'd never, ever, anticipated Eva having kinks. With how strict Clara was, I only ever pictured her as demure. Evanna would have obviously only consented to boring sex. Lights off, in a bed under the covers in missionary, no modifications, sex. I was wrong. Eva arched up against me as her cunt fluttered on my cock head. It hit like a train; Eva liked this. She wanted it.

"Fuck, I don't know what I did, what stars aligned to get us here, but thank you," I muttered. For the moment, I relented. I gave Eva a rest from attempting to make her take more dick.

I leaned down to kiss her. It wasn't some gentle, loving thing. I thrust into her mouth within seconds. Her moan while I rolled my hips combined with how her tongue flicked against mine rolled through me. I focused on providing us with friction. That it was Eva who broke the kiss was predictable. But she wasn't back after catching her breath. She instead initiated a coy, taunting game between our mouths.

"Suck my tits, Theo, please?" She dared to whisper the request into a half kiss while she rolled her hips to meet mine.

There wasn't any shame in how I pinned her shoulders to the couch and attacked her breasts again. They were so soft and big. I couldn't get enough of how they felt on my tongue and against my lips. That Eva apparently got off on my playing with them was a bonus.

"Theo. Fuck, it feels good. This is so perfect. I want you like this every night." Eva panted and whined. Her hands held my head to her tits again. She was so damned wet on me; I was doing mental gymnastics. I needed to know how often I could steal her away at night for this.

I was more than willing to finger her until she could take my cock easily. She might have thought it an idle threat, but I was dead set on doing my level best to send her to college pregnant. Eva opened the door, and I wanted to make sure she'd never be able to close it on me.

"Fuck, princess." I pulled away, pulled free of her before I looked down at her. "Get on your knees."

She flipped over and lifted her hips up with a shaky breath. I hadn't yet looked at her, hadn't been able to appreciate the pussy I was about to wreck. So, I did. I put my hands on her thighs and rubbed them a few times before I used my thumbs to spread open her lips. She was wet, pink, and mine. As if on autopilot, I pressed my index and middle fingers against the mouth of her. I rubbed around and against it before my eyes moved to meet hers. "Every night, huh?"

"Teddy, please." Her hips pressed into the touch.

I ignored her and sat up to replace my fingers with my cock. "Do you really want it, princess? Are you really telling me?" I pushed into her with a groan only to stall when she tensed. "You want me to play with these soft tits," I leaned over her and took a handful of her breast, "to fuck this tight-ass cunny every night? You want that? Will you ask me for it, ask me to touch you until you let my cock in?"

"Holy fuck, Teddy, please," she sobbed and gave a non-answer. In response, I gave a short thrust against her. I groaned as I witnessed her swallow a little more of my girth.

"Eva," I didn't intend to be threatening, but to my own ears, that was how I sounded.

She went pliant, whimpering. "Yes, okay? Yes, fuck me every night, play with my tits, finger me open, Theodore. I fucking *want* you."

A little shocked by her reaction, I swallowed, adjusted my stance and took hold of her hips. "Good," I said and began to grind and rock against her pussy. It gained us precious centimeters slowly. Kisses got trailed along her spine while I focused intensely on her every reaction.

"Come on, princess, let me in. Take it like you want it," I whispered it every time she tensed up. I listened to her moan and whine and cry each time, too. The process was slow, but worth it as at the quarter point, she allowed me more movement. I didn't focus on gaining space within her. Instead, I concentrated on being sure she'd want this again.

"There you go," I groaned while my fingers squeezed her hips. "That feels good, doesn't it Eva?"

"Uh huh." Her reply was breathless; her knees shifted open until one threatened to slip off the couch. Her pussy swallowed a little more of my length. The moan that Evanna let out kept me focused on gaining every bit of ground I could.

"God, I'm going to come," I groaned a while later. I sped up, just about halfway inside her. "Jesus, princess. Gonna fill this pussy with cum, Eva."

"Close," was her answering gasp, and I could see her eyes had lidded while her forehead pressed against the couch.

My hands squeezed her hips so hard I had to assume she'd bruise later. "Hurry up, slut. When I'm done, so are you."

I was a self-admitted ass, but I'd never been like this with the women I'd fucked in the past. Evanna, though. With her I wanted, no, I *needed* to control everything, but especially that. Mindful not to go too far, I thrust harder, and gave her ass a slap "Got it? Your hole comes with me in it, or not at all, Evanna."

"Teddy. I— I want to see you, need you to fuck me like that."

I got her flipped onto her back so fast she was breathless. I was too eager to be gentle with her. I guided her legs around my waist and slid back into her. Her face went slack as she groaned, and it was almost better than how she felt wrapped around me. "There you are princess. Here's my slutty girl."

"Theo. More," she bit out the words as she thrust up. I could barely even focus on her instead of the blissful wet warmth of her around my cock.

I tried. I gave her as much as I could. While fucking her doggy style had been great; this was better. I was able to watch as her face reddened, and watch as it moved down her throat to her chest. Her tits were bouncing, nipples hard, they called to me; and I answered them.

I blanketed Eva with my body, hunched somewhat uncomfortably, and she wrapped her legs around me. Like that all her moans, sighs, groans, and whimpers became progressively louder. It was a trial to keep my orgasm at bay. But I needed her to come, to feel it. I was aware I'd threatened to deny it to her if I got off first, but I absolutely had to feel her coming on me.

I worked for it with a hand wedged between us, thumb on her clit. Her hips ground up quick and steady, in time with my desperate thrusts. My awareness narrowed down to the slick sound of my cock, the feeling of her wrapped around me, and the taste of her skin. It could have been minutes, it could have been hours, but as she began moving more erratically, she whined she was going to come. Hips churning, something aligned for us as the rest of my cock slid into the hot well that was her cunt.

Eva screamed.

"Goddamn, princess, that's a good girl. Fuck, yes. There you go, give it to me. That's my princess, letting me in this hot, perfect cunt. God, fuck, Eva." The first words were groaned against her chest before I grabbed her hips to fuck her through it. I couldn't make myself slow down to savor it, either. I took everything from what we'd achieved and came so hard with Eva milking my cock, I would swear I saw heaven.

For a while we were silent. My living room was filled with our heavy breaths and nothing else. I was almost, *almost* ready to pull out of her when her legs squeezed at me.

"Teddy?"

"Yes, princess?"

"Fuck me again, please."

Who was I to deny her what she wanted? Especially when it got me what I wanted.

The Realities of Daylight

Evanna
16 May

If you'd never heard the term *sex hangover*, one…lucky. Two, I hadn't known it was a real thing, and it very much is. Theo—Fucking *Theodore LeClair*, talked me into staying with him for the rest of the weekend. I don't really remember what I told Clara, my adopted mother, about where I was. I knew I used Theo's cell, so there was every chance that I said something truthful, without it having been the whole truth.

I ran my hands through my hair before I carefully adjusted the new outfit I'd gotten. Well, that Theo bought me. Another piece of ammunition for him to have used however he saw fit. I couldn't very well wear what I'd worn at the club, and I couldn't show up at home in Theodore's clothes either. So, 'I went shopping with Dawn'. Not only was it a plausible lie, as we'd been together this weekend as a cover, but true, after a fashion.

"Princess, chill out. You're going to give yourself an ulcer," Theo said. The words dragged me from my thoughts. It was nice. His voice, I mean. That sort of baritone that you never would quite expect from him. One that dropped firmly into bass territory whenever he was angry, or apparently, horny as sin. In my dreams and nightmares, that voice was an equal star.

"I'm as chill as I'm going to get," I replied quietly. In that instant I set aside Real-Eva for Approved-Eva. Real-Eva, she's the one who went dancing in clubs, who wore ridiculous perfumes, who was proud of her body and mind in equal parts. Real-Eva would let her mouth run, and as the weekend proved, Real-Eva would happily let Theo fuck the sense out of her. Then again, Real-Eva had something of a track record there.

Approved-Eva blames Real-Eva's launch into sexuality on having survived the car accident that killed her childhood best friend. Trauma, grief. Grief led Real-Eva into the arms of the girl who'd become her best friend, and the boy would become the bane of her existence. Dawn and Kelly respectively.

The approved version of Eva had relationships, only ever with boys, and nothing more untoward than excessive kissing. Mother's 'Approved-Eva' wanted to focus on nothing more than her tests and her future. Her Eva went on diets like clockwork every six months, because God forbid, she gained five pounds over her doctor-specified lowest acceptable weight. The Approved-Eva spoke softly, thoughtfully, smiled all the time so no one would ask her what was wrong. Approved-Eva never got into trouble in public.

I hated Approved-Eva almost as much as I hated the real me.

"Listen," Theo spoke again and ripped my attention back to him. "I won't say shit about this weekend, Evanna. Clara would rip my dick off, for one thing. Plus, I have a plan, and you know I hate when my plans are ruined." His voice had a light tone I didn't often hear, and even more rarely had it been aimed at me. It was strange. However, the entire weekend had been a rollercoaster of strange, wild emotion.

"I know. I trust you to keep this, at the very least, to yourself." I replied and swallowed down the taste of ash after. I didn't have a choice, but to trust that Theo's cock would overrule his desire to watch me suffer. Though, his cock made me suffer too. I shifted slightly in my seat and winced. It was worth it. The soreness I had to deal with was worth it.

"I'm more paranoid that Clara will just know. I don't even remember where I said I was."

"I do," Theodore said and snorted. "You were pretty out of it Saturday morning, thanks to the marathon of sex. I made you call her. You asked to stay with me to visit Andi. Then I dropped you off at the mall with my card instead of going with you." His eyes shifted over to me, and I blinked back at him. I don't comprehend what he's just said for a while.

"That's why she was there." Well, that made more sense, at least. Andi and I had been close when we were younger. Big sister, little sister roles, for all that we were cousins. We'd grown apart of late. I thought it was sad.

"Yeah, princess, that's why she was there," he laughed, and I kind of loathed him a little.

"Stop calling me that, please," I asked brusquely. Theo didn't give me nicknames. He used the ones that the whole family used. A new nickname would be a dead giveaway that something changed. And any changes between us would've warranted scrutiny. We didn't need that. My crashing at his place so I could see Andi was easily overlooked. Theodore loved his sister more than he hated me. Andi happened to be pregnant, so there wasn't room for me in her apartment. Theo's couch would have been the best alternative.

"Sure, little queen," he sighed, and silence reigned in the cab.

I was glad. While I would've loved to unpack our baggage, that had to wait. Life, my life, had a very specific set of rules. One must always be put together, be respectful, especially when others showed no respect. Be kind with a sharp tongue, so you could make your reprimands polite. Hair straight always – acceptable. Curly hair – my curly hair- was 'too ethnic', too black. Jasmine is your sister, not your birth mother. Don't lie. *Lie so well people never question it.*

"I think I'm gonna be sick," I whispered with my hands rubbing at my face. The weight of the situation, of sleeping with Theo, and having planned to do so again, made my stomach twist. There was rebellion and then there was that. "If Mom figures it out…"

The truck stopped.

"Evanna, baby, look at me."

I took a minute to do so. His brows pulled together, a little v between them. The moment I looked at him, he summarily pulled me from my seat into his lap. Across it, really. The event that 'led to it all' flashed through my mind. I'd never been so stupidly brazen before.

His mouth was on mine. He tasted like chocolate and coffee from our very 'healthy' breakfast of Dunkin's. All the shrill thoughts that bounced around my head started to quiet down. I sank into the kiss-into Theodore. It was so stupid to have given him that much power over me. But I'd done it, I wasn't so stupid or masochistic to refuse comfort either, even in that form.

His tongue swept along my lips to get me to open for him. I did with a sigh as our tongues met. It was slow, the way we twined together. One kiss turned into five- seconds slipped into minutes. I shifted from across his lap to on it. From having sat in his arms into a complete embrace. When we parted, my mind was pleasantly abuzz with silence.

"Better?"

"Yeah." My head bobbed while I moved back to my seat reluctantly. Theo's hands didn't leave me until the point he'd have needed to lean across the center seat to keep hold of me. When exactly had our physicality become *this*?

"Good. I'll figure out a reason to see you during the week," he said, the truck starting as I threw a sharp look at him.

"Theo---"

"Nope," he cut me off neatly. "I won't make it to the weekend without at least touching you. And if I do – you'll go home looking worse than this. Slightly dazed and sort of stiff is a good weekend with lots of movies, late nights, and falling asleep on the couch. Completely out of it will have Clara assuming drinking or drugs."

I had to give it to him. Mom would absolutely assume I was on something rather than having excessive amounts of sex. I stayed silent and just shook my head with a hint of a smile that played over my face.

I pulled down the visor so I could check myself in the mirror. My hair was loose. Theo'd had his fingers in it – *again*. With a heaved sigh, I took out the pony and braided down my hair instead. Without a brush, there wasn't any hope of achieving a smooth ponytail.

Silence stretched between us. For once, I didn't feel like I was being hunted. Silence and Theodore, when concerning me, was bad news. I'd burn that bridge once I was on it, I decided.

Theo dropped me off, and I went in while I prayed that Mom wouldn't immediately descend on me. Typically, at this time of the year, she'd be outside more often than not. She'd be obsessive in her quest to make the garden set up just right. She took her time with it and subsequently took well-earned pride in those flower beds.

She wasn't in the living room when I padded up the stairs. I silently thanked God for it, too. I made a beeline for my room, where I shoved my clothes off into the basket before I ran for my shower. I was that girl, yeah. My bedroom was a comfortable size- not huge, but big, complete with the private bathroom. It had been a blessing and curse in some ways.

As I stood under the spray, I pushed aside cursed memories. None of them would've helped me. Instead, I washed away the scent of Theo's soap and searched for signs he'd left marks on me in places I would've had to explain. His fingerprints were on my hips. There was a hickie on my thigh. I'd need to wear the tried-and-true period panties. They'd cover the finger shaped bruises. Those were the ones that wouldn't make sense. The thigh bruise, however, was just one of those random things that happened.

Especially during the winter and coming out to spring. That was when I was at my lightest. Without the sun, I shifted from a medium-dark foundation to a light-medium. Winter called me 'dusk' like golden hour, and summer called me 'hazel'. Or, as my dad liked to say, I paled from a chocolate spread to a baked vanilla cupcake. I hated when he said that. I've never been edible.

I was, however, able to bruise like a peach. The entire family had that blessing, regardless of melanin content.

"Evanna?" My Mom's voice filtered through the noise of the shower, and I panicked.

"Yeah! I'm here. I'm just getting a shower before doing laundry, Mom. Want me to wash my hair for you?" I really hoped that Clara didn't pick up on how my voice wavered. I wasn't up to properly doing the avoidance dance.

"Okay, sweetheart. I'll do your hair after dinner. Did you have fun visiting with Andi? Was Theodore actually kind to you for once?" Her voice was louder, so I knew she was hanging right outside the door.

With a deep breath, I closed my eyes and pulled on Approve-Eva.

"I did, yeah. She's getting a pretty good bump! I'll bring down my homework so I can check it while under the dryer. For being so far along, Andi is very energetic. Theo was … Theo. No one got sent to jail, nor did I end up in the ER, so I count it as a win." I laughed – that was the definition of a win between Theodore and I. We had a relationship that was infamous in our family.

"I'm glad that boy is getting his head on straight," Mom replied evenly. Where most of the family laughed off Theo's bullshit, Mom, Dad, and Uncle Joe watched us like hawks.

Before the weekend, that was positive. It probably kept me out of the ER more than once.

"I'll be outside. Did you eat lunch yet?"

"Once the laundry is going I'll come outside," I said, ignoring the question about food. No answer was right, and I wasn't about to chance it.

"All right," she called, and just like that, Mom was gone. The tightness in my chest, the rapid thump of my heart, the pressure on my head and tunnel vision all relented.

I loved my mom, I did. I just couldn't keep doing this. I couldn't stay frightened of what she'd say or do. Or what she'd think of what I wanted in my life. When I was little, I always thought Jasmine's stories about mom were odd. See, when she turned eighteen, Jasmine left, started a life, had no intention of returning.

When she told me those stories, I was a kid. Mom and Dad were my heroes. They were perfect humans insofar as perfect was possible. Jasmine though, she described them like the boogie man.

And Oliver, Jasmine's younger brother, my older adopted brother, had never told me stories like that. He never encouraged me to question things when I was small. He just smiled and said he knew once he met his wife, Charlotte, that college wasn't a priority. He wrapped up the way he jumped ship like a pragmatic, if reluctant, decision made for his family to work.

Once I was older, I saw what they both did. They ran the fuck away. When Oliver got married and moved, he didn't come back. Jasmine came back – with me. She tried to leave a couple times after that, too. This town, though, it had away of sinking its claws in and never letting go.

That was why I knew I had to leave. I'd known since I got my license, honestly. I'd probably decided after Tori died, and I didn't. I wouldn't end up being the one who never left. I wouldn't marry a boy from my class, or a year younger. There was no way I could live and raise children here. Frankly, I'd have rather died.

I hadn't told my mother yet. She was all for the scholarships I'd garnered in an academic sense. She wanted me at the state university— close to home, just two hours away. Her thoughts amounted to my getting a trade license first, then working through college exactly like I had during high school. Shit wasn't easy.

The entire reason I sent in every application for every scholarship under the sun was simple. I didn't want to be sleeping less than strictly healthy to manage a job and classes. Not only that, I'd incur out-of-state fees freshman year. They'd need to be covered.

Finished, I shut off the water and left the shower to dry off quickly just to dash to my room again. I threw on clothes quickly. Weekend clothes, go outside and sweat, work, possibly rip them, clothes. I was sure before the day was done I'd be in the garden too. There were to letters on my desk that I glanced at. Both were acceptances. Well, they were the follow ups, asking if I'd decided. I had last week, before Theo. Brown or Howard. I was getting the hell out.

Freedom loomed. To survive the summer, I had to remember that.

20 May

"Grand-Mère! Merci de m'avoir permis de travailler à nouveau à la ferme," I said while I hugged the woman with skin set in deep wrinkles and hair a grey as steel. For a woman of eighty, she was spry. Grand-Mère was never idle.

"Oh, you know I love having you here, Eva. After you finish your work, you come in for dinner, like always," she said, laughing as she patted at my cheeks when she pulled away.

Wincing at the mention of dinner, I started to shake my head. Grand-Mere knew, though. She knew how mom was, and she clucked her tongue at me before I could get my mouth open.

"None of your diet nonsense. You're eating here, Evanna."

"Oui Grand-mère," I said with a sheepish laugh. "Do you want me to start in the barn? Or did the boys get the milking done early?"

"In the summer?" Grand-Mère snorted with a wry look. "They're lucky to start on time. They're still milking, go get your barn clothes on. The garden is for the afternoon. Got it weeded just the other day."

"By whom?" I demanded as I moved toward the clothes we all kept to work in. The garden had been mine for years, though I relinquished it for several. Grand-Mère had taught me carefully how she wanted things. She taught me to grow the food and flowers hardy, and to do so while supporting the trees around the garden.

"Oh, that girl of yours, Dawn."

"Grand-Mère!" I gasped and whipped around. "How many plants did she pull?" My throat hurt from how high my voice went.

Grandmother just clucked her tongue again, her eyes slanted in a look as if to say it's my fault I didn't come directly after graduation to work. "You'll see. Get a move on, girl. Day light's dying."

I rolled my eyes while I absolutely dreaded seeing what the garden looked like. The clothes switched out quick, with a heavy dose of reluctance. The thick proper denim and told t-shirt made me hot, and I hadn't left the safety of air conditioning yet. I shoved myself into socks and boots and ran out the door. It was sweltering, but the breeze was cool. It was helpful that morning.

The barn doors stood open, and I could see Aaron, Joe, and Theo all working. Aaron was our hired farmhand. He was Joe's age, an old schoolmate. When Andi and I were both working, he took vacation time. But Andi hadn't been there in years. At least, not to work.

"Well, looky here! The little queen has returned!" My uncle's voice boomed the greeting as my boots touched the barn floor.

"Uncle Joe!" I smiled and headed over to hug him quickly. "Where do you need me?"

"You're back for the summer?" he asked, a careful look on his face before his eyes shifted between Theo and I.

"Yes sir," I replied with a firm nod.

"Well, let's get you gettin' the girls out to the holding pen before we guide'em to pasture."

And so started the day. My Grand-Père wasn't out with us that day, though I wasn't surprised. He was likely out in the fields. We weren't a big farm by any means, but we had plenty of ground to cover. From the barn, I moved to the coops. It wasn't until near lunch I got the eggs in to Grand-Mère. I was sweating like no bodies business, too. Which meant I headed over to the old barn where the equipment was stored. There were rooms up there, an apartment of sorts.

I was alone, so dropped my clothes outside the door properly, like we all did, before I made for the shower.

My priority was cooling down, then hydrating. Eating was a distant third when I got into the shower. When I got out, food sounded good. Wrapped up in a towel, I went to hunt out my stored clothes. I hoped I was smart enough to have left underwear. To my knowledge, I was blissfully alone. When I made it to the bedroom, however, Theo was there, and crowded me up toward the wall.

"You came back for the summer, princess? Making money or to give me access to you?" He asked while he loomed over me, hands on either side of my shoulders to cage me in.

My heart slammed against my ribs in a staccato rhythm. Teddy smelled of hay, sweat, and the cologne he never failed to wear. Fear and arousal swirled together to keep me in place.

"Maybe it's both," I said quietly. It was a sad way to not boost his damned ego. Teddy smirked in response, as his head dipped toward me.

"Just tell me you want me to be close, baby." Teddy's voice dropped, it made me shiver in response. I licked my lips as my hormones staged a coup.

"Teddy…"

"Yeah, princess? You need something?" He crowded me so I was stuck up against the wall.

While I chewed at my lip, I knew I had a choice. I could attempt to summon up the boldness I'd displayed Friday night, or I could have made Theo coax it out of me. Teddy dropped his head and used his nose to trace along my shoulder to my neck. In the end, I didn't make the choice. Teddy put his hands on me, one at my back, one on my waist.

"Princess?" A question. One that I could answer without overthinking it.

"Yes."

He turned me around abruptly before he planted a hand between my shoulder blades. My hands kept me from becoming completely squished. Teddy's other hand tugged at my towel. I let it drop, face turned to watch him while he looked me over. Somewhere over the course of Saturday and Sunday, he'd found that if he looked at me, it made me uncomfortable.

At least, he *thought* it made me uncomfortable. I was, sort of. Theodore enjoyed looking at me, and when he did, it made my body go all hot and needy. I wanted Teddy to look at me and have his need overrule his common sense. Just like mine was with him.

"So damn pretty," he murmured, having raised a hand to cup my hip. He caressed up over my side before dipping to take hold of my ass cheek. He shifted me open like that; a foot tapped against mine to make me open my legs. I didn't resist, I had no plans to do so. We didn't exactly have the luxury of time.

Which Teddy was well aware of. But he wasn't rushing. He just… looked and touched me carefully. He was waiting. I tried to wait him out. My teeth raked over my lip, I thought of anything but that. I really tried. But I was too aware of where we were. Anyone could've walked up, could've come in.

"Teddy…"

"Ask me," he whispered it with his dark eyes on mine.

My throat was so dry. I had to swallow twice before speaking. "Please fuck me, Teddy."

While that wasn't really a question, it still earned me his fingers working into my body. It wasn't gentle. I squirmed away from the too sudden fullness, wondering if he'd just shoved three into me. The hand laid between my shoulders ran up and down my spine twice.

"Easy, sweetheart. Relax for me." His tone was quiet. Much more than it had been over the weekend. Even so, I focused on the good parts, rather than that sharp sting of entrance. I lost track of how Teddy touched me until I heard his belt jangle, the hand on my back gone.

It was stupid of me. Teddy's fingers disappeared, just for a moment, before he pushed another in. I hissed and turned to press my head against the wall. I wanted this, but I wasn't exactly 'geared up' for it. I struggled to make myself relax. So long that I'd barely started to enjoy him when Teddy withdrew.

"Damn it, Teddy." My head turned and made him laugh.

"Don't get tetchy, I'll give you what you want," his fingers tapped at my lips, the ones that'd been in me. "Suck."

"Teddy—"

"You heard me." My mouth immediately opened. I didn't miss that hard edge to his tone. It was one I knew meant I'd better get the hell out of dodge or do what Theo wanted. His fingers slipped into my mouth within seconds. I tasted sharp, strange, and he watched me like a hawk before the sensation of his head pressed against my entrance distracted me.

"Stay relaxed, Eva." The warning made my eyes widen before I squealed around his fingers. Teddy didn't allow me time to adjust.

He was relentless in making me take his cock inside me. There wasn't a pause until his hips were flush with mine. I was left breathing hard, like I'd run a sprint. It hurt. It was good, though. I wouldn't be able to ignore what we'd done afterward.

Which was likely his aim. Asshole.

"You're such a good girl," he murmured, fingers slipped free of my mouth. I hated myself for sighing at the praise, for allowing my eyes to slide shut. While Teddy gave no respite, he was still then. The moment I relaxed, he started to move. The pace was quick, too quick. His withdrawals were shallow, his hands were everywhere, but his face stayed pressed against my hair.

"Fuck – Teddy, slow down." I tried to keep my voice down, but it was a big request considering I was suffering being skewered by Teddy's dick.

"No, you're taking it so well, Eva. You're good for me, aren't you? Are you going to keep taking what I give you?"

I whimpered, nodded before I could stop myself. Of course, I'd be good. It was sick, I knew that. But when I was good like this – letting Theo be rough, letting him use me, he was pleased. When he was pleased that meant Theo would make any discomfort better. That had been the pattern over the weekend. I held onto that with the hope it stayed that way.

He sped up while he took hold of one of my breasts. Blessedly, he slid a hand down my stomach. Teddy dropped his face to my neck before I could ask him to hurry up and touch me. Hot air washed over my skin, his mouth close behind. His teeth scraped against my skin; lips pressed against my neck. I nearly came out of my skin with a whine as he pinched at my clit.

Teddy did it again, lighter, and it made me feel too hot. My nipple's tugged as I spiraled away from worry of where I was, what he was – we were – doing. My hips pushed back as I made a noise that resulted in him biting at my neck, growling. His cock surged into me just a breath later. I knew my mouth formed his name as a response.

If there was one thing, I was sure Theodore enjoyed, it was making me moan or yell his name.

"That's it, baby. Let it out. Tell me you're mine." His lips moved against my neck; the words vibrated against my back.

"Yours, yours. I'm yours, Teddy, please, more." I couldn't tell if I was still on Earth. There was only the stretch of him inside my channel, the way he kept at my breasts and clit. His breath or lips or teeth on my skin. My legs shook as I yelled.

"Goddamn," Teddy moaned, and I loved the sound of it. He switched the way he was thrusting. His withdrawal was slower, his return faster as I rode out my bliss. "Saints, Eva. You get so wet, makes me crazy."

"Teddy," I whispered clumsily before a jagged sound left me as his fingers tugged at me again. He'd left my nipples and clit alone moments go. A small reprieved before he was back to pulling the pleasure out of me like a job. "Too much."

"You feel like heaven, sweetheart. Don't you want me to feel good, too?" His teeth grazed over my ear as I tried to pull thoughts together. Coherent thoughts.

"Yes, but."

"Let me touch you, baby. You keep taking it so fucking well." Teddy was everywhere. He slowed down so he could make me feel every inch of him move inside my body. I couldn't think.

"My princess is making my cock feel amazing. Remember what we said?" He pulled slowly at my abused, over sensitive clit as he asked. I quaked between him and the wall.

"Toy," I gasped out. I almost collapsed as he did it again.

"Mmhmm. That's right, princess. You're my toy. We aren't doing anything wrong because I'm just using this…" He trust harder while he spoke and I yelped. "Hole," he bit out the world while pushing into me until it hurt. "…To get off inside. Just jacking off, right? Just using my pretty, pink, wet girl."

"God, Teddy." My nails scratched against the wallpaper as I sobbed. He sped back up, his hand clamped over my mouth as I came again. That time, I did collapse, but instead of stopping, Teddy arranged me on my knees and made quick work of stealing his pleasure inside of me.

I was so oversensitive that my eyes burned, and I couldn't stop the tears that escaped. I made noises, loud ones, pained ones. It felt good, but it was also agony. Teddy's praises were distant until he was draped over me, his breath fast and hard against my neck.

"Want to fuck again after dinner?" His question made me squirm, his hands tightened like vices on my hips as he hissed.

"Maybe," I managed. We stayed still until Theo was too soft to stay inside without sitting up. He slipped from me as a soft sigh left him.

"So fucking pretty. Gorgeous like this, worn out, full of cum. I wish you could see it, Eva." The hard edge had returned to his voice. I shuddered. His fingers kept dipping into my pussy. He was putting the cum that leaked from me back in. I didn't realize it at first. But when I did, I bit down on a strangled whine. That should've upset me, instead it just made me want more. He swiped his thumb one last time along my lips, then Theo got up and set is clothes to rights.

"Let's get going before someone looks for us." He walked off before I could even make myself move.

"Asshole," I whimpered having shoved myself upright. With a groan, I slowly rose on shaky legs. I had time to find my clothes and grab an apple before I returned to work. Thankfully I avoided him by working in the garden. But Theo had always wanted me exactly where he put me. He wanted me miserable, or happy at his pleasure.

I wasn't surprised when he found me after dinner. Equally, I wasn't surprised when I gave in to what he wanted after he plied me with sweet kisses. That boy – man – made me stupid. It was a huge fucking problem.

Shifting Emotions*(ish)

Theodore
1 June

"Teddy, no more."

Eva clung to me; her eyes unfocused when I looked up at her. From where I'd stationed myself between her legs, she was a mess; in a good way, her hair was everywhere. She was covered in that fine sheen of sweat we got conditioned into thinking was sexy. On her, because I caused it, yeah, it appealed.

I lazily detached my mouth from her cunt, one last thrust that made her keen. Then I was in a place I could answer her. My hand wiped over my mouth as I shot her a smirk.

"What's wrong?" I asked, while I knew full-well I'd been pushing Evanna into spaces she'd never been in before. Frankly, I'd had to look up exactly what I wanted to do, and how to do it. The day I'd jumped in carelessly had left me with my arms full of a largely unresponsive woman. It startled me more than it scared her. From then on, I started carefully, listened to her.

Even as every touch made her twitch or squirm, I was cautious. The research had paid off. I just needed to keep us in safe spaces.

"Too sensitive," she said, voice little more than a murmur. She struggled to push herself upright, clearly Eva thought I was done. That she'd get a rest. I didn't have a single intention of allowing that.

"Ah, and what's too sensitive, princess?"

I moved to lie beside her. It was easy to play into her idea that I'd let her calm down. I wrapped my arm around her loosely and pulled her to lay against my chest. She went where I led her, far more agreeable than usual, which I noted for future use.

"Everything."

I bit at my lip in order to hide my grin. I urged her up with gentle hands, careful to avoid any areas that would've set her off. She grumbled but moved so she was settled astride me. Eva looked wobbly, but coherent enough I didn't worry.

"Everything is broad, sweetheart," I said and sat up, leaning back against the wall. To throw her off, I lifted my hands and threaded my fingers into her hair. As I massaged her scalp, I watched her eyes slide shut. A soft sigh dropped from her mouth. "Is this too much?"

"No," she whispered and opened her eyes just enough to see me. "It's nice."

"Mm."

I shifted, humming as I took hold of her hair with one hand and tilted her head. My lips pressed gently along her shoulder and neck. I didn't retreat, instead I allowed my breath to wash over her skin. "And that?"

The two words had her squirming, her lips parted in a gasp. I waited patiently to see if Eva would give me an answer sometime soon. When she didn't, I repeated the process. "Eva."

"It's – a lot. Sharp and good but bad." She strung words together in a loose yet understandable sentence.

With a nod, I bit at her pulse. Her back arched as she groaned, her hands flying up. They settled on my shoulders. I let her free to sooth the bite with kisses. I did it again, right under her jaw and sucked lightly. Her hands gripped tighter, her fingernails – silver like that first night – dug into my skin while her hips jerked against mine.

"Teddy. That's – no more."

For the moment, I backed off to press a kiss on her lips. "All right, princess," I murmured, having moved back just enough to say it. The next time I drew her in while I leaned back. Hand still in her hand, I brought Eva with me. The kiss was slow to keep her occupied while my free hand swept over her back. I noted that in random places, Eva would twitch or moaned into the kiss.

That was new.

We stayed like that, stuck in the holding pattern of kissing and my hand finding sensitive spots along her back. She seemed able to deal with that. At least until I lightly raked my nails over a random spot. Then her hips rolled, her back curled against my hand. Twice she broke the kiss.

I kept at it until Eva was rolling her hips along the length of my cock – and she was doing it purposefully. Her kiss changed when her movements did. Instead of running from me and letting me dictate the kiss, her tongue slipped into my mouth. It was fascinating, that brief show of aggression.

As a reply, I pressed my nails into the latest hot spot, and her nails dragged over my shoulders. With a grin, I broke the kiss and licked my lips while I looked at her. That coral against golden brown look that I'd enjoyed so much was in full effect on her face.

"Do you really want to play that game, Eva?"

"You started it," she said, bluffing while she put up a serious front.

"Do you want me to make it hurt?" I asked. I said the words with a deliberate slowness as I brushed my lips over hers. "You know you have to answer."

Her lips pulled into a frown. Eva clearly considered it. Which I was distantly glad of. I was far more pleased, however, when she nodded and said, "Yes. A little."

"All right, princess," I flipped us over and turned her onto her stomach. "Get comfortable."

I hadn't planned on Eva's back becoming her ultimate demise. Not where that session of overstimulation was concerned. I'd thought my tongue would end up being the simultaneous loser and winner. Instead, I bit and kissed along the planes of her back. A dark bruise formed near her hip with my handprints as accompaniment. Her hips buck when I settled my lips there, and I gleefully held her down.

The same occurred just below her neck, between her shoulder blades. There was a minor difference in that she ground up against me, and I shifted into a position I could rock forward against her. Her whines, and the way she shivered as I sucked at the place I bit, prompted me into hauling her onto her knees. Her thighs were slick, the deepened brown of her summer tan shimmered with the evidence of how I affected her.

"Teddy. I don't think I can stay like this, "she said, her voice trembling just like her arms did. I smoothed a hand up her spine with a considering hum.

"Pillow your head on your arms. I'll take care of the rest, princess."

Eva dropped onto the bed with a relieved but shaky sounding sigh. Her reactions to me endlessly fascinated me. Her unwillingness to admit defeat however, was almost worrying. However, Evanna was a big girl. She could deal with what she'd agreed to.

I was aware that this wasn't kosher. That how I treated her was appalling. It didn't stop me. Knowing that just egged me on.

"Stay nice and relaxed for me," I said softly. My hands held her steady before I sank my cock into her faster than I'd ever dared. Eva shrieked as her channel spasmed around me – a protest that I ignored staying still and buried in her pussy.

"You're all right," I murmured while my fingers dug into her skin to keep her hips in place while she whimpered. "It's okay, just stay still, Eva."

It's not the last time she shrieked for me that afternoon.

~

I left Evanna passed out in my bed to meet up with the guys. This weekend had been a surprise, not that I'd complain. I hadn't adjusted my plans either.

Which was how I ended up in Oasis with my t-shirt inside out while I smelled of sex.

Richard, Kyle, and Jimmy were already seated. It made finding them easy. They were also the loudest assholes in the place. I went over and pulled out the free chair, taking a seat. I didn't wait long for someone to say something.

"Look who showed up," Kyle snipped. The irritation oozed from him. He had a look on his face, too. Scolding or something. I didn't know how his boyfriend put up with his shit.

"I unexpectedly had to entertain," I replied with a shrug. I didn't see what the big deal was in being five minutes late. The guys, however, had opinions.

"You're never late unless you've got to work," Jimmy pointed out. He tipped his beer my way, "in fact, you hate being late."

"Am I guilty of a crime, officer?" I asked with thick sarcasm. I wondered when my comings and goings got so interesting.

"Yep," Jimmy said easily. He took a swig and smirked. "Guilty of putting hos before bros."

"Oh, for fuck's sake." I leaned back in my chair with a sigh and signaled the waiter. "It's not my problem you can't get laid, Crane."

"It's your problem when pussy is more important than keeping a schedule," Kyle cut in. "*Especially* when you smell of it. If you're going to be late, wash your dick off before you get here."

"How 'bout you hop off it first," I snapped right before the server came over.

"What can I get you?" She asked, as she brushed her hair over her shoulder in a practiced movement. She'd had this v neck shirt on, Eva had one too, with 'Brunette's do It better' emblazoned on it. But the server's

42

shirt rooted for Redheads. I might've agreed if the server had bigger tits, was a few inches shorter, and far more tan. Yeah. It was like that. I wondered where Eva got the shirt. It was probably a secret purchase, or it'd come from Jasmine.

"Another round for them, please, and can I get a Sam's? Whatever seasonal is in is fine." I said and offered a smile.

She beamed; pearly whites visible for a moment before she nodded. Clearly polite customers were in short supply. While I was a dick, I wouldn't ever pull that shit on a server. Been there, done that, it was a hell I wouldn't wish on even Evanna.

"Sure thing, hon. Food for the table?" She looked around expectantly.

"Sure, the special," Rich said.

"Salad please, double down cob."

"Just the Egg Salad plate for me."

"The Bacon Burger set for me, thanks." I rounded out the table and our server disappeared.

"The Cob, Kyle? For real?" Jimmy shook his head. "When did you decide to skip out on happiness?"

"I'm not," Kyle said while he waved it off. "Worry about what *you* put in *your* mouth. Now, since she was important enough to make you wait, who is she?"

"Are you my mother now?" I asked with a snort. "Doesn't matter who she is, we get one another off, everyone's happy."

"I guarantee she's not," Richard declared. "Not a single damn woman in this tri-town area would be happy as a booty call."

"Pretty sure it's *me* who's the call here and she's the caller, but okay." I leaned back in the chair. I had the option of tuning them out. They'd have gotten the memo. It didn't take much to clue them in, not around me. I either went silent or told them to fuck off.

"Booty or Caller, she was enough for you to be smelling and looking a mess," Kyle stated, not letting it go. That had to be payback for when I interrupted him and his boyfriend that one time. That hadn't been intentional, it was irritating I had to weather a petty punishment over it.

"Fine," I snapped, right as the drinks arrived. I waited until the server disappeared again. "She's younger than us, likes me in charge. Hell, she lets me do as I please, it's good. The situation is equal, no one is in this for happily ever after. Plus, her parents fucking hate me, so dating wasn't ever in the cards. I'm just her rebellion."

"Short list," Jimmy mused. "Not a lot of women we know, younger or older have parents who hate you before they meet you. Which means this is a daughter of a family you know. What'd you do? Fuck her in her room while her parents were downstairs?"

"That was Richard with Betsy Mason three years ago," I snarked while rolling my eyes. I paused to figure out how to say Clara and Jake without using the names. "You've met my Aunt and Uncle, right?"

"Yeah."

Which was to be expected. Most people have what with the three towns funneled into the same schools from pre-k to graduation. Which made the thing with Eva all the more dangerous and gave me a bigger pay off. It'd be glorious when I claimed the kid and tarnished her. Kept her for myself.

"Okay, so this chick's parents are basically Clara and Jake. All about the perfect match for their perfect little girl. It's all about the right clothes, hair, you name it. Clara fuckin' loathes me, and Naya hates me by default." I plucked an exchange student's name from the air and congratulated myself on a lie well spun. "So when we saw each other and wanted to scratch an itch, this seemed easier. Low and behold, it is."

"Right." Kyle looked unconvinced. Jimmy however, leaped onto the mention of Clara and Jake. I should have predicted that.

"How is the fair lady Bishop-LeClair, Theo? Haven't' seen her around lately. I miss the coffee she made at the gas station up in East River. Went every morning she was scheduled." His leer made me grind my teeth together.

Some days I forgot that I wasn't the only one with eyes for Eva. I probably wasn't the first to notice Evanna was beautiful, which irked me to no end. His decision to bring her up in conversation didn't bode well for the rest of the get-together.

"Workin' at the farm, leaving for college come the middle of August," I swig at my beer to cool my temper. "So, you won't be getting coffee for a while, Jimmy. What do you even see in her?"

Continuing the conversation about Evanna was a bad idea. But I was a masochist somewhere deep in my head. I had to know how much interest Jimmy had in her. Had to know if I should've been worried.

"She's damn smart," he replied like a shot. "Fierce with that tongue of hers. She's got a pretty smile, great tits, great ass even if it's on the smaller side. Evanna's the girl you bring home to your momma, no matter the rumors circling. Cause it's well known the nuns never caught her out of bounds even once."

My mouth ran dry, so I picked up my beer to take another swig. Anger swelled in my chest. The girl you brought home to your momma. If you had one. I could see it, though. The Eva that they knew wasn't same the one that shared my bed.

Eva put on a hell of a show for the public. She got the grades, smiled when she had to, took the right after-schools, never missed a day of work, never cancelled plans. On paper, Eva was the perfect girl, set up for a picket fence suburban life.

Even though I knew how her temper could rage, having felt it and having seen her crumble under the derisive comments of family, she was still fairly perfect. She cooked well, never left a mess when she vacated my apartment to go back to the real world. Her insults were sugar sweet and cut straight to the bone when she lobbed them into a conversation, too. I didn't factor in how she was in bed with me, it didn't matter in the total sum of her character.

"On paper, she sounds great," I said. "But you ever talk to that girl?"

I had to do this. I knew that I couldn't *not* insult or demean Evanna in front of these three. Rich would've noticed immediately, and Kyle would've connected the dots too fast. Jimmy would have told everyone if I seemed to have changed my view on Eva. And the cycle would have ended at Clara, who would attack Eva over it.

Like she had every time she heard a rumor.

"Once or twice. Pulled her over a week before her graduation. She was scared out of her mind, which was a little weird until you remembered how strict her parents are. I gave her a warning, she deserved a speeding ticket, but I chatted her up a bit instead. Eva's a polite little thing, and I've heard her cuss you out six ways from Sunday."

"So, because she's polite, you'd overlook the dirty looks you'd have for havin' her on your arm?" I asked, though I knew already he'd say yes. Had I been able to, I'd have said the same. As it was, I was belligerent to anyone who slanted a judging look Eva's way. She was mine, so no one else had the right to judge her. "Can you overlook the rumors? You know they can't all be lies. Say you got her to stick with you. Kids would come up, man."

I hated myself. The words sat heavy on my tongue. But needs must. No one would get their hands on Evanna but me. She was mine, to make cry, to hear moan, to make smile.

"She's pretty light," Jimmy replied with a shrug. "Chances are her kid'd be white as lilies. Hell, she is, if you really think about it. Got her perfect diction, didn't fail out of school or a single subject. She got scholarships galore as your dad loves to brag. It doesn't matter that she's got browner skin than me, she's as far from ghetto as a girl can get. As far from hick as the girls round here can get, too."

I shook my head to keep my temper checked. Eva's a princess, a queen in the making. Jim wasn't wrong. But I wasn't sure her kids would end up ghostly pale like Jim did. Nor did I like the idea of it. Every time I closed my eyes and thought about it, our baby is as warm as Eva was. Freckles all over their little face and arms, dark hair, big curls. Like nature meshed the pair of us together perfectly.

"Whatever," I sighed. "Try her if you think you can pull her, Jim. Not sure you'd be able to, but Jake wouldn't hate you on sight if you showed up in uniform at least." That came out far more bitter than I intended. I hastily took another drink and shifted forward to lean my arms on the table.

"It never made sense to me why you hate Eva," Kyle said after a little while. "She seems like a person you'd want on your side."

"I don't need her on my side," I snap, old anger and habits reared up. I didn't need Eva or anyone who could leave me again. "She just doesn't *belong*, Kyle. Never has, never will. Now, can we talk about something other than Saint Evanna?"

"And there's the anger. Jesus. Wondered when it would show," Rich muttered before he steered the conversation to another subject. I ended up brooding for a while. Methodically I picked apart what Kyle and Jimmy said about Evanna.

She's vicious, I had the mental scars to prove it, even a couple physical ones. All given in self-defense. Eva was perfect, jaded and able to hide it better than most could. The way she'd fit into my arms, into my life was startling. I didn't know what to think or feel or do with her at that moment.

At least with the sex, we both knew how to fit together. The rest of it took a back seat, our bodies did all the talking we needed. Yet there had been several perfectly civil conversations of late. Her arrival had been announced with her anger over Clara attacking her weight. I'd *comforted* her before any clothing had come off.

The fuck.

"You wanna go bowling after we're done?"

I blinked and looked away from the bottle in my hand. "Nah," I said and shook my head. "I've got a girl in my bed, remember?"

"You *left* her there??"

I heaved a sigh to brace myself for another debate with them about my fictional sex partner. Eva alone in my apartment was hardly something to worry about. At worst I'd have returned to a neat apartment.

Never Want to See You Again

Evanna
4 July

I was so sure I had life under control. That it'd never actually happen, and the feeling strengthened as time passed. The sound of my own reassurance crumbling was the sound of tinkling glass on asphalt. Delicate glass, like holiday ornaments. Shattered on impact. That's what I heard as I felt my life shatter because of the test.

It had to be wrong.

"I've got a second," I said, dazed. Muscle memory let me rip the second open to stick it in the disposable cup. I'd read somewhere that the best readings came in the morning. The article talked about hormones accumulating overnight or whatever. It'd changed the way I took pregnancy tests. Not that I needed them often.

One other scare.

And this was just a scare, I reasoned. My fingers pulled the test from the cup after it's recommended soak time and capped it. How that was the peak of feminine testing eluded me. The test was set on the counter carefully. I made sure it was flat, then I had two minutes. In just two minutes I'd know if my fate was sealed or if I'd needed more tests.

I was almost irrationally glad that Grand-Mère and Grand-Père didn't check the trash.

Just that thought had me lean my head against the counter. One sucked in, ragged breath didn't calm me. My family was so fucked. My leg bounced as I waited. I straightened, trashed the cup and contents, washed my hands, brushed my teeth and fiddled with my hair to distract myself from watching the clock. Teddy'd had the idea of spending the night in the little barn. To everyone else, it was coincidence. He said he wanted to be in West River for the carnival that weekend at the East River-Wercen fairgrounds. I'd been 'too tired' to drive myself home. Innocent.

Everything was innocent between us.

Teddy'd already put the sheets in the washer. Earlier I'd opened the windows instead of putting on the AC unit. I wanted to keep my grandparents electric bill down. He wanted to relieve Grand-Mère of an extra chore. We were just a pair of mostly good kids doing mostly good things for their grandparents.

"Eva, you good?" Teddy called from beyond the door.

I panicked. I'm not proud of my mad scramble for the tests. But it was a knee jerk reaction.

"Yeah. Yeah, I'm fine. I just need a bit – I'm sore." I said a little louder than necessary. Which wasn't a lie. It just wasn't why I was still sequestered in the bathroom. I checked the test with a glance. Then another. Pregnant flashed at me from the small digital screen.

My heart plummeted as my blood ran cold. This is what Theo wanted. In full transparency, I wanted that too. But as I looked at the proof, my mind screamed to a halt. It'd been a month and a half. Theo got his way in under sixty days.

I wanted to vomit.

My stomach rolled as if answering that thought. Cold sweat broke out along my arms, along the back of my neck and forehead. Theodore had told me he wanted this so he could ruin me. Sleeping with me was his road to making sure no one would want me. The implications hit me like bricks then.

I could…

This could go away. I was eighteen, I was of age, no one had to know.

That was the thought that sent me to my knees with the toilet seat clacking against the tank. I hated that feeling. I always had. That ruined a six-year streak of not allowing myself to become physically ill. My throat burned. The way I fought against it was instinctual, but I couldn't keep my body from seizing. Not even when there was nothing left.

I coughed, spit twice and flushed before I dragged myself back to the sink. The water turned on as if by magic and I brushed my teeth a second time. I didn't even see myself; I just stared into the abyss. Next month I was set to leave. I'd finally broken it to my parents I'd registered and signed up for my classes. It had been stressful. Dad was pleased. Mom seemed…fine? It'd been harder to read her.

Frothy after effect rinsed down the drain from my mouth and off the brush. The click of the faucet seemed so final as the water stopped. It was like a door closed. I supposed a door was closing.

But it didn't matter. I wasn't staying there. The plan was still in effect. I was leaving and I'd adjust on the fly. My child would be in my life. It'd happen and I wouldn't allow myself to be Jasmine. Hell would've frozen over first. So, I needed to adjust the plan. It needed to be set before I left.

"Fuck," I whispered and looked at the door. Should I tell him, I wondered. Did I give Theo his victory? No, I decided. I couldn't.

The door swung open a few seconds later, tests hidden. Theo waited for me beside the exit. His eyes slid over me twice. Things had shifted between us, Theo's looks were heavier, like his hands were whenever they slid against my skin. The level of difficulty that had developed around not touching him casually was staggering.

Another reason I was set on leaving. Theodore and I – we wouldn't make it in the long term. Our families would've shit kittens if we came out to them. A relationship would've started a feud. Mom wouldn't have forgiven Theo for 'corrupting' me. She'd have stopped going to the Farmhouse and Dad would follow her lead. The prospect wasn't pleasant.

"Are you sure you're good, princess?" Theo asked, his voice jarred me out of my spiral.

"Yeah," I said, allowing a smile onto my lips. "I'm fine, Teddy. Sorry, but I didn't get a lot of sleep, y'know."

It'd become so easy to tease him. I shook my head, both to clear it and set my mask in place for the day. Which Theo seemed to pick up on immediately.

"Ready to act like you're only putting up with me for the family's sake?" He asked, rather than try to anticipate my answer. I thanked whatever Saint claimed responsibility for him dropping the other subject.

"Only if you're ready to restrain yourself from punching anyone that approaches me," I replied while I tossed my ponytail dramatically. Theo grimaced and I grinned. We both had *significant* weaknesses surrounding our entanglement. His were so much worse than mine.

"I guess," Theo said finally.

"Good."

With a nod, I edged past him to open the door. He caught me around the middle to stop me from leaving. I looked at him in question.

"You look great, princess." His thumb rubbed against my hip as he leaned down, stealing a kiss. It was sweet. And I didn't know how to deal with it. "We should stay here."

I snorted and shook my head. "Thanks, Teddy. That wouldn't be obvious or anything."

I shifted and he held me tighter. He actually pulled me up against his body. My hand dropped from the door handle in favor of his chest while a flustered sound left my mouth.

"Then we go to my apartment," Teddy murmured, his eyes having dropped to my mouth. "Your parents won't know. No one will care. We can watch movies or some shit, and I can fuck you on the couch again. You liked it so much last time. I want to hear those moans again, princess."

"Teddy," I laughed softly. "We've been having sex nearly every day. We said we were going to East Run, so we're going."

"Fine, princess."

Theo lifted me up, that kiss longer. It almost made me change my mind. Would it *really* be so bad if I snuck off to his apartment? Would anyone have noticed? In the end, we left the loft together and took our separate cars to the East River-Wercen fairgrounds.

~

"Eva!" Cordelia Cooper called out to me the moment I got out of my car. I had fifteen seconds to find her before she tackled me against it. It was a close call.

"Hey Cordi," I replied and waved to her.

"You look great," she said in a bright tone. Her deceptively thin arms wrapped around me in a hug. "Total summer glow, babe. Come walk with the Cheer team today."

"Cordelia, I graduated. You did too. We can't walk with them," I replied with a soft laugh. She got a gentle squeeze before I removed myself from the embrace. Much as I loved Cordelia, personal space wasn't her strong suit.

"So what? It'll be fun, and way better than sitting on curbs and catching crappy candy. Dawn is here and she's walking too." Cordelia was already producing a bow from her waist pack. The black, gold, and blue colors of our High School caught the light.

"Always prepared," I sighed and held out my hand. "Sure. Whatever. Let's find Dawn and be active."

"We also need you in a shirt," Cordelia crowed. She had a glint in her eyes. That was the fire of spirit week. When school spirit was involved, Cordelia'd always been extra.

"Sure, sure. Remember, we've got to accommodate the boobs. Your clothes are too small for me," I said it for the sake of my sanity and a few precious moments of harmony. My house had been insane lately. So

Cordelia had better have a shirt that fit me. Not fit me like I wanted it to fit, but the fit my mother would have approved of. *Loose.*

"Don't worry about it. Come on."

I let Cordelia drag me to the bathroom. Her backpack was retrieved along the way. My suspicion that she'd planned this were proven right. To my horror, the shirt she produced is one that I would've worn to practice. It hugged *all* of me. Which made me feel nauseous all over again. Mom was going to *murder* me.

"Cordi, come on. Please say you've got a bigger one," I pleaded. I plucked at the material stretched over my chest to illustrate my need.

"Sorry. Your mom will have to deal, Eva. She survived three years of cheerleading and volleyball without dropping dead. She'll survive this too." Cordi's reply was dismissive. Super. Mom survived my clothing, but did I survive her?

"You look hot, by the way," she threw out as we weaved through the crowd. The plan to locate the others was in motion. "Very sun-kissed glow, not that frosty glow. Thank fuck, you never liked that trend anyway. It would've been heinous on you."

"Thanks Cordelia," I said, eyes rolling at that backhanded compliment. "I've worked at the farm all summer. There are benefits to it – tanned and toned, obviously."

"Oh." Her voice pitched curiously. "You're working at the farm? Does your cousin still work there? I remember you mentioning him a few times."

My eyes slanted toward her as I felt myself stiffen. "Yes," I answered slowly and attempted to push off a sudden tightness in my chest. "Theo still works at the farm, too. He's a dick, but he doesn't abandon the rest of the family."

"He's so hot," Cordi sighed. "It sucks he's such an ass. I'd love to give him a ride. But he told Chris that rumor about you."

That stopped me in my tracks. Over the years, I'd heard a lot of rumors. The ones in my last couple years of High School had been the worst. My throat felt like it was closing. "Which rumor?"

"Oh," she stopped too, blonde hair shifting as she faced me. "It was the one where you were sleeping with our old homeroom teacher. Definitely not the worst of them. I still can't believe *anyone* believed them, ya know? You were the teacher's pet. The whitest Black girl I know." Cordelia laughed while I felt like I should've turned around. Maybe Theo'd been right? We should've just gone to the apartment.

I hated when people did that. The 'whitest Black girl' or 'I'm so tan, I'm almost as dark as you!' People who said that shit drove me mad. Like, what did they want exactly? I could only be what my mother raised me as. It wasn't like we had a lot of people in these damned downs. Even fewer families had melanin or cultures not derived from Europe.

I was just *me*.

"Mister Marks?" I squeaked in question. "Theodore said I was sleeping with *Mister Marks*?! God, what the fuck? That's so screwed. Theodore could have gotten Mister M. into serious shit with that."

"But he didn't," Cordelia replied with a sly smile. For a second, I forgot why we were friends. With friends like her did I need an enemy like Theo? "You were *extra* popular, too, remember?"

I wondered how *that* even fucking mattered. Who cared about popularity in the face of the rumor that could have ruined a life?? In that moment I forgot why Cordelia and I were friends. But blessedly, Cordelia deserted me the moment we found the team and former members. The reprieve allowed me to breathe and greet Dawn who pounced when she spotted me.

We spent the next hour walking. We went through old routines with near effortlessness. My stomach protested, but I kept a smile plastered on my face. I didn't look for anyone I knew; I just kept my eyes forward. Every step I took was one closer to freedom from this terrible idea.

~

I heard Theo before I saw him while wandering the East River-Wercen fair. I'd almost convinced myself to try and find him when what he said hits me. Between Cordelia, the parade, the test and that, I was done. It hurt too much.

"Hey, LeClair. Your cousin was lookin' hot today. Did you see her do those flips? You think she's hot for older guys, for real? I mean, I've heard she's easy, but rumors are rumors." It was a voice I didn't recognize speaking. Not that that mattered. Apparently, I was *still* the talk of the town. I never understood it, I'd slept with *two* people by hetero standards, and suddenly I was the town fucking bicycle.

"She's not my cousin, one. Two, maybe, I don't know. Evanna has daddy issues four miles wide, man. I don't get why all of you are hot for her. She's chubby and mouthy." That was *Theo*. My hands pressed against my abdomen as I stood and listened. If I was fat, it was *his* goddamn fault.

"She's *thick* not *fat*. Soft in all the right places. You know? She'll be easy to hold while railing. I mean, fuck, did you see her shirt and shorts today? That damn ponytail swishing while she walked, too. Eva's a walking 'come fuck me' ad."

"Fuck off," Theo said gruffly. I didn't have an ounce of hope that he'd defend me. "She's a slut. If I were you, I'd keep my dick to myself. I heard she fucked a teacher before I graduated."

"So? There are *four* teachers in this district who married their students right after graduation. All I'm hearing is that if I bag her, I'll have a great time."

God, I hated people. I hated that conversations like this were just part of life. Careful not to make noise, I moved to lean against the stall. Figured I might as well hear what Theodore thought of me, since I was engaging in an exercise in emotional masochism.

"Will you though? That kid, Kelly? He said she likes it bare. She's probably got STIs." Theodore sounded more bewildered than disgusted. While I felt lost. My lungs wouldn't work. Stupidly I'd thought I could handle whatever Theo dished out. I couldn't. I wanted to run the hell away, but I was frozen in place.

"Whatever," his friend scoffed. "If she wasn't clean, we'd already know. This town loves gossip, especially about the hot Black girl. Considering we've got three total, it's easy to keep track of who's who. Plus, if she's been going bare this long, she's useless for kids."

"I wouldn't know," Theo replied. His tone was low, threatening. I knew that tone, but clearly that friend didn't. And it wasn't my problem.

"Damn. At least if she'd have tried for you, you could really call her a slut. If she's got the standards to keep it out of the family, I'd say she's more discerning than she's given credit for."

Gee, Thanks. What a great compliment.

"Who the fuck cares. You want to bone her, right? So, find Eva. Butter her up, see if you get a pity ride. I don't fucking *care*, Peter." Theo's voice raised and I sprung away from where I'd been leaning.

After I'd moved, it was easy to keep going. I didn't stop walking until I was at the farthest booths on the grounds. The section where trees were trying to reclaim the space. I hid there looking at art and shirts.

Hours later, I figured I could start back. In the low light I navigated the shitty trail carefully and nearly screamed when I was dragged from the path into a dark copse of trees. I flailed and slapped at whoever had hold of me. The day wouldn't get worse, I swore to myself I wouldn't let that happen.

"Fuck's sake, Evanna. Stop it," Theo said, a growl in his tone that made me freeze. "What's wrong with you?"

"Nothing," I blurted. "I'm fine. You're the asshole who grabbed me like a damn serial killer. What do you want, Theodore?"

I wrenched myself free of his grasp and turned to look at him. It was quiet for a while before he sidled up to me. His hands found and followed the path of my waist with a familiarity that made my heart squeeze. He smiled the smile that was mine. A little soft, half-cocked with one dimple showing. It was amazing at helping me to convince myself of the lie. Like thinking that smile was mine.

"Obviously I want *you*, baby." He lifted a hand and wrapped my ponytail around it. My teeth dug into my lip while I fought the urge to cry. How could he try to seduce me after saying all the shit he had? Was Theo just incapable of feeling guilt?

"You up for it, princess? I'll go easy on you so we can be quiet." Theo leaned over me, close enough I smelled the beer on him. It wasn't strong, but evident all the same. Enough that it made him turn back into a heartless asshole.

"No. I don't feel well," I snapped and pulled free again. My hand lashes out and slapped at his. "Go eat and go home, Theodore."

He scowled at me. Theodore had the sheer audacity to *scowl* at me. I wanted to shout at him that I'd heard him. I wanted to cry over it. God, I wanted to scream at him we were done, and why. I couldn't do any of that. I knew I had to keep the recent revelation to myself.

"What's wrong with you? You *always* want me. You've been fucking weird all day, Eva." Theo was irritated, it was painted on his face, confusion mounting and softening the black look on his face. The longer we stood there, the more I wanted to be gone.

"Nothing is fucking *wrong* with me, you dick. Go find someone who actually wants to fuck you tonight. It won't be me," I said, voice venomous as I started to turn. I was ready to make good on my desire.

Theodore's arms hooked around my middle and dragged me back against him before I'd gone five steps. I growled, clawing at his arms while I mentally told him to screw off. Him and his stupidly long arms.

"Go find *who* now?" he asked while looming over me. In the dark, with his tone so low, threatening, it was too familiar. My heart sped up as my mouth ran dry. Flight kicked in as the fight drained out of me. His arms retreated, and I went to bolt, only for one hand to return, pressed against my stomach. I could feel how he wrapped his hand in my hair again. One hard pull and I turned, another and I was forced to look up at him. His other hand hadn't left. It was just pressed against the small of my back.

"I want to fuck you, princess. Why would I find someone else when you're right here? Why would I waste my time on someone random when I'm meant to be working on knocking you up?" Theo said it in such a blasé manner that it immediately rang false. He threw my words back at me.

We stood too close, with his mouth hovering over mine. The scent of the beer he'd drank made my stomach turn dangerously. Before I had the chance to make a retort, witty or bitchy, his mouth was on mine. His tongue forced its way to meet mine.

Ironically, the taste of the beer didn't bother me.

While I froze, he turned us and backed me up against a tree. I would have liked to say the only reason he got me lifted and my legs around his waist was because I couldn't stay mad. That wasn't true. It was a damn mystery, but it happened.

Angry, I tried to bruise his mouth. But the second Theodore settled against me, leaving me trapped against the tree, my body took over. I hated myself for it. We fit together well, he and I. Our bodies were well aware of that, conditioned to respond eagerly. I could feel him hardening, my arousal echoed his as he kept on kissing me.

When the kiss ended, I was panting, squirming angrily as he held me. I was even angrier then. Hissing and spitting like I was a bag of wet cats. *Damn him*, I thought. Theodore doesn't get to turn me on, to use me, and brag about his newest whore. Not from that point forward. I wasn't blind anymore.

"I'm—"

"Shut up, princess." Theo ground out the words and caught me by the chin. "Let's make something clear, Evanna. Until you're pregnant, the *only* cunt I fuck is yours. The only man you fuck is me. You're mine, Eva. You should know that by know."

I was his. But he wasn't mine. That was all I heard. He was aggressive that day and didn't give me a chance to cut back at him. Another forceful kiss left one of us bleeding. I couldn't tell who until he pulled away. I licked at my lips to find I was free of a split. *Good*, I thought viciously.

"I'm going to be sick," I said finally. Theodore put me down as if I scalded him. I was so angry, happy, and confused simultaneously. Because he cared and yet was still a dick. At least I was free from his hold.

"I'm not your whore, Theodore," I hissed, watching as his face clouded with confusion. "For the record, I'm not a slut, either. You're the *second* person I've slept with. And if you weren't, it's no one's business but *mine*," I said as I stomped on his foot. My heart thudded in my chest like a hummingbird's wings.

That said, I turned and sprinted away. The tension in my shoulders eased as I heard his swearing fade into the background of far louder sounds. I was confident in my escape once I was bathed in multicolored light. Theo wouldn't come after me. He wouldn't try to catch me where anyone could see us. I was his secret, after all. He couldn't let it get out that he was close to me.

I ignored the few people who said hello as I headed for my car. It was time to sleep. Honestly, it would be relief to be home after the day had ended. Between the test, parade, and confrontation, I was worn out. Or, it *should* have been a relief. When I closed the garage, likely just a few minutes behind my parents, I was greeted by an ominously quiet house.

Immediately, I went on high alert. My heart sped up once again. Frozen, I took a minute to get my shoes off. I adjusted the bag on my shoulder as I swallowed.

There were two, perhaps three paths there. The first, no one bothered me. I put away my things, possibly even got ready for bed before Mom sprung her accusations and lectures on me. The second, my foot would hit the top stair and then the Inquisition began. Then, the last, that by the grace of God, Mom wouldn't be mad at all.

I had to work the next day. If I stayed up late to defend myself I'd be exhausted. It wasn't on my priority list, though that had been rather skewed. While I mounted and climbed the stairs, I prayed for option three. Manifesting was supposed to work so I'd heard.

"Evanna."

Fuck seared across my consciousness.

"Hi, Mom," I said cheerily, as if nothing was wrong. "Did you have fun at the fair and parade? Cordelia roped me into walking for the team. I'm dead on my feet."

My feet kept moving. One step after another while I chanced a glance around to find my mother. My heart dropped to find her in the living room. She was in her favorite chair, without tea, and not a book in sight.

She hadn't even changed into comfortable clothes. I knew then that this was going to be bad. Mentally, I was already crying irritated tears. I was too tired for this. I might've been able to weather it had I slept normally. Instead, I was running on a few hours of sleep and even less food. Fumes. I was working with fumes.

"Want me to make some tea? I just need to put this stuff away first," I said as I stopped beside the archway leading to the common room. My hands stayed clear of the walls, knowing they dirtied incredibly easily.

"No. I want to speak to you, Evanna," Mom said, her tone flat.

My walls went up, slammed into place. I forced myself to act as if I wasn't aware I was about to be berated. The real trial was to not tense up. It was something incredibly difficult to do and it was still my best coping mechanism.

"Oh. Okay, sure. Give me five?" I asked as I observed her carefully. I could only hope she'd not had the time to work herself up.

"Sit. Down."

My stomach dropped and I did it. My ass hit the nearest chair while my bag was sat between my feet. When a storm was about to hit, we'd all learned it was best to just do as Mom said. There was less chance of making it worse that way. That was at the top of our *Rules of Engagement*. Do what she said. Nod when she asked if you were paying attention. Answer only when actually asked a question. All your answers must thread truth into the lie if you had to lie. Don't let her see you get upset. Hold back the tears as long as you could.

All families had rules like that, right?

"Why were you wearing that shirt today? You looked like a hussy in front of the whole town, Evanna," she said, starting off hot while she made herself sound so damn reasonable. That I hated most of all.

"Cordelia roped me into the parade, like I said. They needed people and I still have friends on the team. She gave me the shirt. I asked her for something bigger, but she had nothing. No one did. This is what I had, so I worked with it," I replied softly.

The best part of this was Mom wouldn't go investigate any of this. There wouldn't be any verification process. There wasn't any chance of me winning. When Mom lectured or yelled, you *always* lost.

"You didn't tell me or your father you were walking the parade. Your shorts were inappropriate, shoes dirty, your hair was a mess!" Mom started the list and ignored what I'd said.

With my teeth grit, I took a breath in an attempt to compose myself. If I could have diffused this, this would've been my best chance to cut it off at the pass. "I'm sorry, mom. The shorts are ones you purchased for school, that met the dress code. So, I thought they'd be fine. I wasn't expecting to walk, so I just wore my comfortable sneakers."

Mom sucked at her teeth and scoffed. "Of course, they're inappropriate. You've gained weight, Evanna. Just look at yourself, rolls everywhere. You keep dressing as if you're slim. You're just a tub of lard," she said, the bite of her words made me flinch.

She also sent me careening into a panic. I supposed I was gaining weight. Pregnancy did that.

Oh. I thought, *Oh fuck. God, I'm pregnant. Mom would murder me if she found out.*

"I'm sorry, mom," I whispered in desperation. This was the worst night for a fight. Of all the days, I'd been so twisted and wrecked already. So, I just kept trying to cut if off before it got worse.

"Stop lying," she hissed while she leaned forward in her chair. "You aren't *sorry,* you wouldn't do this shit if you were. We've had this conversation frequently, Evanna. From the refusal to attend Weight Watchers, to you never being home. Now you've decided to leave the state and go to college early! You treat this house as if it's a hotel. Is it a hotel? Should I be charging you for each night you sleep here? Do you even enjoy this home? The one that we built *for you.*"

"Of course not! This isn't a hotel, Mom, I know that. I'm trying to do everything possible to reduce my tuition bill. My clothes all fit; nothing is too tight. I swear I haven't been wearing anything revealing outside of what happened today. I didn't have any choice. You taught me not to ignore my commitments. I thought you'd be happy I made a choice." I leaned forward to rest my elbows on my knees while I rubbed my face.

"You're going out of state, where you'll have *no one.* What happens when you dress this way and someone takes what you're offering, hm? Well? What then, Evanna? You won't even have the family priest to speak to." She said, riled up. When she stood and came toward me, I tensed, knowing what would happen next. "Your clothes *do not* fucking fit. None of them do! You never wear what's appropriate, either. People keep *looking* at you."

Fuck, fucking shit, I thought in a panic. I was panicked for a different reason then, because she'd fixated on my weight. She'd try to grab my stomach, my hips, any place she thought should be thin and I couldn't lose weight. It was what she'd always done. But now... I couldn't keep myself from spiraling. My head pounded; my vision narrowed to only see her. I popped up off the chair and thrust my hands out in front of me.

"Mom, don't. This is ridiculous. You buy all my clothes or you approve of what I bring home! I work, I come home, I do nothing without telling you first. I'll be fine in college. If something were to happen, I'd call you or Ollie immediately. Where is this coming from?"

"Don't you tell me what to do," Mom hissed. My blood rushed loudly in my ears. This same exact shit happened every time I stood up for myself. Unique moments played on loop in my mind. The argument over taking pills from her purse. I hadn't, but I got blamed for it. Then the talk about appropriate behavior when I had a meltdown in class because my friends had abandoned me over a weekend sleep over. They spent three days telling me they weren't there for me. But the most vivid memories came from me saying 'don't' to her.

"Mom, don't grab me, then. I don't do it to you. Please, don't do it to me," I said, doing my best to appear reasonable, like the adult she wanted me to be.

"If you weren't fat and lazy, acting like a slut in public, then I wouldn't need to!" Mom snapped at me. In the same moment she reached out and slapped at my side. It didn't hurt me, but it was inappropriate. I couldn't name all the ways it was fucked.

"What? What the *hell*." My eyes stung while I shook my head. "I don't even have a boyfriend, mother. I haven't been flirting with random people, either. Can you please not hit me?"

I wondered if other girls from the team had to ask their parents things like that. Were they pinched, prodded, grabbed, or slapped while being told they were ugly and fat? Part of me hoped I wasn't alone, and part hoped no one else had to deal with that.

"Francis Long asked me today what we'd do about your promiscuity while you're off at college, Evanna. Clearly, you're doing something." She lashed out again, and that time I dodged it only to smack against the wall in my haste.

"Oh, fuck no, Mom. *No*. You *know* that's bullshit! There've been hundreds of rumors. How many of them had any truth? Did the nuns *ever* say that I was anything like the rumors implied? None of them were true. None of the nuns could say something like that, because it would be a *lie*. That hasn't changed. It's why I can't leave fast enough." I raised my voice to stop her endless rant. It needed to stop, right then.

But my heart stopped beating. That was against the rules. Don't interrupt her, don't push back. Agree, apologize, 'do better', keep your chin up, keep moving on. Her hand wrapped around my wrist while I fought the shock of what I'd done. It allowed her to drag me into my bathroom.

Clara pulled the scale out from where I kept it under my laundry basket. It's slapped onto the floor in front of me. I stared at it, wishing it would just spring apart.

"Get on it."

"No."

"Get on the fucking scale, Evanna!" Her hand tightened until her knuckles turned white and I swore I heard bones grind.

"No!" I snapped and swiped away the tears that fell. "I'm not fat, mother! Just listen to me, please."

"You do not dictate how this house works! This is *my house*. You're my daughter, and my rules are in place for a reason. If you want to end up fat, alone, without a family because you ran off, fine. Be *exactly* like Jasmine. Emulate your *worthless, hopeless birthmother*. I wash my hands of you," she said while predictably going for the softest spot I had. Her eyes gleamed, triumph in the blue depths that reminded me of ice. They were usually so warm, like the sky. For some reason I just… snapped.

"Don't compare me to my fucking sister!" I shrieked. My arm pulled away from her as I went a little insane. "Mom, I am not Jasmine. I will never be my birthmother, so stop. Just stop. I'm leaving in a month. I don't want us to be at war when I leave, but I won't let you walk all over me anymore."

"You aren't leaving," her icy response cracked the little sense I'd held onto. "You're not going to that university. Spoiled, entitled… You're an *ungrateful* little bitch. No, you'll stay here. I'll enroll you in the community college. Which you'll attend and feel *lucky* for."

Clara could do anything about my enrollment. At least, I hoped not. I'd done all the paperwork in my own name.

Shit. God damn it. Fuck, I thought while I stared at her silently for several beats. Real Evanna had taken over. There was no way this ended anyway but poorly. I wondered if I even cared at that point.

"I am leaving in a month; you can't stop me. I'm leaving for the night and you won't stop that either." I interrupted softly while Clara compared me to Jasmine again. It was her favorite bullet in her arsenal. Do you want to end up like your sister? Is Jasmine happy as she is? Do you want to be Jasmine? Fuck. Add in the threats and the scene was so unreal I couldn't truly believe it happened.

I whirled around and made for the kitchen. My bag was still by the chair, so I snatched it up. I returned to my room and dumped out my dirty clothes to deal with later, cramming new ones into it. I didn't pay attention to what I was grabbing. It was all done at random. I stuffed all my paperwork from the college into the bag too. I didn't trust her – especially not with anything university related.

As I left my room, Mom came out of the bathroom. My keys and phone were in my pocket, I was safe to leave. So I did, without a word.

Even as I rushed through the house and shoved my feet into shoes, I couldn't believe I was doing it. As the door wrenched open and I wrenched it shut pausing only to lock it behind me and stall her – it was incredible. I didn't know where I'd found the gall to dare do it. My hands shook as I started my car. I was still shaking as I pulled out of the driveway. I kept waiting on her or Dad to barrel out of the house. It wasn't until I was on the main road I tried to calm down.

Tonight, I'd given myself respite. Tomorrow was a battle on which I couldn't focus.

"A month," I whispered. "Thirty days, I can make it. No. I've *got* to make it." That became my mantra and kept me from pulling over to bawl my eyes out. The words changed when I pulled into Theodore's guest parking space.

"He's using you – so use him. Thirty days and it's done."

The choice to show up at Theodore's apartment unannounced was as stupid that night as it had been every other time I did it that summer. But all of this was idiotic. I'd grabbed my bag, stuffed it with clothing, and left my house while driving like I was a *NASCAR* driver. I'd been a fool. The summer wasn't going to end peacefully, it never could have.

I leaned my head against my steering wheel.

"What am I doing?" I asked the air. Never. Never in my life had I pushed my mother like I did an hour ago. That my default hiding place was Theodore's fucking apartment was more telling than I wanted. But I was there. I hauled myself from the car, grabbed my bag, and traipsed up the stairs to knock on his door.

"Eva?" he said as he opened the door, a scowl in place. "What do you want."

"Can I come in, Theo?" My voice cracked, and I hated it. There was no reason to keep crying. It wasn't a big deal; the fight hadn't been that bad. I was fine, it was fine. I could do this. A month and change. I had to hide it from Mom, from Theo. I just had to hide and survive until August.

"Princess, what happened?"

"Let me in or tell me to fuck off," I snapped, finally looking up at him.

Theodore's face was this mask of irritation and worry. It wasn't one I recognized. However, it also didn't matter. Teddy heaved a breath before he moved aside to let me in. I kicked off my shoes and dropped my bag on top of them once in the door. Usually, I'd put my stuff in his room. I couldn't do it after what happened. His hands took hold of me. I let myself be turned to face him, I was just too tired to fight.

"Gonna clue me in, or what?" Teddy said. The tone was a dare, a demand.

"Clara and I got into it," I replied tiredly. My hands wrung together as I tilted my head back, trying to clearly recall what had happened. Honestly, my mind was a mess. The fight was already starting to blur. "End up like Jasmine. Fat and ungrateful. Using the house like a hotel. Dressing like a whore – take your pick. There's another rumor, apparently. Clara wants to pull me from Uni. She threatened it, so I took my paperwork and I left. I don't trust her."

I dropped my head and looked at Theo. His eyes were wide before they narrowed dangerously. I didn't understand him at all.

"She said you were like jasmine—"

"Said I was being a hussy," I cut him off. Tired as I was, my anger shifted to pain.

Even with the Theo thing, I'd been trying *so hard* to do what was expected. When Theo wasn't around, I was perfect. I'd always strove to be exactly what my mother wanted. Never a silly child, older than my years, an old soul. It was all bullshit.

"My shirt made me look like a slut," I flicked my eyes to his while I spoke. "What's hilarious is I heard some random talking about me. He wants to fuck me, which was weird. Apparently, I'm *safe*. Being one of three black girls in the area, it's easy to keep track of us. Who has an STI and who's fucking safe. As if we're tagged fucking cattle," I whispered, not able to raise my voice.

Theodore flinched. Good, he should have.

"Eva."

"I don't know why I came. You're just as bad as Clara," I laughed mirthlessly, and it was a touch hysterical. "You both love to tear me to pieces. It's like your god damned calling. At least Mom does it to my face…"

"Evanna!" he yelled and I jerked back away from him. My teeth clacked together so hard they vibrated.

"I can't defend you in public," Theo said slowly. "But I also can't be quiet while people around me talk about you. They'd see it as out of character."

"Fuck your character," I snarled instantly. I lashed out carelessly. "Your character is awful, Theodore. It's a joke. Just like us. We're a joke. It's all a big, hilarious, fucking *joke*."

My teeth bit into my lip and I turned away. I had to, to keep from screaming at him, *Being pregnant with your child is the cosmic joke.*

"What should I do, Eva? You want me to punch the assholes who want you? Because I will? I'll fight Clara on your behalf, too. Fuck, I'll move you in with me if you want me to," Theo offered, using a wheedling tone. It was an obvious attempt to calm me down.

"Be a decent human to me," I barked at him. My chest heaved as I took a breath. I closed my eyes while I started to re-bottle my rage. "I don't have anywhere else to go, so I'm staying."

Theo letting me stay the night was the *least* he could do. Literally, the bottom of the decency barrel. Which should've made it easy for him.

"Go shower, get changed, princess," Theo said with a sigh. It was a little like he deflated. "I'll make that tea you drink after a nightmare."

God. What the fuck did I think I was doing?

Yours. Baby, I'm Yours.

Theodore
17 July

To say I was pissed would've been mild. Evanna had been avoiding me. Oh, I saw her, she'd come to work and stuck mostly to garden duty. She'd come just late enough to miss working in the barn. We didn't speak, either.

That was a lie. I spoke – at her, around her, all to try and get her to fucking speak to me. It'd been nearly two weeks, *weeks*, since I'd touched Eva, kissed her, laughed with her. I hadn't realized I enjoyed her company so much. Truly enjoyed it.

Sex was a given with us. We were always on one another. There'd been a single mishap between us, but it wasn't worth mentioning. It was why Eva refused to come near me when I'd been drinking. My pride had been shredded that night. Not that it mattered, ultimately.

She was mad that I had to be myself in public to keep us secret. Mad I dared to touch her after I had a beer, and mad she ran straight into my arms when her mother was a bitch to her. There was a lot of Eva being upset. But I was only responsible for a single day of events. Had I not been hellbent on making that woman mine, I'd have washed my hands of her. The fruitfulness of my attempts to get her pregnant were like guessing the status of Schrodinger's damn cat.

That day, however, she was mine. Eva would end up in my apartment or truck even if I had to tie her up. We worked Friday, but it had been just myself, my dad, and a new temporary farmhand. So, I turned to social media to track her. In the end, it was her away message on one of her messenger platforms that gave me a lead.

Solo movie night at the Old Cinema! Let the popcorn flow. Xoxoxox

Which was how I found myself at the old cinema. According to Gramps, the Orpheum had been open all the way back in the nineteen-teens. It had gotten a few facelifts since. But it still sported gold velvet seats with brown, not-quite shag, but certainly not berbere carpet from before it shut down after the gas shortage. It smelled old, even though it'd been about eight years since the last extensive restoration project.

Why they didn't remove the velvet, I didn't know. Reupholstery was a skill several businesses could have donated. The lobby had been completely restored to its original coming-into-the-roaring-twenties aesthetic. Which I loved about that place. The geometric designs in the lobby appealed to me.

It wasn't difficult to know where Evanna was, thanks to the fact Orpheum only ever did single showings. One twenty-dollar ticket for a double feature of *the Mummy* and *the Mummy Returns*, a cup of Ice, and I walked into the only screening room. I was surprised there weren't more people there. These movies had been fairly popular. Returns wasn't even that old. I wasn't complaining, though. There were just two other people there besides Evanna. The beginning title was just rolling, so I was afforded a few hours.

Evanna had chosen the very backrow. That, I had expected. She spotted me right as I walked into the row, stared at me until I plopped down beside her. The seat creaked in protest, but I didn't give it much thought. Instead, I moved the arm rest from between us, and neatly hauled Evanna over against me with an arm around her waist.

"Princess."

"Theodore," she whispered tersely. She sat ramrod straight against my side. "What the fuck?"

"Well, someone's been avoiding me," I replied.

"If you hadn't been an ass, I wouldn't be avoiding you," she growled like a kitten and tugged, trying to get free. I pulled her closer.

Not happening tonight, princess. I thought to myself as I hauled her onto my lap. *We're talking.*

"As I recall, you also showed up to the apartment in tears. I apologized after I let you in and you showered. Or did I hallucinate that?" My eyes took her in greedily, noting her hair was up in a messy bun, and she'd worn shorts she'd have reserved for her cheer or volleyball practices.

"*Super.* I'm still mad." Was her brilliant response.

I rolled my eyes and shifted both of my hands so they slipped under the hem of her shirt. She was warm, soft, *mine.* Eva stiffened some more, but I stayed quiet, not moving either hand. We sat in silence as I held her.

"Forgiving someone and then holding a grudge, is fucked up," I commented casually as the movie started. Was it a dick move? You bet. I was full of those.

"So is regularly sleeping with someone while calling them a slut in public. Yet you don't hear me complaining, do you?" Eva moved again like she wanted to be free, so I wrapped an arm around her waist.

"*Theo!*"

"Shh," I whispered harshly into her ear. Her back was pressed tight against my chest, her head at the perfect height to speak like this.

"We're going to talk, Evanna. This is fucking stupid. I can't tell them to leave you alone. I can't say *stop looking at her before I murder you,* either. If I did, your mother would know. Take a wild guess what Clara would do if she heard something like that."

Eva's shoulders were so stiff, I was worried they might snap. I watched her jaw work as she chewed on what I said. I knew I had a point, and she damn well knew it too. We were constantly trying *not* to be caught. All hell would have broken loose if we were. Worse if anyone caught on I'd started sleeping with her for the express purpose of *breeding* her.

"I'm sorry I hurt your feelings, princess. But you knew the score when we started this. You're not just my secret, I'm yours. Unless you've been warning people off of me? Like that girl you used to cheer with. What the fuck was her name? The airhead who always came to tell me hi like I gave a fuck." I rested my cheek on the nest of her hair while I spoke. I kept it casual, low enough the people down front couldn't have heard.

"If you have a 'but' in a sentence everything preceding it is bullshit," Eva snapped, her head shifting even as I squeezed her waist to keep her still.

"Maybe. But not right now. I *am* sorry I made you upset. There's no if, princess. Or is this whole avoidance game your way of finally telling me to fuck off? Are you done with me? You don't need my cock anymore?"

"Theo," her scandalized tone made me laugh. She sat so stiffly in my lap you'd have thought I threatened her. Even unwilling as she was, her perfume wafted around my face. That stupid ass cupcake-sweet scent. My dick didn't get the memo that the conversation was serious and got hard. It wasn't just the perfume that set me off, either. I'd walked into a bakery two days ago and experienced the most awkward as hell erection because vanilla frosting had forever been associated with having had Evanna underneath me.

"Well?" I asked as I bounced her with my legs. The grin I wore when she squealed wouldn't quit, either. "If we're done, then I have places to be."

"Fuck you, Theo," she said, making that same kitten sound as she had earlier. I lifted my head away from hers and she snapped to face me. Eva was livid, and while I'd known what that looked like for years, *this* version of angry made me want to kiss her. Someone was jealous – and I hadn't even implied those places were dates or hook ups.

"I would, princess, but you don't want me." I shrugged, and she looked at me with her mouth open. Still, she didn't say that that wasn't the end. My heart squeezed and I needed to be somewhere else.

"Got my answer, huh?" I tightened my grip on her to lift her off when her hands slapped at my chest. It got me to stop, just for a moment. When I looked at her, the tightness in my chest eased.

72

"You aren't going *anywhere* and you aren't fucking anyone but *me*," she said and didn't bother to keep her voice at a whisper. Her gaze was black, forbidding, as she looked at me. It was the hottest fucking thing I'd ever seen. I hadn't realized I wanted that, until she did it.

"Someone's possessive. Still, move. I was only here to get you to talk. I own the damn movies; I don't need to be here." Now that I knew where we stood, I didn't care about watching the movies. But Evanna didn't move.

She'd gotten a calculating look in her eyes. Intrigued, I sat back in the chair and raised my brows. The silence didn't bother me. Eva would get herself together, or she wouldn't.

"We're leaving." She decided as she stood up. I watched her walk halfway down the aisle. She didn't wait for me. As if she knew I'd follow her. And with a frown, I did.

Eva walked her little ass right back to my apartment, which was both fascinating and confusing. She may have said I wouldn't be fucking anyone but her; but that hardly meant we were going to do it right then. At least, I figured we weren't.

I was proven wrong as I witnessed her pull off her tank top just inside my door. Which prompted me to hastily close it. There was no chance to ask what the fuck had gotten into her, either. Eva just shoved off her shorts, her skimpy panties and strutted into my bedroom. I was left wondering what had just happened as I locked the door and kicked off my shoes.

It took me a minute to get myself back together. When I got to my room, Eva was waiting for me. She was perched in the middle of my bed, nude and beautiful, leaning back on her hands.

"Someone's awful slow tonight," she quipped as I came to a stop beside the bed.

"Fill a guy in, maybe," I snarked in return. I wasn't used to being thrown so far off balance with Evanna. Her smile, a slow curve of her lips as her eyes flashed while she dragged them over me was. It was something I couldn't put words to.

"You bitched and moaned about how I wouldn't fuck you. Or let you fuck me. So here I am Theodore. Your princess is where you want her, isn't she? Waiting for you do your worst." Her head tilted as she spoke while her gaze hooked me in.

It was bizarre, and oddly sexy.

I moved toward the bed cautiously, not entirely sure what her goal was, or her angle. Imagine my shock when she moved onto her knees and met me at the edge of the bed. She reached out, pulled at my shirt, and I just let her take it. I let her take my belt too, I even allowed her to shove my jeans down.

Eva must have been out for revenge, but it was far from what I expected. Not when she went to lean down, hand around my cock. Her mouth followed close behind it which pulled a groan from me as I gritted my teeth and watched her.

The brat looked right back and wrapped her mouth around my cock head. She kept looking as she bobbed and took more each time. She'd never done this with me. I didn't even care about it. It was fun, but I'd always been too long or too wide. Past partners never kept it up for long. Such was true for her, too.

I had her on her knees before I remembered the important thing. I stopped myself from touching her anywhere but her side. In the mirror while I pet her, I found her eyes; she didn't notice, but I still enjoyed seeing her like that.

"So, princess. It seems like you want something." I acted as if she hadn't been sucking me off. "The way you whipped your clothes off could make a guy think you need attention."

"You," in the mirror, Evanna's faced warmed. She always took on this tangerine pink color first before she deepened to red. My hands dragged up and stalled just under her breasts as she snarled weakly at me. "Just get on with it, Teddy."

"On with what? If you don't tell me what you want, I can't give you anything." I taunted her while I smirked and watched her in the mirror.

I saw little details I didn't notice when I was behind her or on top of her, focused on getting her worked up enough to take me easily.

"Just fuck me," she said waspishly. My response was to hum and look down at her. I tilted my head as if I was thinking it over.

"Why should I? You avoided me for two weeks, Eva."

Eva swore while she shoved herself up. In a swift turn, she took my face in her hands. "I fucking *hate* you," she declared, without heat or conviction.

It sounded startlingly like she'd said she *loved* me.

"Well, right back at you, Eva. I fucking hate you, too." She leaned in after I spoke, the kiss telegraphed a mile off and I took it, meeting her. All the while I wondered how exactly we'd muddled our way to that point.

It wasn't a sweet kiss, not a myriad of small ones traded and stolen while we breathlessly ran toward pleasure. This was borderline frantic once her tongue touched mine. Eva tasted like skittles. It drove me to lean in, to chase the taste of her as her arms wrapped around my shoulders, hands gone from my face.

We didn't come up for air, and I thought of nothing else. I just sank into that kiss, into her. It sped up, slowed down, the pair of us guided it in turn. When she leaned back, Eva's face was a warm red, and her chocolate eyes more like onyx. She brought out parts of me I'd kept buried.

"Theo. Fuck me."

Not about to deny her that request, I got her back onto her knees. I kissed at her back while petting along her sex. She was already wet, but I didn't do what I would have done weeks before. No. I pressed a finger into her first, listened as she sighed, and then another. She shivered, her skin turning to gooseflesh as I took my time to touch her.

"You don't need to do that," Eva muttered while she looked back.

"Princess," I drawled back at her, leaning down to nip at her spine. "I do absolutely *nothing* for your comfort, you know that. Consider me wrecking you all night your apology. When tomorrow hits, I want you still dazed and exhausted. I'm sending you home hung over and stuffed full of cum. Isn't that what you want?"

It was a lie, a small one. That I'd send her home, that I didn't do this for her. But I didn't think about it too much; it fit into our dynamic perfectly, and Eva responded wonderfully.

Her teeth dug into her lip while she watched me watch her. If she said no, I'd have kicked her out of my bed and sent her to the bathroom to wash up. But Evanna didn't make me wait for an answer.

"Sounds fun, but do you *promise*, Teddy? What if I don't go home tomorrow? Would you keep going?"

"If you ask nicely. But you know the rule, don't you?" I slid my free hand up to take hold of one of her breasts and massaged her gently before I concentrated on her nipple. My fingers stayed steady while I watched the brown of her eyes become swallowed by her pupils.

"Which one? Is tonight a permission night?" she asked teasingly as I slid a third finger into her channel. The way she broke off into a moan was highly gratifying.

"No. Not today. But you only have the time that my cock is in your pussy to get off," I replied easily. My fingers spread some to relax her. I hoped I wouldn't need a fourth.

A grunt, and Eva wiggled some which confirmed she wouldn't be ready for a while. I kept working at her, switched which breast I played with, and pressed kisses along her back. The kisses were how I looked for the 'hot spots' of hers that showed up at random. I needed to get her nearly dancing on the bed under me before we went further.

The fourth finger, however, didn't go smoothly. Her hips jolted forward, and I had to steady her when she shifted back again.

"Hurts," she whimpered. I kissed up along her neck in response and curled myself over her until I pressed my lips to her jaw.

"Relax, Eva," I coached her as my hand left her nipple and tilted her face toward mine. "It's been a while; I'd rather not leave you so sore you can't function tomorrow."

Then, I kissed her, like I had weeks ago and dropped the hand I'd guided her face with down between her legs. I petted her lips and over her pearled clit lightly. We were familiar enough with one another that this dance didn't miss steps. We adjusted as we needed to.

My mission was to keep her distracted, my touch constant as she gasped and groaned into the kiss until I worked the last finger into her. Her hand snapped up as it happened, awkwardly sinking into my hair before she pulled it and whined. I gritted my teeth and persisted, a grunt leaving me while I kept circling her clit. My fingers pressed against her harder until she fluttered and relaxed around the fingers inside her.

Then I pulled back. Which was apparently a travesty in Evanna's mind. It made me smirk though, pleased she wanted me close. I didn't examine the warmth that filled my chest whenever she illustrated how badly she seemed to need me.

"You need something, princess?" I asked as innocently as I could. It was far, far too tempting to tease her.

"Teddy…" She only said my name, in a tone edged with desire and impatience. I knew that tone well. I had to bite my tongue to not laugh. Her hips tilted, and I thrusted just a little harder than was strictly needed to watch how her eyes flew open as she gasped.

"You're so damn gorgeous like this, Eva. If I could, I'd keep you exactly like this for the night," I threatened her softly. It was an idle threat and we both knew it. Given the way she huffed and eyed me warily for just a moment before she faced forward. I assumed to be more comfortable. My eyes turned back to the mirror to watch her. It took her a second to realize that when she looked at me next, she was looking at herself, too.

Her cheeks flushed deep crimson, the darkest I'd ever seen them. Delighted, I grinned and leaned down to glance my lips against her cheek. "See how pretty you are, princess?"

"Teddy." She groaned out my name like an answer and turned so her lips brushed over mine. Eva seemed just distracted enough I could pick up the pace. When she didn't tell me to stop, I moved my fingers even faster. Distracted, and too focused on keeping her comfortable later, I had tucked my thumb against my palm and pressed it with the others into her. She'd taken it a few times before, so blissed-out I could have done anything to her.

As I worked it into her, she let out a cry that made me freeze. "No more. No more, I can't," She panted out a plea for respite.

"You already are, baby. I need you to, you know I could hurt you. You're so damn small, Eva. I need to be inside you, but not at the expense of you being able to sit or walk," I crooned softly in an attempt to ease her worry. My movements slowed to allow her to adjust.

"Please," she whimpered as she dropped her chest to the bed and hid her face against the comforter. The softness of her voice is what made me relent.

"Alright, princess," I said while I eased my fingers out of her. Afterward, I urged her to turn over. "Sit back, legs nice and wide for me, Eva."

Eva moved fluidly, suddenly sat facing me, propped up on her elbows while she set her legs apart enough so I could get between them. She was a sight, with all of her lovely tanned skin on display, her face tilted toward me while her eyes watched me carefully.

With deliberate, telegraphed moves, I shifted up onto the bed, boxers shoved off as I went. Her eyes slid over me, and I grinned unable to help myself. It felt good to be looked at that way. It also presented an opportunity to tease her again.

"Y'know baby, it's been so long this'll be like seeing you wrapped around my cock for the first time all over again," I said and tried to keep a conversational tone. I settled on my knees between her legs and adjusted my phallus so it laid against her mound. Then I shifted how her legs bracketed me. They pushed open a touch more before I dragged her closer. "How many times will I need to make you come tonight before I can just fall asleep, and you'll keep me inside?"

Her lips formed an 'o'. Apparently, Eva hadn't expected that, but visibly, she wasn't shying away from me. She wasn't saying no, but not saying yes, either. My hips rocked slowly so my cock dragged slowly down against her lips, her arousal helping ease the way.

"What do you think, Eva? How many rounds will it take for you to demand I not move, to stay inside so you can relax and sleep right like that?" I asked and leaned forward, dropping my voice as I ducked my head. All my movement paused just before our lips met. Her head tilted back expectably, and she moaned then, her legs curled high against my ribs.

"I don't. I don't know, Teddy," she replied with a tremor in her voice.

I brushed my lips against hers gently while I moved my hands to her hips. I wouldn't push her; I never did for things like that. It was always her choice. It had to be. I wanted every desire she had to be her choice, so she had to admit she wanted it. But now that I had her attention, I urged her to move with me. She did and matched my rhythm easily.

"Fuck," I sighed appreciatively, "that's it, Eva."

My hips moved a little faster and she echoed them. We moved fluidly together, so much it was sort of mesmerizing. The slick, heated feel of her against me was maddening. I lost my train of thought, focused on encouraging her instead. "That's it, princess. Christ, you're so soft. So damn sweet. So wet, baby, keep going, sweetheart."

"Yes," she sighed initiating another kiss. This one lasted longer, a little messier. My girl hooked her hand behind my neck to keep me close. One kiss became two, three, and Eva wrapped her arms around my shoulders while she rocked against me eagerly. I had to push my hands into the bed to keep us balanced, her feet pressed into the mattress to keep her situated. It wasn't sustainable, but it was amazing.

"God damn," I ground out as I disentangled her and pushed her shoulders back against the bed. It effectively ended the kisses and the rather acrobatic hold she had on me. My hands took hold of her legs, pulling them up higher while I got closer to her. "That's it, good girl. Keep moving like that. Press that pretty wet pussy against me while you moan."

I smirked as her breath hitched. For once, Eva didn't swat me, she pulled at the hair on the nape of my neck instead. It didn't have much effect, not when I could see how she looked at me as she rode the length of my cock wantonly. She couldn't have convinced me she hated it while she was panting and made no effort to hide it.

"You're disgusting," she said after a bit. The words lacked the heat they needed.

"Is that right?" I asked and slowed how I moved without stopping. My hands found her breasts and I teased her with a short swipe of my thumb over her nipple.

"Is it disgusting to want to feel how much you want me? Or are you still denying yourself what *you* want? You're allowed to want me, allowed to have me." I rolled my hips against her, nice and slow, while I watched her intently. "Princess, baby, I feel how you're moving. I feel how slick you are, see how your chest heaves when we're together. You're so excited, Eva, you're blushing straight to these gorgeous tits."

Two weeks had let Eva revert back into the same shy girl she'd been the second time we had sex while she was fully sober. She acted like she wasn't used to how I spoke to her, even after weeks of it. I loved that. Her chin tilted while a defiant look formed on her face that I hadn't seen in some time.

She pulled me down, kissing me harshly. It was bruising, all aggression without sweetness. One that led to my hands in her hair and tugging her back so she was laid fully against the bed. I'd never stopped enjoying seeing her like that. Pinned and at my mercy. Even on the day she'd fought me about it.

"Stubborn little slut," I chastised her. My head dipped to suck a series of bruises along her collarbones. "You want it and won't say it? That's fine, princess. I'll give you what you want, what you need, soon enough."

"What," she asked breathlessly, "Do I want, Teddy?"

She glared as I pulled her hair again. Finally, she released me to arch up and alleviate the tension I'd created. With a grin, I teased my tongue around the budded deep colored peaks that topped her breasts. Her intake of breath, followed by a twitch of her hips and the softest sound falling from her lips, sent shivers down my spine. Eva eggs me on wordlessly.

"Easy, baby." I sucked lightly at one nipple before I popped my mouth off it. "My little cousin missed me, missed my cock even thought she was mad at me." I ground against her slowly to make my point. "She wants to be stuffed until she doesn't have to think anymore, isn't that right, Eva?"

I freed one hand from her hair as I moved to hover over her. Her eyes slid away from mine, but I kept watching her. I pressed my lips lazily along her skin while I kept rocking my hips against hers and waited for her to react.

"It isn't like that," she moaned after a few rounds of motion. It wasn't convincing at all. But I indulged her – and why not? I'd waited two weeks just like she had. I could have waited hours longer to be inside her, to take pleasure from her as surely as I gave it.

"Oh, but it *is* like that, princess." I shifted and settled myself over her in the most comfortable way possible while we had sex. "You always want my cock, baby. You love having it in your pussy, making you feel good. Just tell me, Eva. You're already showing me; let me hear you say it." With the hand still in her hair, I tugged harder. She arched up, pressed close to me, which left not even a whisper of room between us.

"Teddy," she murmured, voice shaking. Her hands slid up my arms, but I didn't help her to find purchase. Instead, my hips swiveled against her. I groaned as she bucked and yelped. Her hips lifted higher when she moved the next time, legs tight against my sides and it was just right for my head to notch into her hole.

Right where I wanted to be.

"Jesus, Eva. Princess, *say it*." Threat leaked into my tone as I moved in quick jolts, teasing into her. "Say you want my cock, Evanna. Tell me to fuck you. Scream you want your cousin fucking your pussy, making you come, giving you a baby."

It was far harsher than I'd wanted. I'd obviously lost the battle of keeping hold of my frayed control.

"Teddy," she beckoned, and I answered. My mouth slotted against hers as I let her free. I moved slower, pushed harder. Each of her whines and grunts were swallowed until she pulled away from me.

"Fuck me, Teddy. I want it, want you."

"Say it, princess," I demanded as I kissed her temple, feeling the way she shook as I pushed until her body engulfed my crown.

"Oh god. Teddy, please." Eva's hands dragged over my sides to sit against my back, her nails on my skin. "I. I need my cousin to fuck me. Love me. I want…" She paused; her tongue slid across her lips while I watched her. Something passed over her face again. Something I couldn't read. "I want you to breed me, Teddy. Fill me up, make me come. I'm yours, just yours."

"Evanna," I ground out her name and thrust forward before I could tell myself not to. She accepted me, let me in, and we cried out together as our hips met.

"Breathe," I said, or panted, as I made sure we were both comfortable. Eva clung to me as she sipped at the air. "Just breathe, baby. You're okay, you're taking me so well. Let yourself adjust."

"How did I forget in two weeks how big you feel?" she grumbled while I waited for her to relax around me. I didn't laugh but smiled instead as I smoothed her hair from where I'd tangled it.

"You say the sweetest things, princess."

We moved slowly together, careful, lazy. We watched one another like we couldn't look anywhere else. I never pulled far from her. Only a couple inches of my cock ever left her. Eva rolled and lifted her hips to meet me with the quietest sense of urgency.

"Teddy," she whispered, and I hummed, questioning her while I was silent. "Tell me what you're thinking."

My hips churned back, rocked into her harder while I pieced together what exactly was on my mind. "Right now? How you feel and look." I paused to figure out the best way I could've said the next part. "I'm curious about how long it'll take to know if my 'seed' have taken root. I'm desperate to see you carrying for me, princess. Do you know how often I've imagined you like that? So fucking often, Eva."

Her mouth dropped open into an 'o' again. She groaned and her channel rippled around me. Clearly despite my limited vocabulary, it got to her like it got to me. I dropped my lips to her neck and sped up, not able to resist when I knew she liked it. My hands wandered, slipped between us to swirl over her clit. Eva keened as her hips tilted back and her sheath clenched tight around me.

"Christ. Shit, Eva," my head dropped to the pillow beside her as my free hand grabbed at her hip. "Fuck. Relax, sweetheart. Relax."

"Be smaller," she grunted. Her teeth caught my neck, dug in gently before they released me. "God, I feel split open, Teddy."

I'd feel prideful over that later. In that moment, I ground into her, listened as she moaned only to echo it as she twisted her hips. My body felt like a live wire, pleasure coiled at the base of my spine and bult slowly. We slowed and sped up as we needed, unintentionally staving off orgasms that were well within reach.

"It's funny," I whispered to her as I recalled her words from our first time. "The golden girl of the family is depraved. The woman our parents crow about is letting her cousin fuck her, spreads her legs for him eagerly."

Eva jolted under me. I tilted to look at her, caught how her teeth raked over her lip. Her head shook. "No. Not like that, Teddy. It's not wrong to want you."

"To us," I agreed. It was a thought I'd had many times since I realized what I wanted from Eva. Sometimes it made me hot, sometimes it made me feel shame enough to consider confession. And every so often, like that moment, the two swirled together and led to me surging into Evanna.

"To us it's fine, princess. We know," I brushed my lips over hers. "We know there's no shared blood. Everyone, anyone else… they'd see the same last name and no wedding band."

We sped up together and her nails dug into my back. Clearly, the reminder of how wrong this was had aroused us. So, I kept speaking.

"Outsiders see cousins. If someone knew how desperate we are for one another…" I trailed off ominously. "They'd tell you, you're sick, wrong, disgusting, and depraved for needing my cock so bad, Eva."

"Teddy." My nickname keened was just as sweet as my proper name. "More. *Need more.*"

"More what?" I asked and stole a kiss before I sucked harshly at her pulse. "What do you want. Moving, talking? Which is it, princess."

"Everything, Teddy." She rocked against me, squeezed, made me groan and clutch at her. "Tell me everything you want. You won. Show me I'm yours. Prove your mine. Don't. God. Don't hold back."

How could I ever have said no to that?

Good Intentions Can be Wrong

Evanna

16 August.

I knew having lunch out was a bad idea. Since I'd found out, it was like all the symptoms I *could* exhibit with pregnancy crashed down on top of me. I couldn't understand how I was pregnant–I'd had a period. It had been light. I'd been ecstatic and who wouldn't have been?

But I'd realized Theodore had to have gotten me pregnant in May. My luck? Shit. Which I knew, so tell me why I thought this was smart? Jasmine wanted to talk, suggesting we meet at the diner. I'd agreed, stupidly. Everything there smelled of grease, and while I'd been able to start branching back into less bland food, I wasn't ready for this. My stomach was already protesting the scents. I couldn't wait to see what would happen when I ate.

"You've been quiet lately," Jasmine started softly. "Which is interesting given how much our mother's been talking."

"Oh?" I sipped at my water and eyed Jasmine carefully. I didn't trust this at all – didn't trust *her*. The last time Jasmine started a conversation this way was five years ago. I'd been so lost, drowning so completely I'd been caught off guard. That turned into one of the worst days of my life. When I confided in my sister, it ended with my life being placed on review. Every breath watched, every moment accounted for, and why?

"If you want to die so badly, do it somewhere else. Don't thank us for everything we've done by bleeding all over the floor and staining my carpets."

That would never, *ever* leave my memory. Those scars wouldn't fade. Considering it was Jasmine who parroted my words to my mother, and my guidance counselor had disregarded my warning because he was 'worried' I had very little trust to share around. It wasn't in large supply as it was, but especially not with family.

"She's had quite a lot to say about your absence. I think she's hurt you don't want to spend your time with her and dad before you leave." Jasmine smiled, as if that made sense of what she'd been told.

Mom wanted us to be active. Clubs, sports, music, whatever we wanted to do, she encouraged under the guise of socialization. But now, when I was actually living up to what she wanted, work, friends, et cetera, it was a bad thing.

"Jaz," I said cautiously. "Mom's had me everyday for eighteen years. I've spent two months figuring out a life without her as a safety net. What exactly is she expecting of me?"

"I don't know," Jasmine replied without looking at me. "Probably what she wanted of us all. To stay close enough she can reach us, but far enough away to 'grow'."

"Ri-ight," I drawled, drawing the word out as I leaned back in my chair. Not speaking more, I allowed my eyes to sweep around the dining room. When I found no one was obviously eaves dropping, I was glad. Even so, I kept myself at a private conversation volume. "That's ridiculous. Not one university or college that I applied to was even in New York. No hate to the state, but it's not the pinnacle of all things education."

"You know she hates abrupt change. Springing it on her that you planned to leave this month. That wasn't kind or smart."

My eyes narrowed – Jasmine was parroting someone, I had a hunch I knew who, too. "I love Mom, you know that, and so does she. But I don't want to stay here. I thought a gap year would be great, but in my heart, I know it's not. The need to fly the coop is strong, Jasmine. I'm not Mom, I'm never going to be like mom. So, no one can reasonably hold me to her patterns or expectations."

"You could go to State. Their programs are good enough," Jasmine countered.

"Good enough for *what*, exactly? And when have we ever been told to settle for good enough?" I asked her, feeling the rise of my temper. "Jasmine, *come on*, seriously. I don't want to stay in New York. There's no work for me here. I could, *maybe*, get a job with the press or local news. Riveting as that is, I want to do bigger things. They encouraged me to do bigger things."

Driven. Driven was the accurate word that I didn't use. Everything I'd done, everything my parents did, made sure that I could 'be someone'. From ballet to scouts to violin lessons to band camp, all of it served a purpose beyond my enjoyment of it.

"Eva, I don't know. Okay? I know she wants you to stay home, that the rumors are getting to her. She's pissed you seem to be getting along with Theodore. You just keep moving outside the mold made for you," she replied, just as snippy as I was.

I didn't continue the conversation. I went quiet, and because the universe was full of jokes, that's when our food arrived. Bland was my friend, and luckily enough, I'd never been what my parents would've called adventurous. So, the egg salad and fries were within my norm.

One bite, however, had my stomach revolting. I got up hastily, barely kept my chair upright while I power-walked between tables to the bathroom. I wish I could have held myself at the table longer, but this wasn't about to be pretty any which way I cut it.

As I knelt on the bathroom floor of the local diner, I decide I wouldn't recommend it to anyone. If any of my friends had kids, I'd tell them to opt for delivery. I gripped the toilet for all I was worth and tried not to think about the germs that were inevitably all over me.

Shower later, be sick now. I thought as I tried not to resist what my body wanted. *Make your excuses to Jasmine quickly.*

As I silently made my list, I added stopping by Grand-Mère and Grand-Père's house for that shower. I thought that I might've told one of them, or perhaps both of them. I could've begged forgiveness and sanctuary while I was at it, because there wasn't a chance in hell my mother didn't hear of this in the next three days. And then, the bathroom door opened.

While the steps cautiously made their way over, I heaved a few breathes as quietly as I could. I didn't even look at the shoes because I really, truly prayed Jasmine wasn't the one out there. I leaned my head on the back of my hand while I sipped the air slowly.

"Eva?" Jasmine's voice may as well have been an air horn in the dead silence of the room. "Are you all right, sweetheart?"

"I'm fine," I croaked, roughly cleared my throat afterward. I couldn't avoid spitting. "I'm fine, just a little stomach weirdness again."

It's the only time in my life that I was thankful for my allergies. I blessed them every day for being food related to near exclusivity. None of them caused hives, but most *would* make me vomit. It was the best defense I had. Which I realized when I had a second to think rather than fight the urge to retch.

"Didn't you have an appointment with your allergist last month?" Jasmine asked as she leaned against the stall support. Her shoes and shadow loomed like a death knell.

"Yes, I did. And?" I asked more tersely than was advisable. I understood that to her, and many others, I was still a child. Even though I'd never felt like a child, I understood. But I was old enough to vote or to sign up to possibly die for my country. So, by that same stretch, no one should've been questioning why I was ill when I gave a reason.

"Well. I just thought that Mom said."

"Mom isn't privy to my medical visits or records now. She still has to sign off on major surgery in an emergency, I guess, but outside of that, Dad will know when I attend a doctor's appointment thanks to the insurance claim," I said, while I quietly reminded myself that would only be the case if I made one.

That reminder hit me like a runaway train. I knew I needed insurance for the kid to be born, but I hadn't really dwelled on it. That wouldn't be hidden when the time came. Couldn't be. I needed the internet in that moment. I reasoned out that I could go to the library later, there I'd look it up and clear out the browser history, so no one would be the wiser.

"Eva," Jasmine called my name, and I startled.

"Yes?"

"Don't get mad at me. But. Are you pregnant?"

My heart stopped and my stomach dropped through the floor.

"What are you talking about?" I asked quickly in the hope that my pause wasn't so fast she'd have seen it as defensive or secretive. If I achieved that, I reasoned I could make it another two days without the beans having been violently spilled.

"You're eating real careful," Jasmine replied softly. "Mom might not've noticed yet, but I've been at the house for dinner lately. Dad hasn't noticed either from what I can tell. But you're awfully careful around smells, food, and while you haven't gained weight yet – your tops are tighter. It was the same for me."

The irony of it didn't escape me. My birthmother telling me, her adopted *sister*, that I'm pregnant in a public restroom. The drama. I flushed the mess away before I shoved myself back onto my feet. The stall door opened as I made for the sink. Once my hands were washed, I rinsed my mouth, then turned to look at Jasmine.

"Mom can't know, Jasmine. She'll kill me. I'm leaving in *two days,* and I don't plan on coming back." There wasn't a point in denying it. Jasmine would've gone to Mother with her suspicions anyway.

"Evanna, that's the worst plan you've ever uttered."

"I've had time to think, alright? I've missed a major piece, but I can adapt. There's nothing I'm better at than adapting to a situation." I flashed a smile. It was my hope that it would lighten the mood in that dank little room.

"You need to tell her. She'll find out, you know she will," Jasmine said seriously as she pushed away from the stall.

"I'd rather be halfway across the country when she finds or figures it out, thanks." I pushed my hands through my hair before I rubbed at my mouth. This was a disaster. It figured I'd made it within days of leaving and everything went to hell. Why would it have been any other way?

"Give mom some credit," Jasmine started, and I cut her off immediately.

"No. Unlike the rest of the family, I remember what she said when I was at my absolute lowest. I refuse to give Mother the benefit of *anything*. All she wants is the visuals of a pious, , catholic family. That's not us, Jasmine. Not me, not you, not Oliver. And I really don't get why you'd want me to walk into that trap," I didn't yell, but it was a near miss. I was still louder than I wanted.

Jasmine, thirty-eight to my eighteen, flinched. I didn't know if it was because of my words or how I said them. Part of me didn't really give a damn, because I was absolutely *terrified*. My worst probable scenario had come to pass. Someone in my family found out. Mom would find out.

Mom was catholic and she employed the politics of a noble in the French court at its height. Perfection or bust, basically. I was the closest she'd gotten out of her children. The version of me she thought she knew was a lie. No. That was dramatic. That version was *mostly* a lie.

"It'll be worse if you don't tell her."

"How?" I asked, my arms crossed over my chest. "My bank account is no longer joint, hasn't been for a year. My scholarships are all paid directly to the school. My car is in my name, I pay the insurance. My pay-as-you-go-phone? She can have it if she wants it. I'll buy another. Mom can't do shit to me over this, Jasmine. I made sure of it."

"How can you have plotted to leave us like that?" Jasmine snapped, finally. She proved she was just as much her mother's daughter as I was. "You've got it all figured out, and have for a while, huh? Leaving the state, pulling your roots up one by one. You're just going to abandon us as if we're nothing."

"One, I was never staying, Jasmine. Never. Two, *of course I'm jumping ship*. You did. Ollie did. Then you did *again*. But as a bonus, you left *me* behind, gave me up! You let me be raised in a series of towns so small that it's a miracle most of the population isn't their own second cousin. And let's not forget the rampant racism. It's not exactly a selling point. I don't feel bad about this. I'm leaving, no one is going to stop me. Not you, mom or dad, and not the baby I'm currently cooking," I told her. A touch of pride flared when I didn't get in her face or yell.

"If you don't tell mom, I will," Jasmine said, quiet and cold as the worst winter. It didn't even shock me.

"*Fine*. Let's go then. Let's trade places, you and I. You can be the golden girl, finally, and I'll play the whore," I said before I swept past my sister, leaving the room. I took all of three minutes pay for my food while I cited a terrible stomach bug I thought I'd gotten rid of. Damage control.

~

I managed to beat Jasmine home. Mom and dad were still in the garden, so I did what I did best. I careened into my room to snatch up the last of my things. Anything I knew I'd need later. My journal, laptop and accessories, my dirty clothes. In the bathroom I dumped it all into the removable bag, along with toiletries and reasoned I'd deal with it later.

As I came back in from tossing the bag in the car, all my keys – the spares I knew mom had included – were stuffed into the pockets of my shorts. I was ready to run, ready for her to do her worst. Mom had already proven that she'd disregard my boundaries, as had Jasmine. Dad was my last hope, and that wasn't exactly a high bar.

"Eva," Jasmine's voice was eerie. Calm, without its usual spritely, almost manic edge. Her betrayal of me, forcing me into this, was something I'd neither forget nor forgive. Ever.

"I'm here. Are Mom and Dad?" I asked as I slid off my flip flops and walked upstairs. The kitchen table was the chosen battle ground. Jasmine hovered by my seat, the one on the same side as the stairs. I immediately scowled. That wasn't fucking happening.

Gently, I shoved her away, and sat quickly. Mom and Dad were already at either end, frowning while they watched my sister sit opposite me. Seconds ticked by as I sorted the words I needed to use. I banished Theodore from my mind all together. Neither of us needed that. Not with what was about to go down.

"Jasmine said you wanted to talk to us, kid," Dad said with a smile, though is eyes were wary as I looked over at him. My smile in response was wan.

"Sort of. Please listen until I get to the end, okay? It's important that you let me say everything, or you won't fully understand what is going on," I said, the urge to slip into pidgin French pushing at me. Mom was terrible at it, having learned Parisian French as a kid. She had to take time to translate some of the off words or phrases. I'd moved past conversational into fluency, but it was Dad's first language. It would've bought me time. But I didn't.

Their silence prompted me to start talking.

"I met someone in May," I began carefully while I rearranged the facts of my life to suit the story. My aim was to be as truthful as I could be. "He's a little older and works in Lake Mouth. My weekend job at the bookshop? He works nearby. We went on quite a few dates when I said I was working. I didn't have that many shifts. But things were going really well."

I took a breath and didn't look at anyone. I didn't want to see their faces or even hear their reactions to what came next. "We decided we were ready to be intimate together just a little while ago. It… I made sure that we were safe. I bought the contraceptives; I even watched him put it on. But… It failed. And, well, I'm pregnant. It isn't my proudest moment, but that's the truth."

Mostly the truth. My anxiety roared in my head that my parents would see through the parts that were a lie. It wasn't as if I had bank records to back me up. Cash was king, and it kept me from over-drafting. The room's silence didn't help to quiet my roaring thoughts either.

"You're pregnant," My mother repeated what I'd told them slowly. It made the hair at the back of my neck stand on end. I looked at her, feeling like a rabbit ready to bolt. "How many people have you whored around with?"

My jaw dropped. I couldn't believe that came out of her mouth. I couldn't believe that was what she was hung up on, wanted to know. The number of people I'd slept with was… superfluous, and not her business.

"One, Mom. I… Don't understand why *that* is what you're focused on," I said while I glanced as my dad. His face was a mask of neutrality. It made my heart sink. It was possibly more terrifying than my mother's manic rage.

"Well, I thought I'd confirm which rumors are true and which aren't. Pregnancy isn't a rumor I've heard, so we have time to do damage control. No one needs to know you gave your virginity away for nothing." Her tone made my hackles rise. My patience had been thin on the best of days. With my anxiety dialed to one hundred, I had no time for that.

"Damage control? You're worried about how this looks. Fuck me, I guess, right?" I said and shifted my eyes to Jasmine. "I told you. *I fucking told you* that this would happen. They don't give a shit unless it'd make them look bad."

"Do not speak that way at this table," Dad rumbled, finally deigning to speak. My immediate thought was that he could go straight to hell. He and mom could've shared a personal buggy and it would've been beautiful.

"Dad. Seriously? I'm leaving in two days. Forty-eight hours. Mom is about to go off the deep end for no reason. No one is going to see me or know about this."

"Of course, no one will know. You're getting rid of it," Mom snapped at me. The impatience was clear in her tone. "We won't have people talking about you like they did when Jasmine brought you home."

Across the table, Jasmine flinched. There it was. The same song and dance about my wayward birthmother. The black sheep, the child who did nothing right. I was the child meant to do no wrong, that's why she resented me. I had to be against her. There was no reason for me to ever feel anything about Jaz beyond disdain or hate, according to Mom. I should've focused on having as little to do with Jasmine as possible. So, I wouldn't end up the same. As if Jasmine was a virus that could've infected me. I pitied us both. We shouldn't have been like this.

"I'm not getting rid of the baby. This right now? This is a courtesy, one that Jasmine *blackmailed* me into. No one's going to talk because no one will know. No one has a say in this but me," I spoke slowly, because I wanted everyone in the damn room to hear me.

It needed to be clear that this was my body, my life, my child, and my decision. I'd had weeks to get my head where it needed to be. I was going to college, and I'd do the best I could in class and at home with said child. With luck, I hoped I wouldn't fuck it all up. I'd promised myself that if I couldn't be good enough for this kid, I'd be responsible. I'd put them up for adoption, not in the general system, through a private firm, a catholic one.

"You are," Mom said, voice near a whisper. "You're getting rid of that worthless lump of cells. You'll withdraw from your college, and you'll enroll at the community college. You never should've been allowed to apply out-of-state. We should've known you'd be a stupid, *stupid* little slut, taking the first dick that would have you. You're no better than Jasmine… Worse because of your father."

I reeled. I lurched back so hard and fast I almost toppled with the chair. She didn't… She wouldn't… Mom had some messed-up views, but that had been the most racist thing she'd ever said. Jasmine made a strangled noise across from me, her face sporting spots of livid color high on her cheeks.

"What the hell do you mean?"

"Evanna. You know *exactly* what I'm talking about," Mom said, her rage made her accent thicker. "You, like those other girls, just spread your legs for 'love' and to secure yourself a future. I raised you better than that. To use your mind. That's why I dressed you so carefully, never letting you wear those horrible fashions that are so popular. Until you demanded I let you choose some things. Then it was only a matter of time before your body got you into trouble. As a child, you were so modest, but it melted away."

"*Mom,*" I said her name like a plea. This couldn't be reality. She wouldn't have said that. She loved me. Mom was narcissistic but she *loved* me.

"I tried, Jacob. I did," Mom went on dramatically. "We got so close. A good girl. Obedient. Smart. She knew her place and strove to overcome it. Jasmine married down; she defied all our lessons. I knew it wouldn't be good. We should have let your parents have her."

Me. She meant *me.*

"Tell me you didn't say that," I said, desperate in that moment for Mom to take it all back. I needed to know my Mother of all people wasn't a lie. To realize that Oliver was the only person in my corner was devastating. "Tell me you didn't mean it."

The silence. God, the fucking *silence.*

And my supposed father? Dad was silent too, once more he avoided everyone's eyes. My heart shattered. I felt it crack inside my chest. Those people. They were supposed to be my parents. My blood. And they lied. They *lied* about having loved me. Lied about their expectations. Lied, and lied, and fucking *lied* to my face.

"It's hardly detrimental," Clara said with a scoff. "The truth sets us free. Do as you're told, and you'll redeem yourself. You don't have to be loose, Evanna. A small life is obviously what's best for you. Out of sight, with a good husband. I shouldn't have indulged you in fantasies of becoming more. Perhaps that's what ruined you. Maybe your boy will take you … provided he isn't black, too."

"You horrible, racist *bitch*," I breathed out in shock. My eyes stung with tears. "You – who told me *repeatedly* I wasn't different from you? That my hair was beautiful, that *I* was beautiful with my skin color … Did you lie to me, Mom? Whenever I came home upset over someone having said something ignorant, you went on the warpath. You didn't care, did you? Didn't care what it did to me. All you wanted was to keep your perfect image. Is that what was? Was that the reason you did anything?!"

I screamed the last question as the photo I'd kept in my mind of my family ripped. What really killed me was that Theodore had been my villain until that moment. That he still wasn't a good person didn't escape me. Theodore, my Teddy, the father of my child, who *hated* me, *tortured* me, spoke about me like *trash*, was the most truthful person in my life. Oliver, I hoped, could be placed on the same level or higher.

"Don't raise your voice." Dad's voice cut through the pounding of blood that drowned out everything else. I turned to him, not knowing if I was about to cry or scream. "You'll show respect at this table or stay silent."

"Daddy. Seriously? *Respect*? You honestly want me to be respectful? No matter that what she said is tearing me to pieces? That's what you want? How can you even look at her? How? You're supposed to defend me, to love—" My head snapped to the side as his hand collided with my cheek.

The tears that stung my eyes fell as pain burst through my awareness. Jasmine yelled, and Clara was saying … something. Dad had never hit me before. He never spanked me as a child. They lectured me, at length. Every little wrong or slight had been likened to a grand and terrible betrayal. They'd made me feel as if I were a bug under a microscope. All the while

96

they demanded I grow up, that I understood and managed *their* feelings. If I hadn't, I'd have always been in trouble. So, I suppressed myself to manage them.

But hit me? Never. I guess the possibility of bruises was too much of a risk before.

When my ears stopped ringing, I stood up and walked down the stairs and slid my shoes on. There wasn't a point in staying. What was there to fight about? Was there even anything left to say? In my head were a litany of *'don't forget to let me relax your roots, don't wear your hair frizzy, don't wear your hair in braids. Don't wear those colors, that brand… Wear this dress, that blouse, these shorts, those shoes…'*

I'd never questioned it. I realized it as I slipped behind the wheel of my car, the door slammed shut.

The key turned in the ignition before I threw it into reverse. I almost hit a car that came screaming around the curve. I didn't even feel scared. Nothing mattered. I was *done*. I was out, I wasn't staying. I couldn't and coming back wouldn't ever happen. That wasn't my home. Those people in that house weren't my parents, weren't my family.

They never had been.

Part II.
NOW

When You're a Bastard and You Love Her

Theodore
20 December 2014

Evanna Nichelle Bishop, Bishop-LeClair, officially. She's my cousin, in a legal sense. She should be by familial standards too but, it's complicated. Let's just start there. As I sit in my truck, so similar and yet completely different from the one I drove in our hometown, I'm on the road toward my family— our family. States pass me by, and my mind is full of thoughts about Eva. Stuck on her.

But who am I really kidding? That woman has lived in my head rent free ever since we were kids. And it wasn't in some bullshit romantic made for TV movie way, either. We were the epitome of toxic, and most of that rests on my shoulders. I didn't know how to handle her. Therapy wasn't popular in the 90s to early 2000s. I just wanted her gone, so I did my best to make her unwelcome.

In the end, I got my fuckin' wish. Evanna left home at eighteen after previously expressing her wish to take a gap year. I gleaned from hushed conversations that there had been a knock-down-drag-out fight in the Bishop-LeClair household. Her adoptive parents, her actual grandparents, hadn't said a word about what the fight was over. They also haven't seen or heard from Evi in ten years according to my sister, Andi.

The word is that Aunt Frankie had convinced Evanna to come home for Christmas. While it's not the ideal holiday to be stuck with people you haven't seen for ten years, I can hazard a guess why Frankie leveraged Christmas. Eva loves our grandpa to death, they share the same birthday, and Grandpa had been an outsider in our community too.

Were I Frankie, I'd use Grandpa's age to get Eva to relent. I'm just lucky I have the excuse that I didn't want to hear Andi bitch continually. "She hasn't seen me in 'forever' ". It's an easy cover for the fact that I am on the highway. All for Evanna.

It was sudden, when Eva left. There one day and gone, the next sudden. The rest of us hadn't known until a week later. I was absolutely livid that she'd essentially run away. I realized how shitty things were when I moved to an actual city. Not just between me and her, but between her and her parents.

As a kid and teenager, I was a shithead. I own it. I thought I'd gotten better, gotten over it as I moved into my twenties. By the time I 'connected' with Evanna, I knew I had to break some bad habits. I was wrong. So fucking wrong. In Alexandria, I made friends. Those friends took it upon themselves to educate me. It was a crash course on just how fucked up I was.

Aunt Clara would've said I was a 'good old boy'. I was straight up racist and abusive to Eva. To more than Eva, I didn't realize it. Our little corner of the North Country is insulated. So much so, there wasn't much to learn or know in that regard. But Clara and Jake— they had years on us, *decades*, and they were so subtly abusive and racist that it shocks me. I can't figure out how Clara acted that way to Evanna. How Jacob let her abuse their daughter that way.

It is neither here nor there. Not yet.

I watch as the snow gets heavier, frowning. The road has salt on it, at least. The plows will be out soon. Pulling off the road at three in the afternoon isn't appealing. But, just in case, I call my dad, tapping at my hands-free headset.

"Hello, Theo?" My dad's voice sounds distracted, which doesn't much surprise me.

"Yeah, Pop, it's me. It's started snowing in Pennsylvania, I might have to pull off. I wanted to reach Albany before then." My fingers tighten on the steering wheel for a moment.

"It's still a few days until the festivities. Don't rush, Theodore. I want you here alive, not in a matchbox," Dad's suddenly serious tone makes me sigh. I'm thirty-some years old and Dad still acts like I'm sixteen with my brand new license. It has to be the State Trooper in him.

"I'm not rushing, Pop. If I was, I wouldn't have called you," I reply patiently. "Is Andi with you? She never said where she was when she called."

"Yeah, she's back in the house. Both kids too."

Wincing, I make a mental note to not ask after Andi's likely ex-husband. She's never had an outstanding track record with men, but when I received the invitation to her wedding, I thought her story was done. Given that they held it at her husband's parents' farm in Idaho, that didn't count as going home. I'd flown in and flown right back out. She never let me forget it either.

"She okay? Or is it a Grandma's hiding all the liquor kind of year?" A valid question, given how I'd spent the first two Christmas' after Evanna left. Not that anyone knows about the second.

"She'll be fine, probably. Kids'll be at the farmhouse so there won't be any proper nog, anyway." My laughter drowns out my dad's put-upon sigh.

"I've missed Grandma's eggnog. The bought stuff just isn't the same," I say when I collect myself. My fingers flick my lights on as the sky shifts from mostly sun-behind-clouds to grey as far as the eye can see.

"It's an old recipe, she's only given it up to Eva, same as she only gave up the cocoa recipe to the pair of you," Dad gives a tonal equivalent to a shrug. "I got her pies, Jake got the maple candy, Frankie and Candace got the meat for that one dish you'd never eat."

"It's called blood pudding," I sigh in exasperation. "I was ten! That Eva and Andi ate it and liked it is frankly unnatural."

"No," he laughs, "the girls just have good taste. You were always picky."

"Mm," my lips quirk. I really was. "Ah, well. For now, I'll let you go. I'm going to find an early dinner and a decent hotel. It isn't getting any better."

"Be safe, son." It's the closest my dad gets to I love you, but at least I can recognize it now. Progress is progress.

"I'll see you tomorrow, hopefully." Hanging up, I pull off the road. My thoughts inevitably turn to Eva. Is she driving home too? My fingers tap against the steering wheel in a roll. I can't imagine frugal Eva taking a flight, but it has been a decade, she might have changed. Inevitably, she will have changed.

Finally, the one thought I have avoided like the plague slips past the others. Will I meet a child with my nose or laugh? My heart skips a beat, skips ten. I don't know if I want her to arrive with a child; or if I want her to arrive alone.

"Fuck, get it together," I grumble, pull into a Cracker Barrel. Not my preference, but it's that or a Taco Bell and I've had my fill of that for this road trip.

Still, I can't push down the remembered desires from ten years ago. I can't help but pull up one memory from the days I kept realizing I was in love with that girl. In early August, I'd gotten the courage to take Eva out – on a date.

It was our *single* date before the nuke went off that sent Evanna out of state. I saw her one other time before she left. It makes me question my life every time I think about it. But that dinner, the sensation of wanting to rip anyone apart who told Eva she wasn't gorgeous? I learned I was in over my head. How I felt about her leaving. It was an enormous flag, complete with flashing lights.

Her leaving was the big damn voice in the sky.

Dinner ends up being just fine when it comes. Nothing special, nothing to write home about for certain. But it gets the job done that I need it to, namely filling my stomach and passing time I'd rather have been on the road. Snow covers the truck in a fine layer that builds rapidly.

I pull down and use my jacket sleeves to swipe the hood of the truck before the glass and then shove myself inside behind the wheel. Two hotels later, I've got a room. It's a standard room. I don't give it more than a look. It's tempting now to try calling Evanna's old cell number, just to see if it's working. I hadn't when she left. I thought at the time that she'd be calling me.

The phone gets left on the bedside table to charge. I won't act like this. I'll be in West River within twelve to eighteen hours. Then, I'll be back home. Eva will be too.

I might get some answers if God's listening.

The Problem
with Family

Evanna
21 December

Walking in the ankle-deep snow that's accumulated since I walked into the service station, I'm plagued with memories. It makes the distance between the station and my car seem triple what it is. It might be my anxieties taking hold of me, but I am not looking forward to my birthday or Christmas.

The fact that in less than ten hours I'll be in Lake Mouth is daunting enough. In twenty-four hours, I'll be sitting in the church with people I haven't seen in years. In twenty-six hours, I'll sit in the farmhouse with him. Theodore James LeClair, my worst nightmare, my cousin, the father of my child. He, at least, I know how to handle, more or less.

It's everyone else that I'm worried about. My so-called parents, my 'sister'—I have to play nice with them, even though I'd rather not acknowledge that they exist at all. Acting like the last ten years hasn't happened is impossible. I swore to God and heaven that I wouldn't return. That vow, it can't be laid at the doorstep of everyone who will be in the farmhouse. Grand-Père, Grand-Mère, Uncle Joe, Aunt Frankie, and Aunt Odette aren't to blame for my abrupt departure. Grand-Père, especially. With this most likely being one of his last Christmases, I can't stay home. He's turning one hundred, and I'll turn twenty-eight. Ten years. I made it ten years alone, shut off, shut away from everything that happened in northern New York. When I got the letter, though, things shifted.

Aunt Frankie had sent me a pointed message some six weeks ago. I want to curse her for it.

Hell, I want to curse myself for not finding an excuse to stay the hell away from the towns of Pinehall, West River, East River, and Wercen. Except, I couldn't. All I could do was make sure I hid what was most important to me instead.

Grand-Père and Grand-Mère have always had my back. They've always been good to me over the years. Frankie, Odette and Joe, my aunts and uncle, Ollie, my brother, they've never said a bad word about me or to me. They're the only people who even knew I intended to leave, after the fact. Frankie, Joe, and Ollie were the only three to have my address.

My plan back then was flawless. As flawless as a spur-of-the-moment, spite fueled decision can be. It's no less perfect than Theodore's had been. Fuck. I sigh as I try to come to terms with the fact that I'll see him and have to speak to him.

Why couldn't I be a bitch?

That would be too easy. I'm going home, but not like my birthmother had, to stay. I'm only visiting. When I decided, I knew I couldn't just show up at this family event. Not after a decade of absence. I had to make people aware of it, at least some of them. My parents, sister, my brother. The entire fucking disaster family filled with disaster humans.

1 December

"Oh, I'm so happy you're coming home, Eva! I've missed you so much," Jasmine says. Her voice is full of excitement on the phone. I force myself not to pull it from my ear to stare at it incredulously. Missed me? Jasmine missed me? I bet she missed me so much she never asked if anyone knew where I went.

"Yeah," I say without enthusiasm. "It'll be… something."

"Are you bringing the baby, too?"

It's an innocent enough question. However, Jasmine may as well have slapped me. I exhale sharply while I fight back an instant and all-encompassing rage. Ten goddamn years. Yet it still hurts that no one attempted to find me. That Jasmine hadn't tried to contact me. It's something I know I should have expected.

"No. I will not be bringing my daughter and don't want to talk about it," I say, trying to accomplish a firm tone, and ending up sounding rather forbidding.

"Oh," Jasmine says. "Okay."

And that was the death of the conversation with the woman who'd birthed me.

~

"Ollie, tell me you're going home for Christmas." I all but beg my brother for some positive news when he picks up.

If Oliver goes home to East River, then everyone will fawn over him. If he brings Charlotte and the pipsqueaks, I can fade into the background. Everyone loves Charlie. Everyone loves Ollie. He's the perfect distraction, and a perfect ally to have at a dinner table. Especially over a holiday.

"Sorry, Eva, I'm not. If I'd known you were planning to go to West River, I'd have taken time off. I'm scheduled to be on-call the whole holiday. Charlie and Brit already went to Charlie's parents' place for the holiday."

"Fuck," I say with a put-upon sigh. On the opposite end of the phone, Oliver laughs sadly.

"You can do this, Evanna. You've done much harder things already. Don't let Mom get under your skin. All you need to do is smile, nod, and lie through your teeth. You know how to do this, how to survive." His voice is comforting. The reiteration of the survival strategy is even more so.

My therapist, however, would be appalled by learning how I'm willing to do exactly as Oliver advises. They're adamant that I need to face my mother, to say my piece. I'm adamant that I'd like to live to age thirty at least. We don't always get what we want.

"I'm a phone call away, kid. We can get you a ticket back to DC. I'll ship the car back to your place. No fuss, no muss. If it's bad, remember, you're not alone," Ollie says, calling me back to the present. His voice has taken on a serious tone. It makes me want to cry. Oliver lives a life of avoidance, but he never left me in the lurch. Not one, single time.

"Thanks, Ollie." I choke out the words, and he does what he always does. The comfort helps, but I still quickly end the call. I'd left our parents for last. This is the call that worries me the most. This is the call that I dreaded that kept me up at night. Mom and I had gone at one another ten years ago, and Dad just stood by. He watched, like he always does.

Rubbing at my face, I get up to get water. I make tea, grab cookies, and circle back around to my desk. I have to make this happen. So, when my ass touches the chair, I set out my things and get to dialing. The sooner this is done, the quicker I can talk to my therapist.

At the very least, they'll be gratified I didn't run for the hills. It feels pathetically small, but I've learned wins are wins.

"Hello?"

My mother sounds old. That's likely a mean, or even traitorous thought, but it's a shock. In my head, Clara is still in her mid-fifties. In my head, nothing's changed. Out of sight, out of mind.

"Mom," I ask, a croak in my voice. "I was hoping to speak to you if this is a good time?"

There's some movement on her end of the phone, making me brace myself. Things go one of two ways with Clara. Either she has an explosive episode at you, and that's the end. Or you're shut out for years at a time. She'd once changed our landline number just so Jasmine couldn't call anymore. I think I was eight. And, yes, it hasn't escaped me. I am my mother's daughter.

"Yes, of course it is," Clara says. The curt, almost rude answer makes me sigh in relief.

Still, this isn't making me hope for reconciliation. Mom would have to admit she was in the wrong. She'd have to admit she was an asshole to me, had said some racist shit to me. It won't happen. Not after all this time. Call me a pessimist, call me jaded, or whatever, but I just… I don't see it happening. I don't think she's there yet. If she'll ever be there.

"Aunt Frankie wrote to me," I say, starting out carefully, keeping my tone even while I choose my words carefully. "She invited me to Grand-Mère and Grand-Père's for Christmas. I wanted to let you know I plan to be there from the twenty-third until the twenty-sixth. I'll be leaving that morning."

Now, with that verbal vomit over with, I wait. I don't have to wait long, either.

"You're coming to New York."

I realize that I've been avoiding using the word home. It also hits me square in the chest that Mom isn't using the word either. That shouldn't hurt me. I set the precedent. Still, it cuts.

"Yes. Just for Christmas eve and Christmas." I reply, already tired.

"And where do you plan to stay? Or is this call to ask if you can come stay at the house?" Her question's laced with expectation and disdain that makes my blood boil even as my heart drops out of my stomach. The house. Clara said the house, not home. It really isn't my home anymore, and I feel as if I'm suffocating.

"No, no. I booked a room at Lake Mouth. I didn't want to impose my presence on anyone," I say, praising the big guy in the sky that my voice doesn't waver. Instead, I sound irritated to my own ears. It shouldn't make me pleased to hear her take a sharp breath.

"And you can afford that? I'll send money, a little loan, if you need it." Mom–Clara—is so businesslike that I wonder if I did actually call the right person. That she asks if she needs to loan me money tips my blood from boiling to boiling over. Ten years. I haven't needed help in ten years, but apparently in Clara's mind, that must mean something sinister.

"No," I reply, a little tersely. "I've got it. Like I said before, I didn't want to impose my presence on you. No one likes a scene."

I can't help the digs I take at her. The phrase defined my life: don't make a scene. I doubt that mother will even notice.

"Yes," Clara says in a murmur. "That's a smart decision. Scenes are an annoyance and at Christmas, of all holidays, the most embarrassing. They're always the ones best remembered."

I exhale slowly. My chest hurts, my eyes burn, and I grind my teeth together to keep from yelling. I wasn't ready to make this call. I shouldn't go. There's no way I can sit through three days of this. "Sure. I'll see you at Grand-Père's then, I guess."

"Make sure you have clothing for Mass, Evanna." Clara almost barks into the phone and I grind my teeth yet again.

"Yes, of course. Bye, love you."

"Goodbye," she says blandly, the dial tone following.

I have to force myself to not throw my phone clear across the room. Instead of breaking my most expensive piece of technology, I call Keyanna. Tonight, we're were getting a babysitter, and forgetting the bullshit that is life.

~

Wading through the crowd that just disembarked from a tour bus, I send a brief prayer of thanks out to my best friend. Keyanna has gotten me through some shit. From the moment I met her at Howard in our dorm room, we clicked. We have histories that are disparate and yet eerily similar to one another.

Hell, Keyanna is the only person I've told the truth, the full truth, about Theodore too. I can't even bring myself to tell my therapist the full scope of what he is to me. It's easier to just … avoid it. I was in a vulnerable place when Theo found me that night. I ran headfirst into a situation that would only hurt me.

Thinking about it, about Theodore, even just his name, makes me swallow hard and my body heat. He might have found me when I was vulnerable that night, but I'd been harboring thoughts and feelings long before. It's uncanny how he could make me absolutely livid, and yet I would still blush. Not a rage blush, either. The full body, this-is-attractive blush. Sweaty palms, even the back of my knees, kind of heat reaction.

Theodore makes me nervous. Full on, flippy, twisty stomach, heart palpating, nervous.

Why? There are so many reasons, but at the fore is the fact I didn't tell him. I never told Theodore when I left that I'd had a knockdown, drag out confrontation with Clara that tilted my world view. He didn't know where I went. Theo'd had absolutely no idea that when I left, I was pregnant. At that point, I just couldn't. Couldn't chance that he'd played me like a perfect fool.

In my heart, our relationship had shifted. It felt like love. It felt so much like we were in love. I was, I am, utterly terrified to learn that it's not true. Ten years. I still don't want to know if he created the perfect lie.

It's better in the end that I don't know. And that I didn't know then, too. With the sheer amount of stress I was under, thanks to the revelations concerning my parents, heartbreak on top of it may have killed me. As it is, the stress alone almost got me, almost got our baby.

The hand that's not holding my Starbucks cup falls to my stomach as I remember the terror I felt that day. It lances through me now. The sharp fear-pain that takes my breath away. That it had been a sustained feeling for three weeks makes me wonder how I survived. How did I stay *sane* feeling that way?

Suffice to say that my nineteenth birthday had been a nightmare.

I wanted Theodore with me. For months, I wondered if having Theo at my side would have changed anything. If the outcomes would have been different if I had his support. I wondered more than was healthy. If Theo were with me—would things have been so bad?

It doesn't matter how often I tell myself there's no point in could-have-beens. I still wonder. I've played out many scenarios in my head about that birthday. Ones where Theo being with me meant I didn't become ill. Some scenarios where I think of still being alone and losing Xaria. I've thought of Theo being there with life going to hell anyway. I've had dozens of intrusive daydreams about things going well. Somehow, everything went right both with and without Theodore there.

With a dash of luck, and double the grace, this year's birthday won't rack up as my second worst birthday. I've tried to cover all the bases that I can. My parents are expecting me, after all. It helps to know that I'll have allies in Grand-Mère and Grand-Père, I can't help wondering. My inner monologue fills with what ifs when it comes to the idea of being in a house with my parents.

I brace part of myself to have to listen to whatever comments they'll inevitably throw over dinner. Which is exhausting. I'm not even there yet and I am utterly exhausted. I know snide, cutting remarks are in my future.

After Xaria was born, I kept some of the baby weight. Gone was my size six dress. My new normal was and is a size twelve. It helps that right after her birth I had my last growth spurt. Though with the extra couple inches my hips are still *wide*. My ass is still just *there*. My bouncing baby made the thicker waist complete with heavier breasts. The milk left; the rest stayed. Which means I am going to be called fat, eight ways from Sunday.

I need to make peace with it.

It's not going fucking well.

Returning to reality from my mostly disassociated state, I notice the crowd thinning. The crosswalks are clearer, thank God. My car is even in my sightline. As I step into the slush again off one of the raised areas between the garden boxes, God seems to sweep in. They have to have their eyes on me, given how my cellphone goes off as I return to spiraling down into an anxiety attack.

Fishing the device from my jacket pocket, I answer without looking at the caller ID. I have exactly ten contacts. Twelve people or organizations have my phone number. The likelihood of this being an unpleasant call is slim to none.

"Hello, this is Evanna Bishop-LeClair speaking," I say clearly, moving my scarf away from my mouth. Just because I know who could be calling, doesn't mean I should toss aside phone etiquette.

"Hey, Eva. You good?" Keyanna's voice makes my shoulders drop out of the tense configuration I've been holding them in.

"Yeah, Key," I say, smiling slightly as I reassure her. "I'm good. I'm almost there, actually. Lake Mouth is five hours away. Are you and little bit okay?"

I have to wade through a new flood of people who'd just left a bus that parked. Tucking my phone to my shoulder while finding my keys, I juggle them with the travel mug to unlock the car. Sliding inside, the silence that envelops me is bliss.

"Well, there haven't been any meltdowns. There are also no billionaire hotties in the Parrot café to whisk me away on a spontaneous trip to the Maldives where we'll fall in love either. So, I guess we're fine. Xar is happy, but she misses you." Keyanna's usual level of energy is suspiciously absent from her statement.

Sighing, I figure I may as well bite the bullet. "We should have gone on the girls' trip, Key."

I loathe when I'm wrong, and I detest admitting it. Passing up a perfect opportunity to travel abroad to drive to Upstate New York–through to the edge of the border? That hadn't been the right choice. My stress levels aren't exactly waning with each mile closer I get to West River.

"*Bi-itch,*" Keyanna says, really drawing out the 'I', giving the word a whole extra syllable. "I *told* you not to go home. I told you we weren't on that level yet. But no. You had to let yourself get guilt tripped into driving fourteen hours north to a place you don't even consider home. Worse! The guilt trip happened by letter! *By fuckin' letter.* Who sends letters anymore, Eva? *Who?*"

"Well, my Aunt does, clearly," I drawl, sipping at my caramel apple drink and letting Keyanna get her frustrations out.

This is how things work with her and I. We vent, we accept, and we move. Sometimes the vent and accept portions of the cycle have to happen a couple of times, but isn't that just the nature of life?

"Man," Keyanna says, sucking at her teeth, "I can't say anything bad about your auntie outside of the fact she crafty as hell. But it's *still* messed up that you're there and we're here, Eva. Xaria's never experienced not having you at home with her, Evanna. I know we spent the entire month talking to her about this, preparing her for it, but it still feels shitty."

Keyanna, if possible, sounds more upset than I feel about me going home. Frowning, I lick at my lips. This isn't normal for Keyanna or me. The melancholy, the lack of energy in her voice. I'm worried.

"Keyanna, are you okay?"

"*Fuck no*," she says with a groan. "It's hitting too close to home. It's giving too much prodigal daughter. I'll be okay, though. I'm worried you're going there for a few days, and you'll come back home broken. You don't need that kind of setback. Xaria, sure as shit, doesn't need to watch you have to wrestle with that either. Now, little miss loves my cousin's house as much as anyone, but it's not the same as having you here. Not to mention, you left me here to deal with all the shit *my* aunties are gonna give me."

"It's going to be fine," I say as soothingly as possible. I'm quite glad, really, that I can focus on Keyanna here rather than myself. "Do no harm, but take no shit, babes. Just remember that. Tell your sisters, cousins, brothers, and aunties to go to hell if they try or say some stupid shit."

"Easier said than done," she replies evenly. "Or you'd be holding the same philosophy much closer to the chest. When are you gonna tell Clara about herself, hm?"

"A week from never," I say quickly, meaning every word. "God, I could never, even though I want to. I am on the do no harm train, though. I can't. No. I *won't* let someone make me feel bad for leaving. If I hadn't, I wouldn't be where I'm about to be. You're going to be a whole ass Doctor, Key. I'm going to work for a damn Senator. We made the right choices. Doesn't matter what precipitated them, doesn't matter how family took it, we did *exactly* what we needed to do."

My therapist would be so proud of me for saying that. While it will be damn hard to remember this when someone inevitably questions me, I'm clinging to it. It's my armor. It's the answer to the question. That's all anyone needs to know.

And my job, the one I'll be riding home to, is exactly what I wanted. It's better than what I'd thought I'd achieve once I finished college. I'd made it through without help. Everything I have right now is mine. Mine because I put in the work. That's the most important thing I can remind myself and others of. I worked for this life; I earned this life. Earned it for myself and for Xaria. We're living a life free of toxicity; we're breaking the cycle. I might have anxiety, but I spot my own toxic bullshit and fix it.

Ain't a lick a time to let old wounds reopen. I just need to remember that.

"Yeah, yeah," Keyanna huffs. I can almost hear the way her eyes roll. "I hear you, you're right." She takes a deep breath on her end of the phone and lets it out slowly. "Easter, girl. We're out of here come Easter. The U.S. of A will have to say goodbye to its most dynamic trio. We've earned that with this stunt."

I laugh, enjoying that and agreeing wholeheartedly. We're due some time to relax. "Where do you even want to go?"

"I don't know," Keyanna says thoughtfully. "But we've got plenty of time to figure it out, given we have to time it right with Xaria's spring break. We should start looking up locations that people don't flock to. Make it an experience for the lot of us, not just beaches and lying around."

That's more like my best friend. Keyanna might want her fairytale whirlwind romance, but her head has always been on right. I hear muffled voices and a card reader in the background. It's quiet. Key's quiet for a while. She must be getting food. I should let her go so she can eat and feed Xaria, too.

"Oh. Didn't you say Kelly's going back north, too? He was from around the same place you lived, right?"

Groaning, I start the car and wipers to clear the snow on my windshield. Of course, she'd bring up Kelly. That boy is *almost* as bad as Theodore, for me. After Xaria was born, I was–*again*–in a vulnerable place. I'd bring her to class with me. Some of my professors even took her, walking her when she was fussy. Not all of them, but most were willing to help me. It was a blessing. One I don't know that I'll ever be able to pay forward.

Kelly, however, *wasn't* one of those blessings. He swept in, seeing easy prey, and strung me along. Theodore had at least legitimately wanted me, even if it was nefarious. Kelly couldn't make up his damn mind if he wanted me or just enjoyed fucking me. When I wised up to what was going on, I stopped our dance of will-they-won't-they.

"Yeah," I reply after a pause. "He's from around my way. Before you ask–no, I didn't inform him I planned to make the pilgrimage north. I have enough shit coming my way already without stirring that drama pot."

"I was just asking, shit." Keyanna defends herself while sounding far too pleased. "I'm glad you didn't tell him. That boy is bad for your heart and health. Even Xaria didn't like him. And last time she saw him, she was four."

That had been the only time Xaria met Kelly.

"Maybe stay far away from tall, dark, and dickly the entire visit to New York, Evi. They're not worth the hours of mediocre sex you get from them." Keyanna finishes her thought decisively. In my head, I can see Keyanna nodding along with her own advice.

Brows raising, I can't say that Keyanna is wrong. Kelly hadn't been a wonderful decision, even throwing Theodore into the mix. Still, I'm not going to let that comment sit.

"Listen, I've got a different tall, dark, fair, and confusing to deal with at the farmhouse. I don't need to add another. One will always be enough for a single holiday." Good God is one more than enough to deal with.

Theodore haunts me. The what ifs, the longing. I think he'll always haunt me.

"True," Keyanna replies. I hear the rustling of bags. "Hey, let me let you go, though. I got food, Xaria's coming back from the bathroom, too. I'm adhering to your 'it's not cute to eat and talk on the phone' rule."

"Good," I say with a snort. "Add the 'it's not cute to eat in the car when you have time to sit there' rule, too. Keep an eye out for your billionaire love interest, get my baby fed and tell her I said hi, too. I've got to grab gas, some drive-thru, and get to this hotel. I'll call before Xaria's bedtime and text you once I'm checked in. The faster this starts, the faster I'm back at the apartment planning the farewell party, the move, and Easter."

"From your lips," Keyanna laughs. "You go play the prodigal daughter as long as you can stomach it. The life you earned is waiting for you here."

"Talk to you later," I tell her as I pull out of my parking spot. "Be safe, be smart. I love you, and tell Xari I love her too."

"I love you too, bitch. Stay safe out there, Eva."

Phone call ended; I get on with it. The gas station makes my wallet cringe while I shiver in the cold, running the odds of me making it through the holiday unscathed. The chances seem slim, upsettingly slim, with Clara within an arm's distance of me. That's not factoring in Jasmine's mouth and Jacob's complacency. Theodore isn't even put on the roster. I can't. Part of me still wants him to have wanted me. I still love that asshole.

I have the worst feeling that I'll leave New York with more emotional scars than when I originally left.

However, that non-zero chance that I might make it is the hope I cling to. That keeps me from turning my car back around and saying 'fuck this'. It's also what keeps bringing up memories of Theo. Hope. It's a nasty little bitch.

Gas tank filled, wallet pleading for mercy, I flip on the radio and turn up the heat a little more. A random 'smash hit' fills the car as I navigate myself through the nearest fast-food chain. I absent mindedly order, pay, and retrieve the food before driving off. While I should pay close attention to the world around me, my mind knows these roads, and I'm stuck on Theodore.

We spent four months desperately fucking on the sly. That's all it took to make me think he could have loved me. Four months is all I got before reality came calling. The shit hit the fan, and my life crashed around me. But what does my mind bring up? The pet names, the brief moments that made my heart speed up.

"You know, princess, you're going to be even more beautiful after I breed you. I didn't quite think it was possible, but now, I'm sure."

"Fuck, baby, you look gorgeous. We should go out. Except, I don't want anyone seeing how slutty you are for me, how perfect you are. I'd end up in jail for assault if someone else saw you dressed like this."

"Princess, don't let her get to you. Clara's bullshit is her problem. Come here, let me make it better. Let me love you, let me chase it away."

"You don't think you're leaving already, do you, sweet girl? I haven't seen you in a week, haven't been holding you at night. You're staying in this bed for the weekend and you're going to be my good girl, aren't you? Fuck, I missed you so goddamn much."

The words drift through my mind. Some still have the same effect on me. I take a vicious bite of my nugget as I recall how his arms would twine around me once we wore ourselves out. Theo would tuck around me like a shield against the world outside. He'd wake me up with kisses and caresses, or we'd chance walking downtown with me tucked against his side.

I blindly feel for my drink, lifting it to sip. The caramel-apple sweetness makes me relax a little. The moment I got to Maryland and tried it for the first time while pregnant, it became my comfort drink. One of the few things I craved that didn't remind me of what I thought of as home.

Worrying my lip between sips, my eyes follow a truck that passes by me on the road. Inevitably, I think of him again. He's a curse.

"Hey," I whisper one night while wrapped in his arms. I'm half asleep, still breathless, too. "What names do you like?"

A whole two months have passed since we started sleeping together. Theo's still on his bullshit, too. He still tells me he's only fucking me to knock me up, to ruin me. The tone is different, though. Sort of fond. I don't tell him that he's got the job done. Mission accomplished. Theo won. I'll never willingly say those particular words.

"Hm?" He nuzzles into my neck, clearly stalling as his brain boots up.

"Names," I say in a whisper, laughing at him. "For when we have this kid you want so bad. Y'know, the baby you're still hell bent on giving me."

"Mm," he nods against my neck. "Not the popular ones. Remember school? Six kids turning when one name is called. Fuck that. Need t'be able to yell it and get the kid right off," he murmurs while sliding his hands over my sides.

"It's gotta be unique, like Evanna."

"Wow," I say with a huff, a pleased flush warming my face. "That's so helpful, Theodore. No popular names, no weird ones I'm assuming, but Welsh names are in? Guess it's my job to keep your kid from having a shit name."

"You'll be too tired," he says, voice a low rumble that twists up my insides. "It'll be me filling out the birth certificate so you can sign it."

"Oh, you'll be there?"

"Like I'd be anywhere else."

Shaking my head, I scowl and shove a nugget into my mouth. I chew viciously. Back then, I'd wanted him to want me so badly. I wanted him to the point of stupidity. The hormones had me so willing to overlook the fundamental fact that we were a secret; I was a secret. A dirty secret. I'd willingly overlooked that my parents would have had an actual cow if they figured out it was Theo who got me pregnant.

They'd have done something irreparably stupid.

Just thinking about that, about the conversation I'd had with them, makes me want to scream. They're why I didn't know, or want to know, if Theo would have left me had I stayed. It would have broken me.

God above, I got so sick after the stress waned. In the hospital, while I was terrified, staring at my belly and willing Xaria to stay where she was, I wanted Theo with me. I *needed* him there. I needed him to help me through thinking I'd killed Xaria. Then, when she finally decided she couldn't wait longer and came early in February, I still needed Theodore with me. I wanted him there. He should…

"For fuck's sake. What is wrong with me?" I ask the empty car and put aside the empty cup of nuggets. "He wasn't there. He won't be there now. Get over it."

It's harsh, but I have to think about it. I have to say that. It doesn't matter anymore that he wasn't with me. What happened, happened. It's all history now, and there's no changing what the past wrought. I'm going back to the farmhouse. I'll stay there until Boxing Day and then I'll leave again. Boxing Day I will leave New York and return to my life, to my daughter, alone. He is my past. New York's just where I grew up.

Theodore is my past.

Reunions

Theodore
22 December

Pulling into my grandparents' driveway is strange. The farm hasn't visually changed. The sugar bush is beyond the big barn and up the hill. Garden's still down the hill by the water pump. The sugar shack peeks from between ancient maples at the forest's edge. It's almost as if no time's passed.

But there aren't any cows anymore, the coops are gone too.

Finding a place to park is easier than I'd thought it would be, considering it's the day before Christmas Eve. I sit in the car and get my head straight. I'm far from worried about seeing everyone again. This is a triumphant return. Sort of. Might not have the girl. But I have a good life, a company. There is no failure written in my soul.

Not pertaining to my choices after Evanna left, at least. I don't know when Eva will arrive. She might already be in the house. I need to be prepared for her.

I locked the door when I left the cab. The old house had some work done. New Porch, new windows, fresh paint. Nana must have gotten Gramps to give in and have improvements done. They had replaced the old door. After the new handle turns, I'm back in my old life.

There aren't any boots laid out covered in mud, just a neat shoe rack beneath the coats. Not everything has changed, though. The house still smells of old wood. Stalling, I stand in the mudroom, just taking it in. I don't linger too long. I'd rather not alarm anyone that heard the door.

Shoes off, coat on a hook, I knock on the door.

My dear old Gramps tosses open the door, and I can't help but smile. He's the same as ever, portly, bald, and ready with a bright smile. For a second, he's quiet and then,

"Well goddamn, Theo, it's about time!"

"Yeah," I say without thinking about it, "I 'spose it is, isn't it?"

"Get in here." Gramps moves to the side, and I step into the warmth of the house.

"You put new flooring down," I say, blinking as I look around. The same knickknacks are everywhere, but the wood's refurbished, the flooring is shining, the table has clear repair signs. What in the hell?

"Sure did. It was all Jake. He comes around a lot. Been getting your grandmother to accept some fixin' here and there." Gramps talks like it doesn't look like a new house under the same beloved wrought iron decorations. It's even warmer than I remember it being.

"Got in new insulation. Jake did a new roof this summer. He wants to knock down the old extension, but I'm not sure." He shakes his head and I just chuckle. What else can I do? Last I knew, Jake had a job. Maybe he retired early? He is the eldest of their kids.

"How have you been?" Gramps doesn't miss a beat, waving for me to follow him down the hall. Here are more signs of gentle care and update. Color me very fucking intrigued.

"I've been good, Gramps. Just living my life, getting it together. My company is doing real well, but I'll save that news for when everyone is around to tell it. I don't want to bore you by telling it a hundred times," I say with a fond smile aimed at him.

"Oh hell, you couldn't bore us if you tried," Gramps huffs, opening the common room door. The brightly lit living room holds the sea of people I'd anticipated seeing. Andi, nameless man with Andi, two kids now, Dad, an unknown woman with dad, Odette and her wife, Frankie and her wife, grandma. Jasmine, Clara, and Jake are missing. I can't say that I'm upset about that, either.

"Theodore!" My dad is up and gets his arms around me in a split second, hands thumping on my back. "My boy, my boy, you stayed away too long. It's good to see you with these old eyes of mine."

"Oh, come off it, dad," I laugh, hugging him tightly for a moment. "I talked to you yesterday."

"Aw now, talkin' ain't the same as seein' and you know it," he drawls, letting me find a seat. It's easy enough. I plop down on the empty ottoman, leaning forward with my elbows on my knees.

"Yeah, yeah." I wave a hand. "Don't let me interrupt. What're we talkin' about?"

There is a moment of silence I'm not used to. Andi, though, I can always count on her. She opens her mouth and all the gossip, good, bad, stupid, n'ugly comes out. That hasn't changed. I end up smiling even though her response makes my heart feel like I've filled it with lead.

"Evanna is supposed to be here tomorrow, y'know? So, we were speculatin'. Jake and Clara don't talk about her and haven't for years. Aunt Frankie had to go send a letter to get a hold of her! That can't be good. I figure she ended up in the military. They'll take anyone, and she was smart enough." Her shoulders shrug as she trails off.

Eva— our Evanna, in the military? There's no candidate less likely to enlist than Evanna. That girl would rather chew glass than run. The enlisted guys said certain things. It's doubtful she'd ever make it out of basic. Eva's not made for that.

"I doubt that," Nana says quietly from her seat beside Gramps. Nana's got her knitting out. "Evanna was too ready; too happy about college to do something reckless. I saw her, I assume the day she left. She stopped in to return the keys to the loft. That girl was pale and grey. When I looked at her, it'd been obvious she'd cried. But her face had that expression of being set on it. You remember that look, don't you?"

"Our little queen, when she was certain what she was doing, was right? How could any of us forget, Ma." Aunt Frankie smiles warmly. "She's got a stubborn streak a mile wide. She's Jake's through and through."

I cringe. She's not Jake's. I will never understand why they insist on saying that. Evanna hadn't liked it either. But she's not here to be pissed, I guess.

"It's more likely she's been doing exactly what she planned to do," I say after a while of everyone offering their theories. The nunnery prompted me to say something. Considering that was as unlikely as her enlisting. "Eva was planning to pursue a communications degree, right? So, I bet we'll see her up on the news somewhere. Or we'll read an article with her byline on it. I don't think she's gone to the extreme of joining a convent or the military. Her friends are all posting how excited they are about Eva visiting. So, she didn't get married. One of them would've let it slip." Yeah, sue me, I stalk her old social media page. If she's got a new one, she's hidden it damn well.

"That's boring," Andi whines. "Eva disappeared! She ought'a be doing something adventurous. Honestly, why even leave if she wasn't planning something great?"

"Andi," Nana shoots my sister a warning look. "Evanna decided, and no matter how curious we are about why, they're her decisions. I'm sure she's doin' just fine wherever she is. It'll be good to see her again, that's the important part. That's what I really care about."

Nodding absently, some of Nana's words flip in my head. She'd been crying when she came to give up her keys. My brows furrow as my lips press together. She'd been crying a lot from July on, as I recall. Had been touchy, too. A hair pin trigger on her temper, a libido that was soaring.

Eva always came running when someone or something upset her. At the time, I didn't much care why. I got extra time with my girl, that was enough for me. She always cited fights with her parents, Jasmine, a friend. I didn't think about it.

But I'm thinking now. I don't like how this math is adding, either. Was she told to leave? Did her parents find out about us? I can see Clara blowing a gasket about it, but Jake? Jake loves Eva more than the moon.

"You seem to be thinkin' hard," my dad says, and I jerk out of my staring contest with the floor.

"Oh, I guess. First real vacation. I'm just used to working until I can't see straight." I wave my distraction off easily.

"You never threw yourself into work like that on the farm," Gramps teases. I shrug and smile sheepishly.

"Ah, Gramps, I was neck deep in wanting to be out in the world spreading my wings. I just didn't realize how badly I needed to do that until I did it. Moving was good. It made me rearrange my world view. Made me learn some harsh lessons, too."

"What lessons were those?" Odette asks, looking up from her magazine. Aunt Odette, of all the family, is the most critical outside of Clara. With good reason.

"For starters, I was a real ass—I was a real *jerk*," I amend myself hastily, remembering Andi's kids. "I had learned some real awful sh-stuff here, and it's no one's fault, really, outside my own. I didn't care to see that I was verbally abusive. And I was. Also had some real racially based issues I didn't know about until some friends took it upon themselves to educate me."

"So, you finally saw how you were treatin' her?" Nana looks up and I swallow the lump in my throat. I don't need to ask who she means. I know, everyone in the room knows.

"I owe that woman about a thousand apologies. Frankly, I don't even want her to forgive me for all that ridiculousness. I was awful to her. Knew it then, but I didn't know, if you follow. It was logical to me. I was just broken. Which is part of why I'm home. I figured if Eva came home, I could make those apologies. Along with apologies, I need to give ya'll." I keep my head up, making eye contact with everyone in the room.

"That's very mature of you," Odette remarks. "It's good you finally see what you were doing. My opinion? Evanna left because she'd reached the end of her tether. People treated her awfully and hid it under a fake smile. Wouldn't surprise me a bit if that's what made her leave. The rumors were especially awful that summer."

"Rumors?" My brows pinch again, eyes narrowing. "I know I didn't start any, so I'll have to ask you what you're talkin' about, Aunt Odette."

"Couple of boys apparently saw Eva with a young man that summer. According to the story, Eva was seen while intimate with him. Apparently, they were sayin' all manner of things to each other." Her face is red, and I feel my stomach roll.

We'd been careless, but not *that* careless.

"One of her friends thought she was pregnant. Her partner didn't want her, or the baby, so Eva left. It makes the most sense. You know Evanna. She wouldn't give up a baby for love nor money," Andi offers at last after a tense silence.

While it's a probable scenario. Hell, it's the most likely. I want it to be a lie. If Eva left because she was pregnant, she never told me. Evanna wouldn't have done that to me. Not without a reason. Swallowing, I stretch to get comfortable and to cover my absolute despair. I don't know what I'll do if she walks into church tomorrow with a child. My child. Our child.

"Well," Gramps says and slaps his knees. "If the little queen had a prince or princess, we'll be overjoyed. Anyone who doesn't like it can leave. Anyone who says a word cross wise about her will hear from me, too. That girl deserves to be welcomed home."

"Here, here," Nana and my dad echo.

All I do is nod. I can't seem to work around this lump in my throat. Nor can I seem to dispel the pit in my stomach. Why would she run if she were pregnant? We wanted a baby. I made it.

Fuck. I close my eyes for just a second.

I don't think I ever told Evanna I wasn't playing to hurt her, not anymore. I was playing to keep her. She'd pegged me right that night in the cab of my truck. I didn't want anyone to get Evanna's attention but me. If I could have my way, she'd already be just Evanna LeClair. We'd be happy… and gone.

I know I hadn't been courageous enough to make it clear. We had a lot of time, I thought. I was so sure.

"Theo."

"Hm?" I shake my head, and my dad looks at me with minor concern.

"I called your name about five times. Are you tired or hungry?"

"A little of both, I think." I scrub my face with my hands, trying to remove any expression from it. We're alone in the lounge. I notice it when I look around again. My head is clearly not in the damn game today.

"Well, we can fix the hungry," Dad says in a drawl. "We can't fix the rest of it."

"Rest of what?" My lip curls toward my nose as I scowl. "I just need some sleep."

"Seems to me you've needed sleep since Evanna left," Dad remarks bluntly. Unlike Evanna, I never really worried about my dad knowing. He'd never disown me over her. We've got no blood ties. We sure as fuck lacked a familial bond.

"Dad, seriously, "I get cut off before I can even weave a lie to keep Evanna safe. I'm not worried about me. I'm always worried about her. Her safety, happiness, whereabouts.

"I saw you, Theodore." He sighs and runs his hand through his hair, looking at the door. "That summer, you and her didn't hide as well as you thought. Eva's got lungs on her."

He looks a little green, and frankly, I feel ill. I knew by August we'd gotten too comfortable here. My instincts had been right. Fucking shit.

"Do Nana and Gramps know?" I might as well start here. Then I'll see how badly the shit'll hit the fan later.

"No. But your Nana has a feeling. Same as Clara's got a feelin'. Clara, she's had you pegged since about fifteen. While I saw you floundering and tryn'a look anywhere but Evanna, Clara just saw you lookin'. She never realized that you didn't see each other like family." He has a look on his face. I know far too well. It makes me feel like I'm sixteen again.

"*Dad.*"

"It's true. As a child, you never liked that poor girl. Not even when you met her. While you like her just fine now, you were cruel. Don't think I didn't know. I did and tried to mitigate your bullshit."

"I was stupid."

"Well," he sighs, deflating some. "At least you've learned that. Now… tell me your plan. What're you going to do when Eva shows up at Mass? How're you going to approach her? If you look at Evanna with an ounce of longing-they'll all know."

"Fuck, I don't know." I rub at my neck. "Listen, there's no plan. I just knew this was my one chance at catching her. The logistics weren't a priority, getting here was."

"Good thing you're not in a job that needs you to plan," dad says deadpan. For a couple of seconds, we're both quiet. Dad's chewing on something, and frankly, I don't think I'm ready to answer whatever questions he's got.

"Did you get her pregnant?"

"*Christ.*" I look at the ceiling, praying for an intervention. "I don't know."

"Do you not know because you practiced safe sex, and it was an accident? Or are you sayin' you don't because Eva disappeared?" There's a hard edge in his voice that I know. I emulate it when I least expect to.

"Because she never said she was pregnant, and she disappeared," I reply. Grandma always says to tell the truth and shame the devil. Well, tonight, I'm telling the truth to shame myself.

"*Goddamn it,* Theodore! Evanna is precious to all of us. Why the hell—" I have to cut him off.

"I know," I grind out. "I know she's precious. What we did… What I did with her… it's our business. But I wanted her, thought that if she was…"

It's difficult to admit, but I force myself to. "If I ruined her, and tethered her to me, then she'd be mine and I don't know, somewhere, we'd be happy? My frontal lobe was just finishing cooking, Dad. It wasn't smart, it's haunted me. Eva's leaving… it was like having a piece of me ripped out. I love her. So just… Just don't."

"Fix it," Dad says sharply. "If Evanna shows up with a child in tow, you fuckin' fix it, Theodore. You love her? Prove it."

"What do you think I've been doing for ten years?" I ask him sarcastically. "All this time, I've been trying to prove it to myself. I had to prove I had business wanting her still."

The Problem
with Christmas

Evanna
24 December

The fated day dawns, bright and horridly sunny, and with it my anxiety takes hold. I've changed three times this morning, switching the black lace dress out for blue silk. I trade blue silk out for festive red velvet. I've put on my stockings, made sure the dress is long enough to cover me demurely for Mass and checked my make-up four times. My hair is curly. I refuse to pick up an iron today. I can look how I want especially near and on my birthday.

Still, my stomach is rolling, my chest is plaguing me with a rubber band stretched too far.

Why? Well, you tell me. What's more awkward than seeing your family for the first time in ten years? What's more awkward than being in love with your cousin, who's six goddamn years old than you, who secretly got you pregnant? Any guesses? Being in a fucking cathedral with them all.

Fuck. Fuck.

Sitting in the pew, my personal prayer book clutched between my hands, I feel like bolting. I could stand up, excuse myself to the restroom and no one would know. We're five minutes over the Canadian border. I can grab my sister's keys, she can ride with mom and dad, and I can leave the car at Grand-Mère's house before calling an Uber. I can disappear again, I can. It would be simple.

Except I am stuck to my seat. I'm absolutely incapable of leaving this damned cathedral. I want to for a lot of reasons. The first communion I took was here. They baptized me in this church. I held Andi's daughter, my goddaughter, in this church and swore I'd be there for her to usher her into God's word. Had fate not fucked me, this is the church I would be married in. It holds so many memories.

My mother's laughter bounced through this place with mine echoing after. We shared little jokes together here when the sermon was too tense. I played piano, violin, and flute here. I sang here.

My nails dig into the leather of my prayer book. I numbly go through the motions of worship, never missing a beat, never fumbling with a single word. What should be a comfort barely keeps me from breaking down.

Jasmine is next to me. Her hair is ridiculously long now. She's wearing something so painfully hick that I can't make sense of her. Jasmine was the fashionable one. She'd always been the one who looked the best for everything. I don't need to ask why she's traded styles or philosophies. It's the same thing that resulted in me calling her sister and not mother.

Someone caught her eye, and Jas left home. *Again.*

That evens me out a bit, at least. That one thing hasn't changed. What's honestly shocking is the bitter taste it leaves in my mouth. But if I can make it through mass, I can make it through Christmas Eve dinner.

The urge to pull at my hair or pick at the hem of my dress is overwhelming on the car ride from church. Jasmine keeps shooting me these brief looks, like she's worried. More so when I ask her to detour so I can get my car, the paranoia in me winning out over the kindness. Maybe my emotions are too obvious now? Had therapy made me transparent? Fuck, I hope not. I'm relying on my mask to keep things calm at dinner.

I worry right until I step foot into the farmhouse.

It still smells the same. Like maple syrup and tobacco. Grand-Père's favorite cologne lingers around the coats as I hang mine. Grand-mere's yell brings me back to the present.

"Oh, regarde-toi, Evanna! My princess! You look gorgeous." Her weathered hands cup my cheeks and I smile despite the anxiety still roaring through me. Her blue eyes are bright, her freckles paler than they were when I left, and her hair. Oh. Grand-Mère's hair is a cloud of white. When I'd left, it was steel grey.

"Bonjour, Grand-Mère," I whisper, voice a little thick. "Tu m'as beaucoup manqué"

Five words cut through me and seem to cut through her too. She wraps me up in a tight hug. I love her for it; especially when she doesn't let go. Not even as Mom and Dad edge past her into the dining room.

When she lets me go, her hands cup my face again. "Never again, Evanna. You don't leave us behind," the directive is whispered, but I know an order when I hear one.

"I promise," I smile, clearing my throat a moment later.

"Est-ce ma Eva?? Ma petite reine est rentrée??" Grand-Père's voice cuts through the soft chatter. I'm swung from Grand-Mère's arms into Grand-Père's. From there I'm passed to Aunt Frankie, Uncle Joe, Andi, my goddaughter as she jumps into my arms, and then ... him.

"Prodigal daughter, returned from parts unknown," Theo rumbles and my heart stops. Traitorous bitch. Past. He. Is. The Past.

"Word is I'm not the only prodigal child," I reply evenly, letting him sweep me into a stilted hug. Stilted, because I want to hold him longer. From the way he's holding me, he feels the same. Instead, we hurry away from one another.

Odette arrives late with her partner, and I'm swept into more hugs and introductions. Andi's partner, Frankie's partner, Joe even brought someone. It's ... well, it's pretty goddamn wild in the farmhouse on the big bend of the road into and out of West River.

I reflect back on my question of what could be more awkward than coming home after a decade and all the drama of my past. I've found it. It wasn't sitting in a cathedral with them all scattered.

It's sitting beside him with every immediate member of both our respective families. Families that know we're vaguely civil toward one another, but otherwise still hate one another. Our history is well remembered, apparently.

The table groans under the weight of the sheer amount of food there is. Roast tonight, because nothing but Turkey is fit for Christmas in this house. It's a tradition that keeps on going. And another part of me that's felt adrift since crossing into New York, anchors again.

Looking around, part of me doesn't remember why I left. At least not until I meet eyes with Clara. *Mom.* Suddenly every single Christmas gathering I've ever been to flashes through my mind's eye. I can, if asked, describe in minute detail the times Theodore pushed me into Grand-Mère's Christmas tree, when he pulled my hair, made me trip into the presents to see what his was. I can remember the years I went with Grand-Père to choose a tree, Theo would hide in the sugar bush just to scare me, nearly sending me toppling off the tractor. He'd do it during sugar season too.

Staring at my mother, it's impossible to forget every hissed nickname, comment, or look of triumph in Theodore's eyes when my word was doubted, as they held him up as sterling. But it's not just Theo's comments and hissed words I remember.

It's hers.

How many times have I sat at this table while my mother lamented my appetite? How often did she make a comment that my bust was too big, my hips too wide? I was putting on too much weight, my hair was frizzy because I sweat too much. Whispering I'd gotten lazy when I dared to decline those few years of working here.

As if I hadn't had a job somewhere else?

During the years before I graduated, Theo tried to tear me apart. Mom, she always said because Theo wasn't able to come to terms with his mother leaving him, that he took it out on me. She just…accepted it. And, sure, that explains a mean kid when he was thirteen. It didn't hold up when I was nine, ten, or eleven and he was fifteen, sixteen, and seventeen.

When he hit his early twenties, he hadn't changed. I was a goddamn middle schooler, and my mother sat back and watched him make me cry.

I have to avoid looking at them… at Dad. I know what I'll see there, quiet longing and remorse. The same look he gives Oliver. That leaves me with Jasmine. Not exactly better. Jasmine once told me that Theodore was just pulling my pigtails, that it was *innocent*.

When we were younger, maybe. There'd been a distinct lack of concern then. Now, I bet if I mentioned Theo behaving oddly around me that Jasmine would just shrug her shoulders.

Mentally, I scream *bullshit*. I did then; I do now. At fourteen I knew it, when he sent me to the ER with a broken arm. At eighteen, I knew it wasn't what men did, that he wasn't pulling pigtails, even as I slept with him. I knew it when he made me cry, and I accepted it because if I was good, he would be kind. I knew Theo was a problem. Just like I knew Kelly was a problem at twenty-four.

Suddenly, never having talked about Theo in therapy is showing me a lot of gaps in what I thought I'd healed. I've gone on dates with men who never pulled my hair for attention. The dates didn't amount too much. Part of me says, 'that doesn't mean a thing'. The other part is giving me the stare down of my life. Knowing that, however, doesn't help me while I'm sitting here with my family.

Fuck. With family like this, who needs enemies?

Plates, dishes, and baskets are being ferried around the table. Everyone is all squished up against one another tonight. It'll be the same tomorrow, too. I should be happy, tossing a roll at my goddaughter, or at Andi, trading stories like I was here just last weekend, but I still need to update everyone. Instead, I feel like a stranger, like the plus one that came but the family member meant to bring me forgot to show up.

Theo won more thoroughly than he'll ever realize.

As the dishes stop moving around, and people eat, I realize I failed to consider how the table, the tablecloth, and the sheer number of people around it made the perfect recipe for covert ridiculousness. When Theo's hand settles on my knee under the table, I almost come out of my chair. Frankly, I applaud myself for staying seated. I stiffen up, almost throwing the rolls at Dad's son, from his first marriage, who would never greet me.

Theo's fingers slide along my knee, right up to the edge of my stockings. I hadn't smoothed out my skirt when sitting. I hadn't thought I'd need to. The galling thing about it all is his touch is comforting.

I ghosted this man a decade ago. Yet he's touching me as if we've been together for years. Why? Where is the logic?

Is Theo remembering what I'm remembering? It is an attempt to make me forget those memories? Can Theodore still read me?

I shouldn't have spoken to him. That night in his truck when he told me his plan, I should have been silent. Instead, I eagerly blurred the lines with that challenge. Theo fucking obliterated them that night and every single chance he could afterward. I welcomed the man that tortured me emotionally into my bed. Some twist of fate led me to love the man, determined to ostracize me. Like a lovesick fool, I ignored when he said he'd get me pregnant to ruin me.

Theo looked at me like he might have loved me. He'd whispered he'd visit me in college, as long as I let him. Teddy told me I was beautiful, looked ready to murder someone when I said mom wanted me to go on Weight Watchers. Would he? Does he still see me the same? I don't dare to look now.

It's practice that keeps me passing bread and the various drink pitchers around the table when they're called for. This is something I can do. I can go through the motions. Masking the truth is a cultivated skill. As long as I'm paying attention. So, maybe it isn't such a bad thing that Theo knocked me out of my anxious, spiraling daze.

Conversation continues, time ticks by. Finally, I sneak a look at him. Theodore is as handsome as he's ever been. His hair is longer, his skin is still swarthy. It makes him look like he works outside still. But his hands are softer than I remember them. He doesn't have facial hair, but there is a definite shadow over his jaw.

His sweater is older. I can only tell because I've hand washed dad's wool sweaters a hundred times over the years. It looks brand new. That means that wool is expensive, and he's taking wonderful care of it. That's not quite the Theodore I know.

"Well, little queen, our prodigal daughter," Uncle Joe crows boisterously at me from across the table, grabbing my attention. You're a real professional gal now, eh? Your Master's program ended with the semester, didn't it? The way Dad keeps bragging, I have the idea you made the top of the list. So, what're you gonna with those degrees?"

It's an innocent enough question. I know that. I'm fully aware that Uncle Joe just wants to talk. My immediate reaction is to be rude. Even with the sweetest, most playful smile on my lips, which wouldn't fly. So, I squash it down ruthlessly. Not today, Satan, Loki, or Anansi. We're not telling truths today.

I put on my big girl panties, paint my patented out with a very important company smile on my lips, and prepare an answer. A breath in, and I let my words flow. "Well, I did work in an internship position last summer in DC under one of my sorority sister's siblings. We were staffers for Senator Kairn. I actually wrote several of her speeches. It was the most amazing opportunity, one that bore rather significant fruit for me," I say proudly. Taking a breath, I get ready to go into more detail. This, my job, it is my pride, and not quite, but close to all of my joy. I want to rub it in all of their faces, too.

But Andi cuts in. She clearly woke up this morning and decide it was a fuck around day.

"Fruit like you got a job, or fruit like you got a man, finally? Though, since I don't see anyone here for you … that answers that. If you got a job, is it an actual job? You know, one that pays, not like an internship. Or are

Clara and Jacob going to pick up your slack again?" Her voice is nasally high, complimenting the look on her face. Smug needs a new goddamn dictionary entry. Andi really thinks she's doing something here. In a way, she has. She just doesn't know what.

My eyes involuntarily swing to Clara and Jacob, narrowed as my temper simmers. Since I left, I've paid my own way. I scrimped, saved, used every single program I qualified for to put everything I could back into my loans. I ate more ramen than is strictly healthy for anyone to eat, especially pregnant, even in the goddamn dormitories.

I did it because I was bound—determined not to call them. Nothing on this earth would make me a failure. I'd do whatever I had to for my baby and our future. Pick up the slack fucking where? My mouth opens. I'm ready to give in and let it all come out.

Theo saves them. Theo saves *me*.

"Christ, Andi, do you ever think before you open your mouth? Evanna's been gone ten years. Do you really, honestly, think that the girl who worked on this farm for three summers in middle school and two in high school while having a job down in Lake Mouth would let someone else pay her living expenses? If she did, you don't have a leg to stand on. You've lived with Dad on and off since you graduated from Lakeside Community College. You treat our childhood home as if it's some halfway house between not-so-significant others. Evanna finished her Master's degree with no support system, however far away from us it is that she lives. She was alone. What have you done alone, Andi?" His voice is sharp, dangerously so. It's a tone that makes me flinch because it used to be reserved for me.

I think my heart stopped beating when Theodore lit into Andi. It's impossible to process the last forty seconds. I'm all over the place. Warm because he defended me. Confused, because Theo shouldn't feel that urge. I'm irritated that he pulled this while having his hand on me. He's… he's comforting me. Theodore has the audacity to protect me when I plan to put him in my review mirror again.

I peek quickly at Andi. Her face is ghostly white beneath her makeup, her blush having turned into two livid spots on her cheeks. Habit has me looking toward Mom who stares daggers at Theo. She's looking at him as if she's trying to set him on fire right now.

I swallow quickly, licking my lips nervously. I never said who got me pregnant. Mom, she can't suspect Theo. That's insane. That's… She can't think it's him.

"Well," I say slowly, "As I was getting ready to say, Uncle Joe, the internship opened up doors. They offered me two different staffer positions. I took the position with the House Speaker, actually. Over the next four years, you'll hear a lot from me."

My best friend, Keyanna, she's my roommate, finished her degree, too. When I head back, we'll be going to DC together. We'll room again until we're stable enough to find reasonable places of our own. She'll be going to American University, a doctoral program. We're jumping into the deep end, but we're acting as one another's safety nets as well. I did have the option of coming to Albany to work for the local government, but I can't stay home forever."

"From the sound of all that, little queen, they'd have squandered you here," Theo says smoothly, cutting off any naysayer neatly at the knees. My heart flips while my stomach fills with butterflies. I wish I wasn't reacting like this, but I can't control it. What is happening?

"That. Uh. That's kind of you, thank you, Theo." I smile, hoping that I'm not obvious about how this is all really affecting me. His hand squeezes my thigh, though. It's difficult to stay still when I'm given the comfort I've yearned for then and now.

Joe prompts me to pay attention to him with another question a second or two later. We studiously ignore the silent half of the table where my immediate family sit. It's horribly convenient and awkward, right until Mom decides she won't slip quietly into the night.

"You're out in Maryland, aren't you, Theodore? Or is it Virginia? I can't ever remember. You have some sort of start up there, don't you? What is it you're doing, exactly?"

I cringe, mentally and physically. Mother dearest has the uncanniest way of making people fully aware she's kept up with them; while also intimating that she doesn't care enough to remember what's important to you. All so it's clear she cares, but not that much. You're important, but you're not that important. There's so much subtext of *'you aren't worth it'* in four sentences, it's staggering.

"Virginia, Aunt Clara. It's easy to get it mixed up, especially this far down the road. I live in Alexandria. I bought a beautiful little house on the Potomac last spring. My 'start up' is a cyber security firm. We specialize in virtual and artificial intelligence, deep fakes, and the usual suspects for network security."

Theo smiles benignly at Clara and I stuff a carrot in my mouth. Theodore seems to have learned some tricks while I was gone. It's hot. Goddamn him.

"Our office is in based in Arlington. The rent prices are reasonable until we find a suitable spot to break ground for our own office." He offers that with a shrug. I blink, shoving another carrot into my mouth.

I barely taste the honey on it. We've been living that close for a decade. I go to the city with Xaria often; she loves the museums. I doubt he has reason to be in that area of DC, but...the fact stands. He could have seen us without realizing so many times.

"Since you'll be in DC proper, you're always free to come crash at mine. The city is intense. I have plenty of rooms, so you'll have your privacy. Before a place opened in Alexandria, I was living on the outskirts. When I saw I could afford it, I all but ran for it." Theo chuckles, and the laugh actually reaches his dark eyes. I am transfixed for a moment before shaking myself out of it.

"That's really kind of you. Thank you, Theo." I aim for politely disinterested with my reply.

I can feel my face warming, however, and I know I must be glowing. Maybe I can pass it off at shock and embarrassment. Theo thinks I need a place to escape? The smile I'd placed on my lips falters as he glides his fingers up my leg. My skirt bunches at the tops of my thighs. His fingers pause when they feel the catch of my garters.

"I wouldn't want to impose on you or your privacy," I say seconds later, pleased there wasn't too much of a gap between me speaking. "I won't be able to keep steady hours. Certainly not nine to five. But my door is open when you end up caught in the city. The traffic is murder once the sun sets. We'll be in a quieter area at least. I'm not sure exactly where. We've narrowed it to a few options."

The conversations around us shift, as I'd hoped, by rambling on about the inane. There's no way to reestablish my sense of equilibrium with Theodore. His fingers dig gently into my thigh for a moment, releasing when Grand-Père cuts through the other conversations to speak to us.

"I'm glad to see the two of you are past your differences." His eyes flick to Theodore for a split second. "I'm proud of you both. You've far outstripped my expectations of you."

I smile even though this has taken a turn for the weird. That alone makes the rest of what I'm going to endure worth it. No one else comments, but there are scattered smiles around the table. It's then I realize Theo's hand is gone from my thigh.

With his hold on me literally removed, my shoulders relax. The flow of the conversation shifts. Now that I'm no longer sitting ramrod straight, things seem less tense.

In the end, even with Andi's crap, and Theo's completely mystifying behavior, this is the most enjoyable, laid-back holiday I've attended. Family or otherwise. *Ever.* It's, shocking, given how I left my parents' house, how I'd cut off most of the family.

It's almost too soon, when all the cutlery stills, placed on plates, and the drinks stop getting passed around.

"Alright, we're fed. Off to the living room. Go on, get. I'll get these things away, and then—" Grand-Mère says, making the traditional announcement. I don't let her finish; there's no point. It's me who's been away; I'm younger and I'm here for Grand-Père and her.

"Go with them, Grand-Mère. I've got this." I say firmly. While I want to make her life easier, I've got alternative motivation. I need space from Theodore. Cleaning all this up will buy me plenty of time to get myself together.

"She's right, go relax, Nana. I'll help Evanna. Many hands make light work." Theodore seems to just materialize beside me. He's invading my space subtly, likely not even trying to. It takes a lot to not shriek at him. To tell him go sit down, to leave me alone. But Grand-Mère's face blooms with a smile.

Not her everyday smile. It was not the smile she focused on me when I arrived. This smile lights up her face, shows off the wrinkles that have deepened significantly, and just radiates happiness. She reaches out to us, cupping Theodore's cheek while patting my arm.

"Look at the pair of you. Mature now, like your Grandpa said. I'm so proud of both of you and overjoyed you're here with us. Don't forget to make the cocoa, Theodore. Bring it with the cookies once you're done."

Neither of us say anything before Grand-Mère turns, practically floating down the corridor.

I'm alone with Theo again. The lounge door clicks ominously down the hall. I'm safe to spin toward the father of my child.

"What the hell are you playing at?" I'd never been one to mince words or dance around a topic with people outside of my immediate family. Doesn't matter where I am, school, university, work, even church when I was a regularly attending member, I get to the point. That hasn't changed since we last saw one another. If anything, it's become more ingrained in me.

I watch him expectantly, waiting for an answer from him.

"I'm spending time with a member of my family I haven't seen in years, and taking work of an old woman's hands," he replies evenly. Turning, Theo picks up serving dishes with left over portions of food in them, moving into the kitchen to store.

"Why?" He asks, straightening once he has about four different serving dishes in his arms. "Is something wrong, Evanna? Something I need to know?"

I look away from him, lips pressing together before I sort dinner and bread plates, and the soup bowls. I scrape remains onto one, stacking the rest for easy transportation. His question. It makes my palms sweaty. He can't know.

"I'd like to think that I'm not unintelligent," I say finally, keeping my eyes on my work. "So, I'm referring to your hand on my thigh. And the way you defended me when Andi was rude. Why don't you just tell them what —we were."

The words catch in my throat. I focus on working methodically and ignore Theo. I hear him walk away, returning twice before he says anything.

"What are we exactly, Evanna, hm? What were we then?" His hand brushes over my side as he returns for the third time. "Am I not allowed to have done some soul searching, self-reflection? Is the idea so impossible to you? I identified and was told all about my toxicity— not to mention the racism. Do you think, Eva, that perhaps I know I was wrong in how I treated you? That perhaps I've missed you? That you leaving, disappearing overnight, might have hurt me?" He poses his questions so casually, his tone low so his voice won't carry, while working beside me. Gathering cups, bowls, and silverware between helping me to ferry the plates into the kitchen.

I don't know what to say. I had hoped that Theodore would get over himself. When my internal biases against myself became exposed, I'd hoped maybe someday Theo would change. In case he met Xaria.

Suddenly, I'm wondering the same things. What if I had told him, gone to him, rather than Dawn that night? If I'd called him after I left, told him where I'd gone, would it have gone differently? What if, what if... What if?

This man wearing Theodore's face isn't someone I'm equipped to deal with. I desperately want him to do something. Anything. I'd defined Theodore as too good to be true. Especially before we started fucking. He'd had a chipped shoulder; one few people seemed to see. After we started sleeping together, I found him to be gentle and quite attentive.

His features are the same. Evenly proportioned, he stands a little taller. He's perhaps more toned without looking like a muscled corn chip. His voice is almost the same. Lower, more thoughtful? Before it was just deep, and sort of nice.

But his attitude, the two faces he showed to me, the way he acted made him ugly. My libido ignored it. I ignored it. But I never really forgot.

So, I lean on old grievances.

"There's no way you missed me, Theodore," I say, sorting the food to be saved and tossed. "I distinctly recall you saying I was a chubby slut about three weeks before I left." My tone is vicious, as mean as I can make it be.

"I did," he says, nodding in acknowledgement. "I called you my chubby, *glowing* slut, actually. If I'm thinking of the right event, I was praising you. You were good for me that day. Honestly, you were stunning."

Theo chuckles, turning the taps on and plugging the deep sink. I carefully lower the plates into the steaming water before he puts the soap in. It's so mundane. I can't help but fixate, considering I feel like I've walked into a new world.

What's worse is he's left me speechless again. That day, when he'd said that, I hadn't known how to respond. I had known what he was referencing, of course, but he didn't. I stay quiet, finding Tupperware for the food that's savable, possibly incorporated into lunch tomorrow.

"You're still stunning," he says in a whisper as I spoon green beans into a container.

"You may not be glowing in the same way, and I may not have imagined you with different color hair, but you're stunning. The blonde suits you." Teddy gives me a once over. He still makes me feel like he's dragging his hands over me when he looks at me. How is that remotely fair?

"Yes. Still stunning, princess, especially in your demure-at-first-glance dress. I certainly wasn't expecting to find what I did under that outfit, and when I realized it was backless?" Theo whistles softly.

"This very well might be the sexiest I've ever seen you dressed. That's counting when I was a hormonal idiot teenager and you discovered tight shirts, skirts, and jeans you had to paint on to wear."

He reaches behind me unnecessarily to open the drawer where the washcloths are. Theo's so goddamn warm; his cologne washes over me. It's the same spiced scent he's always worn. The one I associate with sex. I'm not stone, much as I'd love to be. There's no inherent imperviousness I can call upon in the face of his compliments.

I'm as weak for Theo now as I was then.

"I missed you, princess." His breath fans over my ear, making me shiver. There's no suppressing it, and no getting around having this confrontation.

"Stop it, Theodore. We're cousins, and we've not seen one another in a decade," I say, argument feeble but voice strong enough. Though feeble, it still stands. Even though Theodore never claimed me as family. I wonder suddenly--is this why?

Theodore invades my space now. Not just a hand behind me, not just his breath ghosting over my skin. His chest presses to my back, a hand settles on my waist.

"Only by marriage, sweetheart, we've never shared blood. Even if you did, we're twice removed. You know what that means, or have you forgotten?" His words vibrate against my back, and I hear that condescension edged tone of his. It's an argument we had the morning after we spent that first night together. "We've *always* been free to fuck one another until we can't move."

Theo's in my space now. Not just a warmth that brushes along my back, not just a ghosting breath. I'm softer now, and I can't help but wonder if he's noticed. It's momentary, a brief reminder of how we were before Theo's moving to the sink again. Our close orbit, or whatever you want to call it, isn't new.

I never fell into a Christmas tree because I just tripped on air. And I didn't sport bruises on my waist for two full weeks after Thanksgiving when I was fourteen because Theodore had an aversion to touching me. I damn well didn't get pregnant alone.

"Just do the dishes, Theodore." My voice is too soft for my liking. My heart is going a mile-a-minute. I have the urge to throw myself at him. To tell him everything. Part of me wants to beg forgiveness before this trip turns into a disaster. But, I can't walk this road with him again, either.

I turn to him, hoping to drive the point in with a droll expression. I falter instead as he smirks at me. That damned smirk is even more dangerous. His arm snakes around my waist, pulling me against his chest into a hug. Sandalwood, patchouli, musk— I drown in his scent the whole time. When I'm released, I scrunch my brows and nose at him in question.

"Someone's gotten bossier since they were away. You missed me too, princess. I didn't suddenly forget how to read you. Some part of you still wants me," he says it so declaratively. I hate it. I especially hate how his voice deepens. My blood pressure spikes in reaction to how he sounds, and I have to turn around.

I'm deliberate as I pick up the remains of the cornbread, then the regular stuffing, placing them into Tupperware. I can't deal with this. How can I talk to him while he says things like that? When we never ended, truthfully. When I miss him.

Every time Xaria smiles as she laughs, I miss Theodore.

Silence falls as the sink fills with steaming water. There's barely any noise outside of breathing while I finish putting away the food. I stack things into the fridge carefully, so they don't impede the airflow. I don't need to worry about space, really. Everything in this house is slightly larger than average. Certainly, compared to the houses I grew up in.

I've always liked this house better. It's older, well loved, covered in a thick layer of memories. It's far more inviting than any new home with pristine walls and floors. The dull clink of plates and silverware as they're washed helps me breathe easier.

Theodore doesn't speak either. Which I count as a blessing. We need to be civil for a day and a half. Once dawn hits the twenty-sixth, I'm out of here. I'll arrive home for Xaria at dinnertime. As I review the plan, I leave the kitchen to sweep the dining room for stragglers. There are a few which I pile beside the sink with the serving dishes.

Stationing myself beside him, I take the rinse and dry post. Dishes stacked into the rack, glassware and mugs dried immediately and put away. That quiet, that's so comfortable, breaks while I'm trying to get a soup tureen into an overhead cupboard.

"What did I do to spook you so badly? That wouldn't have happened before you left." Theodore leans against the sink, watching me. I can feel it and see him from the corner of my eye.

Swallowing, I pause for a moment to consider an answer. If I have one at all. "Spook me?" I say slowly, "No. That's not it. It's been a long time, Theodore. That familiarity feels out of place."

Shrugging, I focus back on replacing the tureen. So focused, I miss Theo making his move. I'm ready to climb onto the counter to put the dish away. He becomes a wall of scent and heat against my back. Freezing, I don't even turn my head toward him.

Like Calls to Like

Evanna
24 December

Both of his hands settle on top of mine, guiding the tureen out of my hold and into place. The door snaps shut a breath later, and his hands guide both of mine back down to the countertop. His fingers lace between mine while he crowds me against the counter.

One of his hands disentangles from mine, lifting to swipe my hair up and over my opposite shoulder. That same hand is placed on my waist. "But this isn't out of place, is it, princess?"

"Teddy," I say becoming instantly annoyed. My voice shakes. All of me is likely shaking, though I don't take time to check. "The past is over; it's gone. It never even made sense! I always thought you'd rather me dead than in your company.

I'm flustered, out of sorts, completely unable to hide it. So, I turn, *try* to turn in what little space I have. Ultimately, finding myself leashed effectively to the counter.

"It makes sense, Evanna. It made more sense than either of us probably wanted." Theo sighs. "I was an angry, stupid kid who made myself hate you because…"

"Because I wanted someone to hurt like I did. If you were hurting, I wasn't alone while drowning in the misery. That was a kid who didn't want to understand what he was doing. Once you started settling into your skin, shifting from child to teen and then young adult, I was too horny and willfully blind. Enough, I wasn't thinking straight. Falling right back into pushing you around to touch you, doing whatever I could to keep you on the outskirts of my family, so what I felt wasn't wrong. I know you haven't forgotten any of that. How could you? I was cruel, and I apologize. It may be too little, too late, but we both need those words."

Teddy's face presses against my throat at the end. He's waiting. I know he is. He'll be waiting a while, because I don't have a clue how to start. How do you deal with things like this when you'd built a wall based on protecting yourself from it?

"Theodore. That part of our past. I— can't help but resent you for it. Even with therapy, talking it out, I don't know how to just accept that you're saying you were wrong. We're very different now. When we were together... you hurt me."

The last words slip out before I can stop them. My head hangs down for a few moments before I startle. The hand he'd placed on my waist moves to my stomach, sitting low. He pets me, slow movements that start just beneath my bust and continue to where his hand started.

"Little queen, I didn't start that to be kind. I'll admit it, but when August hit, things were different. I was changing. My feelings weren't at all what they had been. We were on a collision course with one another, princess. We crashed into one another. I wasn't ready to let go when you left me." He speaks against my skin, the words half muffled. Each one creates sparks along my nerves that I can't ignore.

Theo laughs then, a rich deep sound that vibrates against my back. It settles between us like a dark promise. But he follows it with a kiss, light, barely there against my pulse that makes my breath hitch. That's my demise.

With the bastard so close, he can't possibly miss it. He proves it as he places another kiss on the same spot. The hand that had been petting me sits low on my abdomen and guides me back until I press flush against him.

"See, Evanna. Now, if you want me gone, out of your space, all you have to do is throw an elbow. Or just use those wicked little heels on your pretty little feet to get me to let you go." Theodore croons to me like he would whenever I was half asleep, yet he was ready for more. The same damn thrill runs through me, too. I'm sure he's smiling as his hand runs up along my stomach. He lays that hand against my collar, not quite crossing any lines.

"Tell me to fuck off, sweetling. Tell me there's no chance. You've never been shy about cutting to the heart of things," Theo says, and he has the barest hint of a warble in his tone.

"Theo, for fuck's sake, we're in Grand-Mère and Grand-Père's house," I willfully ignore his actual question. Along with how my voice shifted, low with desire, an edge of distress. I move in the space I have, trying to wiggle out of his hold. It only serves to find me pushed up against the countertop securely, the Formica digging into my stomach.

"That's not your issue, Evanna. I've fucked you against the barn and in the guest loft, eaten you out in the shower upstairs, made love to you in in the garden. You don't avoid questions, or you didn't. So, tell me why you're being obstinate. And attempt to do so plainly." The demand is accompanied by Theo dragging his teeth along the curve of my neck.

My knees go weak. The feeling I had just two days ago driving here that I should have gone on some trip with Key and Xaria blooms in my chest. I don't know how I thought I could do this.

My skirt moves and my eyes drop in confusion. Abruptly, I realize both my hands are free now, the one that was holding mine is bunching the burgundy velvet up. My mouth runs dry while my blood runs hot.

I should have worn pants. Why couldn't I go against my instincts just once? Next time I will. I don't care how loudly or long Clara bitches.

My thoughts stutter to a halt as Teddy's fingers brush along my inner thighs. I missed that touch, and it's a little different now. He doesn't have the same callouses he used to.

"Teddy, don't," I plead in a whisper. "Not here, please." The struggle to retain my will to not fall into his arms is real. I want to. I want to just let him sweep me away from the realities of this holiday, to tell him what I should have nine years ago. That is truly the *only* storm I think I could weather right now.

"Eva," he breathes my name over the same spot he stopped when he'd used his teeth. My legs shift to press together unconsciously, needing to ease the ache forming. However, Teddy's hands are in the way. The flicker of desire I feel gains strength as his hands push my legs right back into position.

"You're warm, princess," Teddy says, daring to move his hands farther up my legs. He's so close to my lips. It's so dangerously similar to how he would get when he was feeling feisty. When he wanted to tease.

"I almost forgot how warm you get. You were always so sweet, but tonight I saw a whole new level. The way you were talking about your job, sitting beside me with rose painted cheeks. It was pleasantly shocking to find that garter strap."

He sounds the same, exactly the same as when we hid in his apartment, taking one another apart in pleasurable pieces. I can't stop the whimper that crawls from my throat. Nor can I do anything about the heat that crawls up my neck to settle in my cheeks. Biting at my lip to force some clarity through my cloud of arousal, I drop a hand to grab at one of his.

Teddy just takes hold of it, placing our hands back on the counter.

"It's only a reaction," I say, voice soft but harsh. "It's not one that I can control."

As ever, his hands never really stop moving while I speak. His hand cups my sex, stealing anything else I have to say. Wildly, I wonder at how Theodore can say I am the one who's heated, yet his hand radiates it. My free hand lifts to shove him away - because it's wrong. This isn't meant to happen again. It can't. Falling into his arms— no. I can't. If I do, that summer will just repeat itself.

But I betray myself. I don't push him away. My hand buries itself into his hair as he presses the heel of his palm against my clit. Clamping my legs around him, I force myself to swallow down a whine at the same time. Not that he lets me gather myself at all.

"Open your legs, princess." His teeth nip at my neck as he asks - demands it of me.

The worst part is that I do it. How is it, it's been ten years, but one mumbled directive has me moving? It's done without a single thought to the contrary, and I don't realize it either. Not until his fingers drag along the gusset of my panties, right along the line of my lips. Theo varies the pressure as he touches me, as he always did. He's waiting for me to react.

In response, I squash and swallow every sound I can, right until Theodore remembers the right way to touch me. The right pressure to use against me paired with the right cadence.

A breathy sound of pleasure leaves me. Involuntarily, I drop my eyes until I can see his hand moving - my skirt shifting off to the side. His fingers rub at me slowly, the pressure enough my eyes slide shut as I lean back against him bonelessly.

"Good girl," he murmurs. "So warm, baby. And so much softer than I remembered."

Teddy kisses and bites at a new spot high on my neck. "Do you know how often I think of us? I remember all the times I had you in my arms, watching your face as you shattered for me. God, Eva, do you know how often you're on my mind?"

Biting at my lip, I don't answer him, my throat too tight to speak. I hadn't thought that he would think of us. Or that he'd remember fondly all the times we were together that summer. Teddy should have forgotten. I wet my lips to speak, but all that comes out of my mouth is a whimper as his hips press up against my ass.

He's so hard.

It sets off a chain reaction in me. From the second I acknowledge Teddy's arousal, mine fires hot enough I ache. His fingers hook under my panties, pulling them aside when I shake some of that haze off.

"Teddy, wait." I have to say no to this, even though I want it desperately. It isn't fair to him.

"Evanna, I've been waiting for you for almost a decade. You disappeared on me, but now you're right here in my arms again. You're here, letting me touch you, kiss you, letting me feel how wet I make you. And you want me to, what? Walk away? I can't, not when I've been dreaming of this, of having you back. I've spent weeks' worth of time wondering how you'd changed since that summer. Are you more of a brat? Do you like power struggle games more, or less? Or, and I hope it's this one, are you still my best girl, doing exactly what I ask of you?"

"Teddy," a shock like feeling has me gasping out his name. His fingers press against my lips, finding that I'm slick. So, slick it might be shameful, if I could feel shame where Teddy and I are concerned. "S-stop, we need to make cocoa. Remember? If someone comes looking..."

That would be an unmitigable disaster. The absolute last thing I or he needs right now is for one of our family members to catch us. It would lead to a fuss and bring this to Clara's attention. Then all the secrets would spill out. We wouldn't be able to deny a thing, not like this... with Teddy wrapped around me, his hand playing between my legs.

"Better stop riding my hand then," Teddy growls, biting at my neck. He does it with the right amount of pressure to keep me moving, my hips rocking back against him and bucking forward into his hand. I bite my lip so hard to keep quiet I'm certain I've made myself bleed.

"Teddy," I whisper, a deluge of babble following. "I need... I need you. Missed you. Can't think with you touching me like this."

His hands withdraw, and I let out a plaintive sound that has him laughing against my back. Teddy shoves me down against the counter a moment later. While I catch myself with a quiet yelp, hands slapping against the counter, I'm still pinned there.

My heartbeat ratchets up in cadence as he kicks my legs apart. My skirt's draped high around my waist, his hands petting along my hips and thighs. I'm past thinking that I can deny him, or me, or any of this. I wish, fervently, that I weren't so damn gone on him. If I didn't miss him like I had, I could truthfully, forcefully tell him no.

Teddy's thumbs settle on my lips, spreading me open, and I spiral away from the present back into the past. Pressing my forehead to the counter, I moan softly while his hands settle on my hips, keeping me open. I'd forgotten quite how much this affects me. I don't move, to track what he's doing, even as I feel his eyes on me, his thumbs running lightly up and down my lips.

My breaths are shallow as I swing between wanting to die and needing Theodore to do something to me right now. It's so silent, we're both so still, locked in a holding pattern.

"Princess?" The question I've dreamed of in a thousand different scenarios.

"Yes," I answer almost immediately.

His mouth meets my pussy. I clap a hand over my mouth to stay silent. Every vestige of reluctance I may have held melts away as his mouth presses against me. I barely swallow my sounds as Teddy licks into my cunt, kissing me, sucking at me until I'm laying limp on the counter. His mouth doesn't draw away like I expect it to, thinking back on old patterns. No, Teddy keeps at me, lips and tongue making me spiral as he teases. There are no thrusts that send his tongue sliding deep into me, just small ones to make me ache. My face shifts against the counter to press against one of my hands. When the teasing, the ache building in me becomes enough I might go mad, I lift onto my toes to be free of it - be free of him. Exactly the same way I used to.

He stops then, standing behind me while I try to catch my breath and make sense of what's happening. Teddy's hand threads into my hair before I can, turning me so he can see me, and I, him. *This is insanity*, I think blearily. We'd been reckless in the past, but this ...

His head presses warm, and so very hard, up against my entrance. I think the world's stopped turning as everything narrows down to his gaze and where he's touching me. Licking my lips, I wait for him to ask. I'm not disappointed.

"Princess?"

"Yes," I moan with a brief nod.

Teddy's crown notches into my entrance and he thrusts home. It's a fast slide that takes my breath away. It should hurt… it will make me sore later. But for right now, all I can wonder is why this is better than any tryst we had here over the summer?

He's so silent as he feeds his cock into me. His thrusts are smooth, searching, shifting. The angle of them changes each time he pushes back into me after leaving. I know what it is he's doing. There's no hope or way for me to hide when Teddy's cock drags over the spot that sends shocks through me. Squeezing around his length, I hide my face against my arm, muffling whatever sounds I make in my throat.

I resolve to ride it out while his cock makes room for itself in me. Teddy won't see sense. I'm losing what little I had.

Letting myself feel him, feel this; I get lost in it. In the slide and retreat of Theodore's cock in my body. It's been so long; I've forgotten exactly how he fills me. I forgot how damn possessive Theodore is over all my reactions. Proven when he uses my hair to tilt my face whenever I've hidden too much for him to see me.

His thrusts into me viciously. I can't hide my whimpers or how I rock into the punishing movements. Teddy doesn't hide his half-whispered curses. He doesn't stop himself from pressing into me deeper until his hips are flush with mine. I feel as if I've swallowed him, not like he's fucking me. But I am full, and he's everywhere, over me, the scent surrounding me. A contented sigh escapes.

But we can't be here long. The both of us know that. Teddy's thumb finds my clit, slides over it in slow circles and I half forget where we are. I ride him while he watches me. Panting, I feel myself pull tight on his cock when the moment shatters.

A creak rips through the quiet of the kitchen and dining room. I can't tell if it's the door to the lounge opening, or the house settling, but the pair of us freeze. Five seconds pass, ten. Teddy hauls me up by my hair, his thumb circling against my clit furiously as he thrusts against me.

"Come, princess. Right now, come nice and wet for me on my cock, baby. Be my good little whore." Those words and five harsh, unforgiving thrusts are all it takes for me to tip into oblivion. I gasp, a harsh and loud sound, rather than moaning while Theo rides me faster.

"Fuck. That's it. Goddamn, Princess, you feel so perfect. So good. You want it?" Theodore presses his mouth against my jaw as I nod drunkenly.

Teddy draws out the aftershocks of my orgasm with how he moves. I register him grunting 'good', before I'm pressed against the counter, hips pushed to the edge with more than enough force to bruise. It's been so goddamn long since someone's been like this with me. I missed it so much, too much. The low, wanton moan that leaves my mouth while Theo grinds hard against my cervix is evidence of that.

There's a shock of pain, but it's drowned out as Teddy thrusts and grinds out his own orgasm. That liquid feeling of warmth comes while he groans my name, leaning over me for a precious few seconds.

When he's finished, Theodore unceremoniously pulls from me, tucking himself away. His hands replace my underwear and skirt before he's standing in front of the sink again. I can't do more than watch while leaning heavily against the counter, while Theodore puts together the cocoa. He doesn't bother me to move once. He also doesn't speak.

But, when the cocoa is in the thermal pot, the double boiler set into the sink, Theo comes back for me. His hands urge me up gently, surprisingly so. He fixes my hair, the gentle movements continuing. It's something he'd done before and it's too much like he cares for me to deal with.

"You're spending the night with me, princess. Here." Theo poses it like a casual request. Like we haven't seen one another in a few days. Like we should catch up, so why not spend the night together? But his hand slipping beneath my skirt, a finger sliding along my panties, tells me it's far from innocent, not a request.

Strangely, I don't mind. It feels like I've finally regained my equilibrium, and we need to talk.

I Can't Walk Away

Theodore
24 December

Of all the ways I've imagined today proceeding, I didn't count on fucking Eva in the kitchen. Not with the entirety of our family sitting a dozen meters or less away. We fell into old patterns with new flavors.

Eva took my cock as if we've been having sex for a decade. This had been fucking exquisite, even quick as it'd had to be. I knew I was gone on her, but this? This shit is insane. I want her in my arms, sitting on my lap where I can let her sip at her cocoa while the family talks about whatever they want.

It would require coming out to the family. Which Eva never wanted to do. I suppose Dad's knowledge of us makes us sort of out, but I refuse to cross that line without her. So now we have to play politely social.

I hate it, but I do what's required while keeping a keen eye on Evanna. She sits primly, looking every inch the attentive young niece or granddaughter. She's damn good at looking unruffled, but I can't help thinking that she's leaking my cum while sitting there.

All I can think about is Eva and how needy she must feel right now. It's weird to see her hiding. Most won't notice, but I do. I see how she makes little shifts of her hips, how her responses sound distracted.

My Eva has grown into a different person. I'm half proud of her, half horrified that the woman I knew before is gone. There's something else about her I can't explain. It'll have to wait until later. Shaking my head, I engage the first person I make eye contact with.

It's a mistake. Speaking to Jasmine during good days is unwise. We don't classify holidays as good days. Tense, precarious? Yes. Good? No. Not until after the fact. Still, it happens. My mouth gets ahead of me.

"How're things, Aunt Jasmine? Clara mentioned you got a new job, a new place?" Aunt tastes like ash in my mouth. It's never sat well with me. Jasmine is my cousin – brought in when Jake married Clara. However, as she's twenty years my senior, she's become a 'beloved aunt' instead. Clara's conventions have twisted the family tree into a mess of confusion.

"Oh, I love my new place," Jasmine says with glee. "New York would've never been my home. I realize that now. Even with the memories and familiar faces, it wasn't...mine. New Hampshire, though, is perfect. Lawrence is perfect. As perfect as any human can be. He's everything I've ever wanted. The firm I work with is cozy. There's no bullshit or drama there. It's nice to use my degree now. Life is quieter, simpler. I'm *finally* happy."

My teeth grind together, I feel ill as Jasmine speaks. *Easier?*

She brought home a child, abandoned said child, and thinks life is easier now? Evanna is in the goddamn room for fuck's sake. One glance allows me to see Eva gripping her mug so tightly that her fingers are bloodless.

I should have chosen someone else to speak to. Now I've got to finish the conversation quickly. I pray for the luck of having a polite out before the conversation turns ugly. May God's eyes look kindly on me.

"That's great. Surprised that Lawrence didn't come with you today," I say, choosing to combine a slight with a conversational exit. I've never given a more polite or pointed we're no longer speaking than this.

"Oh, well, it is Christmas Eve. Lawrence and his kids are at his relatives' house in Vermont. The kids love their cousins, and it's a tradition. They're wonderful, by the way. They aren't angels by any stretch, but they are genuinely kind kids. I'll admit disappointment. I thought I'd see a new face tonight. You know, have someone to cuddle, to dote on." Jasmine looks over at Evanna as she says the last part too loudly.

I feel my heart skip a beat before the bottom of my stomach drops. She can't be saying what I think she is. Jasmine has *never* been cruel like this. We're in the middle of a family gathering. Jasmine knows it'll only cause a scene.

Knows and planned, I decide as Clara pointedly clears her throat. I sit stalk fucking still, my heart in my throat. The chatter in the room dies. Jasmine's face twitches, paling for a second before she fixes her smile. I don't know that I'm breathing as my eyes move towards Evanna.

Her eyes are wide like saucers, her back ramrod straight like it had been at dinner. I can't tell why. If it's Jasmine *is* being cruel, or because she should've brought a child home. Everyone looks between Jasmine, Clara, and Eva. No one moves, and silence falls before stretching out.

Finally, Eva takes a slow deep breath. Clara, I see in my periphery, trying not to stare too hard at Evanna, grabs her. Her prefect manicured nails dig into the velvet of Eva's sleeve. I want to rip Clara's hand off Evanna. Though, I'm not sure I'd stop there.

"Don't," Clara hisses, as if the rest of us can't hear her.

"Jasmine brought it up, *mother*." Evanna's voice is so devoid of care, it's frightening. What went on in their house? "It isn't as if I can sit here silent about it."

The glare that Evanna shoots at her sister is one that I've seen aimed at me many times in our life. This feels so odd. Like I've walked into an alternate universe where Eva's family isn't on her side. Eva looks around the room, though our eyes barely meet when it's my turn.

"I couldn't bring Xaria home for Christmas this year. Her school had a pageant scheduled for today, so I opted to allow her to stay home with a family friend to participate. Another factor was that I wasn't certain what welcome I'd receive here. I wasn't willing to potentially expose my daughter to ridicule, racism, and rumors in a place where she should be *safe*." Her voice sharper than a knife as she speaks, a pointed look leveled Clara and Jasmine's way, making things remarkably clear. Some deep shit went down. Deeper than we could have imagined.

"It isn't up for debate or question. I protected Xaria from you. That won't change." Evanna doesn't speak to everyone. She's addressing her mother and sister. I'm proud of her. Proud that her voice doesn't crack as she tells Clara all she'll ever need to know.

School. So, the chi— Xaria, is at least five. Activities she wants to take part in, at least nine, especially for Evanna feel comfortable enough to leave her daughter with someone for three days. Fuck. Three days to learn who Xaria's father is. And to convince Eva I'm not here to fuck up her life. When—*if* we made Xaria, I was far past trying to ruin her.

Xaria is a unique name, adhering to my stipulation about baby names. Eva could call it out and only one child would turn to her. It makes my heart ache.

I tear my eyes away from Evanna and Clara. Clara, who looks murderous now. I don't need to start shit by being caught staring. Once I turn my attention back to the room, dad is observing me. A bushy salt-and-pepper brow arches before he returns to whatever conversation he was having with Jake. Jake doesn't know what to do.

My fingers tap along my mug as Jasmine just picks up her thread of conversation. She launches into telling me about how her new family is simply wonderful. It makes me cringe as she speaks about Zoe, the middle child. The teenager is apparently *everything* Jasmine's ever wanted in a daughter.

I want to reach out and slap Jasmine so badly. I've been an asshole to Evanna, to the family. Fuck, I made Evanna feel she wasn't a part of us and even told her so. When that didn't work, I tried isolating her. I was cruel… but never was I truly heartless.

I've never told Evanna she was replaceable. Nor did I imply that our connection didn't exist. Jasmine, however, is as petty as their mother.

Eva leaves the room with her mug while she murmurs an excuse. For the sake of a veneer of propriety, I wait five minutes. Likely less than five. I make my own excuses, getting up to go find her. The search isn't long. Eva's outside on the porch.

Eva wraps her long coat tight around her body as she sits at the small metal table, staring out across the lawn at the two barns. All I want to do is scoop her up, sit her on my lap and confess my sins against her. Then I want to beg forgiveness before asking if Xaria is mine - ours.

None of that, however, is conversation for this porch. Not where others can overhear us.

"Evanna, baby, I'm sorry," I whisper. "That was stupid. I shouldn't have asked Jasmine anything. I wasn't thinking."

"It's hardly your fault," Evanna replies snappily. "You didn't decide to leave repeatedly and then replace me."

That makes me turn my head away. It's true, I didn't leave her; I didn't replace her. Couldn't, I only tried once. I don't know the story behind Jasmine leaving Eva with Jacob and Clara. No one's sure why Jasmine left so suddenly, or Evanna. Oliver left quickly, not suddenly given his wedding, but quickly all the same. I'm seeing a pattern with a common denominator.

My mouth opens to say anything, really, when the inner and storm doors open. Eva doesn't move, her hands stuffed in her pockets. Jasmine appears and my mouth turns down. What's the chance Jasmine's here to apologize?

"There you are. I'll see you for lunch tomorrow, Eva. Love you, honey. Bye now." Jasmine flashes us a bright smile while Eva makes a strangled, annoyed sound.

"Jasmine, where are you going? It's almost seven at night…did you forget—" Jasmine cuts Evanna off as if she wasn't still speaking.

"I have to show my face at Lawrence's family gathering, Eva. I actually should have left earlier. Tell your baby I said hi, okay? Later, honey."

I watch as her unnatural cherry hair bounces while Jasmine walks down the steps. My eyes don't leave Jasmine until said hair disappears into an

SUV. When the truck starts up the hill, I look at Evanna. Her face says many things.

"Eva."

"It's so fucking ironic," Evanna barks with laughter. Her face twists with resentment. "Jasmine never stops causing fucking scenes, ruining my life, and leaving."

Angry, watery brown eyes lift to mine. I've never seen her like this. Even when she would show up at my apartment all the time. "Better than that. You, Theodore, *you* are the person closest to me who hasn't ever fucking tried to abandon me."

Words stick in my throat while she says that. Eva wrenches a hand from her pocket, swiping angrily at the tears that fall. Her eyes are flat when she looks at me again.

"When I was sad, you were there. I was, ironically, always fucking important to you," Eva whispers it, and I don't actually know if I'm awake or dreaming. I never thought she'd say that to me.

I'm so floored, I can only watch as Eva stands up, heading back inside. Her shoes click against the stone of the patio before the door creaks open, snapping quietly shut behind her. Standing in the soothing, sharp cold, I lift a hand to drag it through my hair, tugging at it some.

"Fuck." I look up to see the orange sunset in the sky. "I didn't know it was that bad, Eva."

The lounge is tense. I'm torn between the urge to drag Eva out of the house to the guest loft; and hauling her to my truck to drive to Lake Mouth. I assume she's staying there, given she's not speaking to her parents.

I want to talk to her for longer than two sentences. Jesus, I am an idiot. Sitting with Gramps and Nana, I'm there for all of ten minutes before Evanna sighs. She looks into her mug, then around the room before asking: "Who wants Egg Nog?"

The reaction isn't proportional to the number of people sitting. Smiling, truly smiling, Evanna stands up. "Right, Theo, collect the cocoa please, then you're driving me to the quick mart really quick."

"How many times can you say quick in a sentence, princess?" I retort without thinking about what I'm calling her. No one blinks. Not even as I almost drop a cup upon realizing it. Jacob gives me a look, but that's it. Clara, who is quite anti-alcohol, doesn't relinquish her glass, nor does Andi's partner.

"Don't worry, this one is safe for drivers. Tomorrow, I make no promises." Eva smiles. It's a smile that I've seen on her before when she was playing her part as the perfect daughter.

I both approve and disapprove, but if it gets me time with her without prying ears ... fuck it. "Let's go, Nog Queen."

Tray in hand, we leave the lounge. We set the cups to soak with the thermos. We grab coats while leaving the house. In the snap of cold, she keeps pace with me, for all she's a full foot shorter than me.

"So," I say, and cut her a glance. "Nog?"

"I had to get out. But I won't let them win, I won't run," Evanna whispers, looking up at me with luminous eyes. "I committed to being here. I'm here. Even if my family is a bunch of assholes."

I suck at my teeth, walking to her side of the truck, opening the door for her. She actually takes my hand as I help her up into the cab. When she's settled, I close her door, jogging to the driver's side.

"Harsh, Sweetheart," is what comes out of my mouth once inside.

"No." she snorts, pulling her coat closer. "It's downright kind, Theo."

"Fair enough," I reply. For a minute, while we get on the road toward West River Center, we're quiet. I'm waiting, honestly, for her to say something... anything. There's a yawning chasm in me right now unravelling my sanity. I don't know if I have a daughter.

"Theo," Her soft call of my name comes as we hit the first light in the town center.

"Yeah, princess?" I glance at her, bathed in the red light from the traffic lamp.

"Xaria's yours," Eva looks at me, even as she curls up to make herself smaller. I want to be pissed; I truly do. I have no right to anger. Not really. I wasn't dating Evanna. We went into our relationship, if you could call it that, thinking it was just for fun. The 'fun' being my attempt to ruin her life. I'm just glad she's willing to be alone with me.

My right hand sits on the console, palm up as the light changes. I'm quiet as the gravity of Eva's admission sinks in, leaving me speechless. A daughter. She's mine. Both of them, hopefully, are mine.

Eva's hand slips into mine and a calm, complete feeling sweeps through me. It's comfortable silence until we pull up at the twenty-four-seven quick mart. When I kill the engine, I turn to look at her.

"You told me that day, didn't you?" I need to know exactly how badly I fucked us up.

"I did. It was terrifying." Evanna sighs. "We weren't on good terms with one another, though it was getting better. You having to be...you in public was killing me."

"I know that now." I squeeze her hand, rubbing my thumb over her knuckles. "I refused to see how I was tearing you down. It was a dick move. When did you find out?"

"July fourth," Eva answers immediately, smiling wanly. "That morning I was taking so long? I took two tests and vomited three times. You got me very pregnant right off the bat."

You've got to laugh at the sheer luck there; I know I do as I shake my head. "I feel like I should get a gold star," smiling lopsidedly at her, I sober quickly. "I— Please let me meet Xaria, Eva. Tonight's been a roller coaster. That's partially my fault. But I want to meet my daughter... our daughter. Hell, if I thought you'd be in for it, I'd ask you to come live with me. Because I'm still obsessed with you, still completely smitten with you, and frankly, unless you tell me you're on a form of contraceptive..."

Eva groans. "God, do not jinx us, Theodore!" She slaps at me. "You can meet Xaria; we can talk about us. But tonight and tomorrow, we just gotta make it through. Or I do."

Her fingers slip from mine as she slides out of the truck. Hopping out quickly, I fall into step beside her, offering my hand to her again. "Make a night and a day? I think we can do that, princess."

Checking Out
to Check

Evanna

24 December

I sit with Uncle Joe, who slings an arm over my shoulders and speak when spoken to. I smile when it's appropriate and laugh softly at jokes meant to lighten the mood, but it's all fake.

I feel gutted, again.

Gutted, empty, angry. Ten years, ten *fucking* years have passed yet Jasmine stills acts like she's in her 30s. She hasn't grown an inch. I've dedicated hundreds of hours into fixing what they broke in me, and Jasmine still fucks up my world in seconds. I said I didn't want to talk about Xaria not coming home with me. What if that meant I'd lost her? Hm? What fucking then?

I want to scream so many things at Mom, Dad, and Jasmine. But I breathe through it; I feel it and I push it away. I've gone to therapy and during that I whispered, cried, and screamed to get the past feelings of rejection and hurt that my family caused. I accept Jasmine will never be my mother in anything other than biology, that my parents are a product of their generation and own ethnocentric biases. I also accept that I didn't do a single thing wrong when I got sick.

I had pushed my body to the limit. The stress reached catastrophic levels. I'm lucky that I didn't lose Xaria. She was in a safe development zone before the worst happened. I don't know that I would have survived losing her. For so long after she was born, I felt guilt. As if I could've kept my body from revolting against me; trying to get rid of the 'parasite' that was seven months into life.

It was Xaria's six month 'birthday' when I finally accepted nothing I could've done would've fixed the damage of my leaving. Being a typical eighteen-year-old trying to make it in college, I tried my hardest. I made it there alone. I've talked about it quite a lot in Therapy.

But never Theo. I didn't think I was ready to deal with those wounds. How I thought I couldn't talk about him, but I could make a fourteen-hour trip to my childhood home, I don't know. Almost forty-eight hours ago, I got into my car, and said goodbye to my family, believing this would be easy. Maybe not easy, but tolerable.

I have a daughter, that's not a minor issue. Walking into the same emotional traps I always had wasn't exactly a great feeling either. I had at least protected myself, making Jasmine take me to my car before I went to dinner. Jas had wanted to bond. I knew better. It felt off. Now I know why.

Looking at those of us speaking, I decide. Jasmine and Clara don't get to have my birthday. They had eighteen between the two of them. I need to talk to Theodore, who is doing so much math that his face is betraying everything, too. So, I announce I'm making egg nog.

I didn't expect Theodore being amenable, or that he'd be so calm. He has maturity that he didn't have before. Fuck, I probably didn't have it before Xaria came along, frankly.

But now, as we hold hands, him with a grocer's basket in hand to get extra eggs, milk and heavy cream, I feel hopeful. Not just the average hopeful. Lighter. I don't have any skeletons in my closet with Teddy. Technically, as far as the family is concerned, there aren't any other secrets.

"I should...Dad knows," Teddy says suddenly as I'm checking sell-by dates.

He shoves his hands into his pocket as I turn around. My brows are in my hairline, and he has the audacity to laugh. I can't quite be mad, but I want to ask, *'what the actual fuck'*.

"He sprung it on me yesterday, okay? Apparently, we weren't as good at hiding as we thought. Prepare for Dad to request pictures. He loves his grandkids." Teddy smiles and I see the boy who I wanted to love when I met him.

I'm a few years late but seeing that smile gives me hope. Hope that it's better late than never.

"Okay," I drawl, closing the eggs and putting them in the basket he holds. "I have to absorb my uncle saw me having sex and let me tell you, that's a trip I wasn't expecting today," I keep my voice low, because we're not the only shoppers. It might be eight pm on Christmas Eve but people still need emergency food.

"You think I was? He told me to fix it, like I wasn't already planning that. Your mom is unaware that Xaria's mine, but I don't know if anyone else suspects. She definitely thinks I had a thing for you."

"Good instincts," I mutter while rolling my eyes. "At least she's got that going for her."

As we move to the cream and milk, Theodore's arm wraps around my waist. I stiffen for about five seconds. Fuck it. If I bring Xaria home, everyone will know. They have the same smile, for pity's sake. There's no hiding that. And Grand-Mère won't let me not bring Xaria to visit.

"We should stay in the loft tonight. I want— we need to talk. I had a plan, and it's gone off the rails, but I'm serious when I say it's still you for me, Evanna." Teddy looks down at me as I look up.

"If it wasn't still you, our kitchen scene would never have happened," I drawl again, grabbing three big creams and milks. I know my family. Eggnog is in high demand, virgin or not.

"Figured, but I won't let things go unsaid. I won't assume again that you know what I feel or where we stand. I have a lot, Eva, a fuckin' *lot* to make up for."

"No." I stop him with a hand up in front of me. "I don't care, Theodore. I don't want to know about it. Nothing before Xaria matters. We were children, and stupid. You made amends for your actions on the fourth of July. Today, you were the only person coming to bat for me against Andi, to check on me when Jasmine slapped a bag of feral cats. We're new, right here, right now."

His smile is slow, eyes worried, but accepting. I'll take it. He takes my hand in his. We stay like this until we get back into the car. The day was wild, but this is still a good Christmas Eve.

Back in the farmhouse, I keep Theodore with me. I officially don't give a shit how it looks. He's my emotional support person. Which is wild, yet it's the truth. I'm giving Teddy a chance, taking a chance for my happiness. If I have him in my corner, I can make it through this.

"Can you separate the eggs for me?" I look over my shoulder as I measure out the milk for today and tomorrow. I could do it in the morning, but we'll have enough going on already that I won't commandeer my grandmother's kitchen if I don't have to.

"Sure." He smiles serenely, the first smile I could ever call that, getting the requisite mixer bowls. We work together quietly. I carefully scald the milk with an unholy amount of clove. Setting it on a cool burner, I get the yolks and sugar together, looking at the bowl he's setting in the mixer.

"One cup of sugar, and then go for gold," I instruct with a smile. He snorts, raising a brow at me while I just shrug my shoulders. It's just as good as saying beat the hell out of them. In the space of thirty minutes, I set the jug for tomorrow in the fridge to cool, while he empties the strainer of cloves. Tonight's jug is much smaller, good for two small rounds, by my estimate.

"Go on in." I shoo Teddy out of the way. Moving to the sink to do the dishes, he hip checks me out of the way instead. Squeaking, giving him a shove, I stare at him. He stares back before leaning down, catching me in a kiss that leaves me dazed.

"Go serve, princess. This'll be ten minutes, tops." Teddy smiles while watching me gather up cups and the pitcher. I feel his eyes on me all the way to the lounge. It might be stupid to start a relationship with him. This may leave me heartbroken, but I'm smiling wider than ever.

Lofty Memories

Theodore
25 December (12:00)

Eva pumps us full of eggnog as soon as I come into the lounge. Her parents vacate as soon as possible. Which begins the stream of exits. Andi left after the first round, her sleeping kids and lover in tow. Those who lived over twenty minutes left next. Aunt Franke and Dad's guest are the last out the door.

Leaving Dad, Nana, Gramps, me, and Evanna.

I know what's going to happen the moment Dad clears his throat. Eva's coming in from the kitchen, and I decide I don't want to weather this interrogation alone. Leaning forward, my hand snags hers, tugging her toward me. Eva sends me a sharp look that I just smile at.

We have a little tug of war before she relents, and I have her seated on my lap.

For a moment, there's silence. Then Nana slaps Gramp's chest. "Pay up, Albert. I *told* you he had eyes for her."

Dad blinks. I blink. Evanna bursts into laughter. It's fueled by her nerves, a little too high pitched, and she takes a bit to recover. Before she does, I join her. Sobering up, she wipes away some tears while looking at me before tossing her hair over her shoulder to look at our grandparents.

"We didn't hide a damn thing, did we?" she asks, leaning back against me while I curl my arms around her.

"Oh, sweetheart, mon chou," Gramps chortles. "Theodore's been trying not to look at you since he was nineteen. It only got worse the summer after you turned sixteen. You wore *the shorts*, as we called them, that summer."

"Oh, you did," Nana cackles, clapping twice. "I ain't ever seen that boy run so fast back to his house. Every single break we gave him, off like a shot!"

My face burns as I groan, hiding in Eva's hair. I'd have liked to forget that. She, however, is giggling, and pushes me back to gaze at me. Her smile is smug, eyes shining when I look up.

"Really, Teddy? The downfall of my nemesis was a pair of shorts?" Her pleased laughter fills the room, warming my heart while I listen.

"To be fair," I say once she's quieted. "Only you and Nana call those things shorts. Me, I called them damn things torture. You couldn't'a convinced me Clara hadn't had a lobotomy to allow you out in them. Your legs looked eight miles long, they were just a little too short, too. I never recovered."

Eva's smile turns pleased, and her lips press to my forehead. Her easy affection is killing me in the best way. This couldn't, didn't, happen before. Not outside the loft, my apartment, or wherever we could hide. Right now, she's accepting our family knows we're together. She's accepting *me*.

I don't know what miracle is at work here, but I'm thankful for it. So much. I'll go to church faithfully for the next ten years to show I mean it. My lips press to her jaw, arms squeezing her while the others look on fondly.

This. It's the most perfect response our family could have to Eva and me being an 'us'. It's the only response I'd take, honestly. I'm not exactly up to cutting my family from my life as wholly as Evanna did. However, for her… for us, for the kid we share, I'd figure it out. I'd do it for them.

It would be terrible at the beginning. But, without their approval, what point is there in keeping contact? Why would I subject the mother of my child, my family, to repeated ridicule? It's counterintuitive in the worst way. So, Nana and Gramps betting on us? I'll take it. I welcome it with open arms and a smile if I can keep Evanna without grief. Providing she'll take me.

Thank you. *Thank you*, Saint Marguerite, Saint Jude, and Saint Valentine, for not forsaking us. We may not be married, but we had trouble in spades. Ultimately, our romantic tie wouldn't dissolve. I'm not so proud as to deny having prayed for this, for their help, a blessing, a sign—anything. And they looked kindly on me. On us.

"I know that you just told us about her, Eva. But do you have photos of Xaria?" Dad asks while looking so cautiously hopeful it makes my chest constrict. Evanna, in true Eva fashion, whips her phone from fuck knows where with a grin.

"Photos? Uncle Joe, I've got *books*. Pull those chairs over because Theodore needs to see her, too," her voice tips into sadness, one of her hands dropping to my knee. For all Eva said, she forgave all the bullshit I've put her through. It sure seems like she's not forgiving herself.

It's not long before we're surrounded with our family. Eva unlocks her phone, pulling up the first photo. Before she tilts it so we can all see it, she chews her lip.

"Before we start. Xaria was early, though not by much. Her due date was wonky because I had a cycle that was light. One tech would say late January, the other late February, one claimed March. Anyway, I was sick, so sick. Stress had me all messed up." Her lips thin into a line, anger putting fire in her eyes before she shakes it off.

"But here she is." Her phone tilts down, the screen bright. "She was still a healthy six pounds when she came screaming into the world."

Sitting up, I lock eyes on the photo of a baby swaddled in white, a pink and purple winter hat on her head. The blanket has a heart on it. Her face is red, mouth wide open, and wrinkly as hell. She's beautiful.

"There's my wrinkly potato," Evanna coos, looking at the photo. "She was so cute. Her due date settled out as the seventeenth of March, but she didn't wait that long. She made her debut February first. I'm really glad she didn't wait for the fourteenth, but it still colors her birthday some."

Gramps gives Eva a conspiratorial look. They've both made their share of complaints about a Christmas birthday. They never complained about sharing a birthday. The weirdos. She taps through photos, filling us in on little details and landmarks.

"This is her six-month party. Little Xaria Ann Bishop-LeClaire." Eva taps at the cupcake in the photo. My eyes aren't on the cupcake, they're on her. In this photo, Eva's a little bigger, but her smile is bright. She's got distinct bruises beneath her eyes. Newborn and Undergrad studies—I don't wish it on anyone. It's impressive Evanna managed it, excelled under the pressure.

"Xaria was always babbling by then, trying her best to sing with me. But she liked when I was studying best. I figured out that week if I read aloud to her, she'd fall dead asleep. So, Xar got the world's most boring bedtime stories until she was two. Then she understood I wasn't telling her about princesses, dragons, or unicorns," Eva regales us with the information, voice warm, fond.

"Is she a big reader?" Dad asks, curiosity plastered on his face.

"Oh yeah," Evanna preens proudly. "Xaria absolutely loves books. She's at a middle school reading level. I'm tempering her expectations of herself as best I can, though. I don't want her to burn herself out before college with recreational reading. She also likes field and ice hockey. She even plays. I have many photos of her in ice hockey gear."

Her eyes meet mine and it's my turn to do a little preening. I loved hockey when I was a kid. Playing it far more than I watched. It had been a better release of the anger that fueled me. No fights, just overly aggressive plays. It's nice knowing I'm connected to Xaria beyond her DNA.

"Is she in private or public school? Where are you living?" Nana asks. Eva turns red then.

"So, I live in Maryland actually. Nearer to Annapolis, but Howard is right inside DC. In fact, we're in the capital district often. Xaria loves the

Smithsonian to a nearly unholy degree. When Theo mentioned he's in DC too, I was panicking. I was sure he'd probably seen us without knowing it. Her school's public. The nuns did real well by me. However, I don't know the church well enough. Not yet, anyway." Eva glances at me and I pinch her side gently. So, they're already close. That makes things easier.

Eva keeps flipping through the albums, showing us the timeline of Xaria's life. She pauses just before a new album. "So, as you can tell, Xaria likes themes. With her birthday in February, we always do circle around love themes. This year, though, she wanted a different theme. Daddy."

My heart stops.

Eva's voice hitches with emotion as she continues. "I didn't— couldn't keep you from her. I wanted Xaria to know you, so I made a habit of telling her all the good stories I remember."

Her eyes turn sly as she looks at me. I wince, smiling sheepishly. Good stories between us are few.

"Even stories about work and Christmas. Xaria always wants to know more. So, I had to stalk your social media for two months. Even dug up old profiles none of us use anymore. Your friend, the trooper? He supplied some stories for me. Got suspicious though, so I stopped asking," she says, shrugging at the look I shoot her.

"So, this party has a Country theme. Country and western paired with country rock music, bowling, and burgers. That's all she wanted. I still convinced her to have a cute cake though." Eva snorts on cute, adding quotes around it. "Xari said she wanted a cake of where I met you. So, I built her a farmhouse."

She slides slowly through these photos. There's a video too. *Freebird* blasts in the background as Xaria, my daughter, totters up to the bowling lane. The bumpers are up, and she has a neon-blue ball in her hands. Not using the holds, the little girl bends and sends her ball off. Granny-bowling like a pro. Her squeals of triumph as she tips a good four pins over makes me smile.

"Oh, look," Nana gushes. "She's got Theo's jaw. She'll be a tall one, Eva. Look at those gangly arms and legs."

The older Xaria gets, the more the older members of the family gush over the photos. Gramps and Dad look a little teary. I know I feel weepy over seeing her in a kindergarten graduation ceremony. Her first grade Christmas pageant, the second-grade choral concert, the third-grade study of the nativity and her absolute irreverence that left her teachers sputtering are all pieces of her I've lost. It hurts, makes my heart twinge in a way I'm unfamiliar with. Even though Eva's clearly recorded each event, I've missed them. I'm living them through the lens of a camera.

Her birthday, though, eight candles on a big red farmhouse. I drink in my kid wearing a flannel shirt, and Carhart pants, her big barrel curls wild all over, as black as my hair, with wide hazel-brown eyes. This is my daughter. I made her, helped make her with Evanna. Xaria's perfect in all the ways I can see.

"I haven't had her tenth birthday party yet. However I want—" Eva chokes and traces Xaria's face for a moment. I look up, watching the profile of the mother of my child. She's nervous. "I… I don't know what Mom told ya'll. But I couldn't stay there with her, with them; truthfully, I never will. For keeping away, I apologize. The thought of what they'd do scared me. But I want you to be there. For Xaria's party, it's the fourth of February every year, no matter what. She'd really love to meet all of you. I'd love for her to meet all of you," Eva says, voice wobbling.

A drop of water hits my hand as Eva sniffles. Which breaks my resolve to not let the water works just flow. I press my face into her hair, wrapping my other arm around her. It's obvious to me that Evanna's been going through it. And this? coming home, seeing me, telling me, has ripped down whatever walls she'd built up. It sure as hell has ripped apart mine.

"You'll have to get me in a cell to keep me away, Eva," I tell her words a grumble more than anything, my voice hoarse. Dad, Grams, and Nana all echo the same sentiment while Evanna just breaks the fuck down in my lap. I'm no better at comforting her than I was back then. Still, I try.

Wrapping my arms around her, I pull her close and rock her slightly. "Hey, shhh, princess. We got you; I've got you. We love you." I drop my voice just for her to hear me. "*I* love you, princess."

Nana pats my shoulder gently. "Take her to the loft, Theo. Go on. Neither of you ought to be drivin' tonight. We'll talk tomorrow, after dinner and before you all head out home, hm?"

"Thanks, Nana," I reply, swallowing to ease the tightness in my throat while I shift Eva around, picking her up. She weighs barely anything to me, even though she makes complaining sounds whilst winding her arms around me. It. This feels right.

"Sleep well, Theodore. Keep Eva safe tonight, eh?" Dad instructs me, knocking his shoulder against mine while getting up. He drapes Eva's coat over her and gets mine around my shoulders. No one follows us out into the snowy yard. Which I'm glad for.

Eva and I-we need some time.

~

"Fuck, it's freezin'," I mutter, setting Eva down on the little couch. With her settled, her sniffles come randomly, letting me know she's calming down. I feel better leaving her to get the heating controls under control. There is a stove up here, one we hadn't used before. Tonight, I truck back down the stairs to the wood stack. I end up juggling two trips worth of wood back upstairs. Between the two, I get the loft started toward warmth.

"Sorry," Eva whispers as I slide down onto the couch beside her, her shoes off to the side, mine back by the door. Settling an arm around her, I pull her in close.

"What're you sorry for, princess?" I press a kiss to her temple. "Being emotional? Eva, baby, you're human. Now, I don't know what happened between you and Clara, but if you felt justified leaving, I can't fault you. It's… I just…"

Pausing, I take a breath, gathering up my composure. This part hurts because I know it's my fault. I made Evanna doubt me. Made her doubt what we'd been slowly starting to build. "I just wish I'd been there. That I didn't just learn about our baby through nine years' worth of photos. I wanted to be with you. You know that, right?"

I work a hand into her hair, tilting her face toward me as Eva sniffles. Her eyes meet mine for a second, then she's looking away again. A little frown is marring her face, brows pulled together, and wrinkles on her forehead. She picks at the arm of my sweater with her nails.

"I thought you would want to join me. But I couldn't be sure, Theo. I just… My world had just inverted, I froze up and instead of fighting, I just ran. Mom, she said some shit to me I will never forgive her for. Dad…he actually slapped me," Eva says quietly, leaning into my hand, eyes finally meeting mine, a wary light in them.

My body goes stiff as Eva says Jacob hit her. He put his hands on her. I'd never raised my hand like that to her. I'd put hands on her, and I still hate myself for it. Evanna has endured stitches because of me pushing her into the fireplace just a couple hundred meters away. Jake, though? Jake was supposed to be her father, her ultimate protector.

"Yeah," Eva sighs, still looking at me. "I think I looked exactly like that. That's what got me actually moving, you know, being slapped. I don't even remember if I said anything. I don't remember a lot of that fight, even less of that night."

Evanna lays against my shoulder, wedging herself up against me. I move around to accommodate us both. It's a small couch. I have to angle so Eva ends up trapped between its back and me. Her hands migrate, inserting themselves beneath my sweater. She keeps making patterns over my chest.

"We're here now, Eva. Whatever you chose that day, you chose the right path. We won't know what would have changed. I've seen my therapist often enough to know there's no use in what ifs. It'll just drive you crazy wondering. We have from here on, though. All our choices from here out, these are what matter." I work my fingers carefully into her curls again, gently massaging her scalp while I speak.

Her eyes find mine and I'm unable to look away from her. Those big brown eyes always held information. Eva's never kept all her emotions from her face. Right now, there's a bit of heat in her gaze, but hope is glowing. There's more swirling in that look of hers. It's been too long for me to pinpoint them all with confidence.

"We are here now," she says slowly as she drops her eyes away from mine. It's as if she's tasting that, absorbing a large part of her life is no longer a secret. Her eyes, big doe brown eyes, find mine. There's a sharpness in her gaze now. "What are we, Teddy?"

An excellent damn question. The way we've both been talking; we could be together still. We could also be fond exes about to embark on a co-parenting journey ten years in the making. What I want is the former. So, I say that.

"We're us, Eva. I want to make a family. You, me, Xaria. It's been what I've craved for years. When you left, everything shifted. Before, I wanted three things: you, a baby in your belly, and the world to know you're both mine. I won't lie. It fucked me up when you disappeared. And when I say that… it's an understatement. Realizing I couldn't find you, that I couldn't have any of it–ripped something in me." Once I start, it's a challenge to stop speaking. It's a ramble that's been sitting on my chest for ages. But it's still the truth. All I want is Eva in my life, sharing it with me.

"That was incredibly…. Unhelpful," Eva drawls, eyeing me with an amused glint in her eyes. "As clear as mud, in fact. "

"I want you to be Evanna LeClair," I announce as my clarification. "Not Evanna Bishop-LeClaire, just Evanna LeClair, with Xaria LeClair."

I watch her doe eyes become saucers as the words settle. She always looks so adorably owlish like this. Not creepy… cute. The expression says I can't possibly have said what I did. I wait, knowing it'll pass. Eva doesn't make me wait long, either.

"Married. You want to *marry* me?" Eva asks, whispering the words while leaning her chin on my chest. There's this quiet awe in her voice that makes me puff up, pleased she heard me properly.

"Yeah, princess. I want to marry you. Got the kid, got a house. I'll live with weird hours, with the inevitable attention you'll draw down the road, so long as it's our bed you collapse in once you're free to rest. I can deal with a lot, actually, if you're in my house, in my arms, as mother of my daughter," I say seriously. There's no point in holding back. She knows that I'm physically attracted to her still. I can't play my cards too close to the chest. I gotta lay 'em out on the table.

Reaching out, I cup her cheek, brushing my thumb along it. "When I say everyone, I mean everyone, Eva. Jake, Clara, and Jasmine can fuck off. You're an adult, you can choose who to spend your life with. Just like you chose what would be best for you and Xaria. They can talk to me if they want to get angry. I'll happily tell them where to put those issues."

"Theodore," Eva huffs at me, but I just smile in response. There's no anger in her tone. No accompaniment of down-turned lips, no narrowed eyes. A smile plays around her lips, her forehead is wrinkle free. My Eva finds this amusing.

"C'mon, baby," I say in a wheedling tone, "We already started the process."

I hope… I pray Evanna will at least agree to trying. We don't have to get married tomorrow–though I would in a heartbeat. All I really need is Eva and Xaria close to me.

Eva takes a deep breath.

"Well," she starts, "your dad, Grand-Mère, and Grand-Père know." Her tone is thoughtful while her eyes flick over my body toward the stove where the fire is merrily crackling. "You really want to marry me, Theodore? You want me *still*?"

When Evanna looks at me this time, the air in the loft shifts. A different tension settles between us. Licking my lips, I give my libido a mental 'cool *the fuck down'*, but my dick isn't listening. The little fucker. Still, I do my best to answer Eva without making it seem like I just want to jump her again.

"I do. If it wasn't clear in the kitchen, I missed you, princess. And not just physically. I've been dreaming of having you back. Of making a relationship with you work, making a family together. Are you sayin' you want me?" The northern drawl I work hard to keep from leaking into my speech is back full force, and somehow, that seems to do it for the woman in my arms.

Her tawny skin colors an inviting coral-pink, eyes dilating in the low light of the room. "Never really stopped. I tried, which was a mess and a half. He wasn't you, and I couldn't do the whole hook-up thing. It wasn't you, so it wasn't right."

Her shoulders shrug. I tug at her hair at the mention of trying to not want me. It means other people in her life. That's never sat well with me. Even when I had someone to chase her out of my system, I wanted Evanna. Which ended that.

"How long did you try to forget, princess?" I ask, noting the timbre of my voice makes Eva shiver.

"Long enough," she whispers, "learned quick I'd never forget."

Eva moves to hover over me. Her curls cascade over one shoulder, my hand on the other side, keeping them at bay. She's beautiful, the mother of my child. Her face is more mature, more angular, her body fuller, softer, her emotions more guarded around people she should trust. But ultimately, this is my Evanna.

"That's not what you want to know, though," she says, pulling me from my thoughts. "You want a number. One."

"One for me, too," I tell her honestly, my hand leaving her hair to cup her cheek. "Been stuck on you a long damn time."

"So, be stuck *in* me for tonight," she whispers cheekily, her face warming as I chuckle. Kissing her nose, I pause, moving back a little.

"Do we need condoms? I should have asked earlier–"

"You never need one with me," Eva says, voice lowered in a rasp. I groan in response. This woman is going to kill me. "But I'm not on anything. I didn't need it. So, if we do this…"

"We're doing this," I growl out, sitting up, hands around her waist. "I missed one pregnancy. There's no way I'm missing this one. From making this baby to you bringing said baby into the world, I'm with you, Eva."

"Jesus, Teddy," Evanna whimpers. I just grin unrepentantly. Standing, I bring her with me, lifting her, guiding her legs around me.

I walk us into the bedroom, the one we've shared at least a dozen times now. It's edging on freezing still, but I don't give a damn as I gently toss her onto the bed.

Eva laughs as she bounces, her sound, that look transports me back years ago. She settles, pushing herself onto her elbows, shooting a wicked smirk at me. "Come on then. I'm right here, if you want me so bad, Theo."

Barking a laugh, I crawl onto the bed and over her until she's got to lie back down. "Oh, princess, my princess, the things I'm going to do to you…"

"What're you gonna do, Teddy?" Eva asks, her hands on my stomach sliding until she has one resting on my neck, the other playing with my hair. Bumping my nose against hers, I take a second to look at the woman I love. To just look at her before I lean in and kiss her breath away.

"Let me show you…"

~

It's been too damn long since I've woken up with Eva in my arms. Waking up with her wrapped around me is somewhere between fond memory and a most desired dream. This kind of intimacy is something I've been craving since… Fuck, it doesn't matter anymore, because I've got it now. Readjusting, with Eva still sleeping, her nose scrunching up, I settle down to look at her.

She's a pretty picture. Her hair is up in a giant bun on the top of her head, her makeup washed away. My girl had grumbled and grumped about having forgotten her bonnet and scarf in her bag–which is still in the trunk. I debate the merits of leaving the bed to go down and get it. It's still dark out, so it's too damn early to be up.

Especially considering we'd barely remembered to call the hotel last night to cancel our rooms. Carefully moving away, I slip out from under her, grabbing my clothes to shove on quickly. Locating our keys is the straightforward part, getting our bags without eating shit thanks to all the snow, less so.

Outside the loft, the world's colored in gentle grays. My breath puffs into a cloud.

Ten years, and I still wake up at the ass crack of dawn. Retrieving the bags, I take them up before returning to grab firewood. We like the cold just fine to sleep. Waking up to it is a damn nightmare. One I won't be subjecting Evanna too, seeing as of the pair, it's worse for her. My coat and shoes come off before I stack the wood in the stove. I'm just getting it started when the floorboards creak.

"You're up at unholy times, Theodore," Eva says, her voice heavy with sleep, making me turn from the stove as the first log catches a light. She's wrapped in the comforter and if I were still even remotely into art, I'd say she ought to be photographed or painted. But I'm not, so I focus on committing the sight of her to memory.

"Morning, gorgeous. Happy birthday," I greet her with a little chuckle. Standing, I close the stove grate, shoving my hands into my pockets while ambling toward her.

"Oh," she says, while blinking. "Right, I'm twenty-eight now."

"Mm hm," I hum and stop when there's a hand span of space between us. Looking down at her, I smile, unable to shake it from my face. "You're one step closer to thirty, baby. How's it feel?"

"Like I have one less fuck to give," Eva says and snorts after. "I'm sure thirty'll be different. Presently, I'm still the mom of a nine-year-old girl. Those are the birthdays I worry about."

"Well, you have an extra set of hands this year," I offer tentatively. "If you want that–"

"Teddy," Evanna drawls my name. The way it rolls around her mouth always gets me hard. Don't ask me why. "I'm pretty sure I was screaming your name last night. You're helping with every birthday that rolls around from now on. You're stuck, Mr. Be-Just-Evanna-LeClair."

The smile on my face widens. My feet carry me forward, I scoop Eva up comforter and all. She laughs, grabbing onto me the moment her feet leave the floor. I kiss her soundly, yet can't banish that inkling of worry that rears up.

"You're serious, right?"

"As fuckin' labor," Eva retorts with a sigh. "I'm yours, Teddy."

Wandering back to the bed, I grin, setting my bundle down in the middle of the mess of sheets. "Good."

Connection, Collision

Evanna
25 December

We 'roll out of bed' at about eight, a respectable time to actually be awake for normal and healthy people. The five am wake up was a bit much. Walking to Grand-Mère's with Teddy to see if we need to go buy breakfast, I estimate this to be my best birthday in a while. Certainly, the best one as an adult.

His hand is in mine, a smile that seems to light up the entire world on his face. I haven't ever seen Theodore like this before. But I like it. While it might not always be like this when we go back to life, making it into some new sense of normal together; I look forward to days in the future where he looks like this, too. Walking in after ditching my trainers at the door, coat up on a hook, I open the door to see Grand-Mère and Grand-Père bustling in and out of the kitchen together.

"Good morning, Evanna, Theo." Grand-Mère smiles brightly as we walk in. "Happy birthday, honey."

"Thank you, Grand-Mère. Joyeux anniversaire, Grand-Père." I dodge around her and her platter of sausage to hug and kiss him. He chuckles, returning the hug and kiss before telling us to sit.

"Figured the pair of you would be staying, so I started breakfast a little while ago. I also figured you had a late night, talkin' and all," Grand-Mère explains when Theo asks her what all this is.

"Oh," I squeak and look over at him. He's looking at me, and I goggle at the fact his cheeks are red! Teddy is *blushing*, he's really, truly blushing. Giggling, unable to hide it, I cover my mouth while trying to compose myself a bit.

"Um. Yes. We were up late talking." I nod, still giggling a bit, not able to look at either grandparent. They just make noises of having heard us. We all eat and chat about what we hope to do once Christmas is over.

It's the first time I'm eager for the end of the day, if only so I can call Keyanna to fill her in. Speaking of which. "Teddy, when we're done, after the dishes. Do you want to call Xaria with me?"

"Of course."

~

"I'm nervous," he admits as we wander back to the loft. I lean against him and squeeze his hand reassuringly.

"I know she seems terrifying, what with being nine, but I promise she's going to be excited. Ready to chat your ear off too, I bet." I pop onto my toes to kiss his cheek.

"Fingers crossed," he mumbles. I haven't seen Theodore nervous about much, so I let him brood until we're upstairs. Then I round on him, hands on my hips.

"All right, Teddy. Get it together, Xaria is about to talk to her dad for the first time *ever*. This is special for you too, but don't be afraid to just talk. Ask her what she likes, mention you heard she likes hockey, hell, ask her if she wants to go bowling or meet you." I throw options at him, and watch as his shoulders slowly slump back into their usual position.

"Okay. Okay, princess. I hear you." He smiles, and I nod sharply, smiling as well before grabbing my phone. I'm almost positive that Xar would have had Key up at six, so we should be safe calling now.

The phone rings and I follow Teddy toward the lounge. He plops onto the couch, catching me around the waist to pull me onto his lap. I shake my head at him, but lean back, getting comfortable all the same.

"Jesus, woman. It's nine am," Keyanna's voice fills the phone and I laugh.

"So, you've been up for what, three hours now, Key?"

"Your child is a hell spawn," she answers, groaning dramatically. "Want to talk to her?"

"Of course. But heads up, because she might lose her whole mind in a couple minutes. Theodore is going to talk to her." I figure it's only right to warn Keyanna. The line is silent before she speaks up again.

"He wants to talk to her? He's not trying to end your life or world for keeping this from him. How is that even possible, Evanna," Key asks, pulling out my full name.

"Long story. Just… plans are going to change so long as Xaria is comfortable with said plans," I offer, giving my friend at least a hint of what's going on.

"Girl." Keyanna sucks at her teeth, the distinct sound making me pull the phone away a bit. "Be careful."

"I am. Now, daughter, on the phone, please."

"God, yes. Xaria!" The yell has me pulling away from the phone again with a curse. Theodore is giving the phone the hairy eyeball. It's funny as hell. This cellphone might as well be a goddamn grenade.

"Mommy?" Xaria's voice comes through, and his eyes widen. I smile, kissing my fingers before pressing them to his lips.

"Hey, sweetie," I say happily. "Happy Christmas."

"Happy birthday, mommy! Did Santa commit a 'B and E' at your grandma's house too?" Xaria asks excitedly and I blink, mouthing what she's said.

"Uh. Well, he left presents, but he didn't— you know what, I'm not going to ask right now. I have someone who really wants to talk to you, sweetie. He's really nervous though, is it okay to put him on the phone now?" I watch Theo as I listen to Xaria.

"Okay! Is it Pepe? Or is it Grandpa? I don't know if I want to talk about toys or things like that with them, though. But you can put them on the phone, Mommy. I'll be polite. Promise." Xaria's energy level spikes the longer she talks.

"Alright, sweetie. Here he is." I chuckle a little as I offer the phone to Theodore. He's a little pale as he takes the phone from me. I cuddle closer to him as he clears his throat, murmuring the first words he's ever said to our daughter.

Theodore.

"Hello, is this Xaria?" I feel a little like I've swallowed two pounds of cotton. If I thought I'd been nervous about seeing Evanna for the first time in a decade, this completely tops what I was feeling then. I keep a tight hold on the phone in my hand, waiting for her to say something.

"You don't sound very old," a little voice says finally. I can't help but laugh, clearing my throat when I realize I sound choked up.

"Well, I'm not that old, so that makes sense," I say reminding myself to keep things simple. Nine… she's nine. How does a person speak to a small human like this?

"Ohh," she hums on the other end of the line. "What's your name?"

"My name's Theodore, but I think your mom told you my name is Dad." I hold my breath saying that. No matter how much Evanna smiles or gives me encouraging touches, I'm terrified. Down to the very last bone in my body, I'm scared out of my mind this kid is going to hate me. Without ever meeting me.

"Daddy?" The whispered word is enough to make my eyes burn.

"Yes, ma'am," I say, going for jovial. "Santa dropped me off to visit with your mom."

"He kidnaps people?!" Her strangled gasp makes my eyes widen before I laugh again shaking my head.

"No, Xaria. He asked, and I said okay. Santa doesn't kidnap anyone. Is it okay that I'm talking to you?"

"Okay," she agrees, still sounding a little suspicious of Santa. "Do you not want to talk to me?"

"Oh, kiddo," I sigh. "I want to talk to you more than anything else in the world. But only if you want to talk to me too."

"I would like that very much," Xaria offers after a little pause. "Are you… coming home with Mommy? Do you want us now that you know?"

"It would be my honor to come home with your mom and meet you, and I do very much want you and your mom in my life, Xaria. I would love for you and her to come live with me, when you're both ready." I am assaulted with memories of Clara hissing over the phone to Jasmine to not promise to visit, to say she'd like that, never be firm and get the child's hopes up. It doesn't feel right to me, but I keep it vague, leave the ball in Evanna's court. Ultimately, it is her decision how this plays out.

"Hm. Did you get Mommy a gift," Xaria asks me very seriously. The abrupt change in conversation has my head spinning.

"I didn't know if she would accept one from me, but Santa had the perfect thing for me to give her." I scramble and thank all that is holy that Xaria believes in Santa. Eva sure as hell hadn't by nine.

Coincidentally, Eva has her head buried against my chest, her shoulders shaking with silent laughter. I narrow my eyes at her. *Yeah, yeah, yuck it up, princess.*

"Would you like a Christmas present from me, Xaria?" Might as well, what kid doesn't.

"Yes!" The shriek makes me blink slowly and shake my head. "Nazeera's Mommy and Daddy got her a little brother. I don't want a little brother, though, I want a sister. So we can play dolls together, I can give her all of my favorites, and I can read to her and stuff."

"A... sister," I croak. Evanna's head snaps up, eyes big. I assume this is the first she's heard of this as well. Kids, man. *Kids.* "That might take a little while, honey. What can I bring you this year?"

"You. And a book, I want your favorite book," Xaria's answer comes after a long pause, and I deflate in relief. Thank God. This is something I can work with.

"All right, one visit and one favorite book. I'll talk to your mom, and we'll see what we can come up with," still no promise. Keep it safe in case today explodes somehow. Even if it does, it'll take someone killing me to get me to let go of these girls.

"Ask her really nicely and politely! And tell her happy birthday before saying Merry Christmas. Mommy thinks people don't see when she flinches or makes her smile stay when she wants to frown, but I do. People are mean, her birthday is important too!" Xaria says, voice edged in a warning. It's very strange to hear out of a kid.

"I will, pumpkin. And I already told her happy birthday, but just to be safe, I'll tell her again. Do you, want to talk to her now?"

"Yes, please. It's nice to know you're real, Daddy, and what your voice sounds like." Xaria signs off like that as I hand the phone back to Evanna. I know I say goodbye and I love her, it's just. It's surreal, to hear her, hear my daughter speaking to me. Asking for a freaking sibling.

I'm so out of it, I miss all of Evanna's conversation with her. It's not until Eva presses her lips against mine, I snap out of it. Even then, I'm not quite sure I'm fully with it.

"You look a little shell shocked," Eva whispers, a fond look on her face. Her hand is petting over my cheek, and I have to agree, I feel shell shocked. So, looking that way makes sense. Her lips meet mine again and coax me back into the land of the living.

I'm not complaining at all about that method of revival, either.

Nine-thirty sees Eva and I getting dressed to go back to the Farmhouse for Christmas Lunch. Capital letters, because this isn't just food, no, this is an event. Complete with cake and boozy egg nog. The latter wasn't always boozy, but I can bet it's going to need to be this year. I won't lie, my Christmas sweater, while lovely, isn't doing much to make me feel like we're going to survive the rest of the day.

No one knows better than me how absolutely evil Clara can be. At least it feels like no one could know better. The truth is, we all probably know and actively try to avoid triggering her. Eva probably knows damn well exactly how evil Clara gets. Jasmine too, much as she's on my shit list, she's been on Clara's longer.

"God, I don't want to do this," Evanna groan, zipping up her dress. Blue isn't the color I'd assume she'd wear today, given her choice of red the day before. I'd have called green, but this is pretty on her. It looks like water as she moves.

"We could just… not go," I say with a shrug, fixing my slacks so they sit right.

"Our cars are in the driveway," she reminds me, picking up bone-colored earrings from a little travel box. "Clara would be over here within twenty minutes of us being late. Even if she's pissed I told the family about Xaria, a snub like this, from me? Unthinkable and unacceptable."

I roll my eyes. "Where the hell did her politics for family even come from?" Because it doesn't make a lick of sense to me. Family is family. Messy, irritating, lovable, hell you may even just hate one another, but it's rarely polite.

"I blame her being very, very French." Eva's shoulders hitch. Facing me she places her hand on the dresser and leans to the side, giving me a slow once over.

"I like that, it's a good color on you. Matches your eyes." She smiles a slow smile, her lips coated in a flavored oil, and I am highly tempted to go over there. But I stay put. Neither of us plans to unveil this thing between us in a visual way like that. It would be our fucking luck, too.

"Thanks, baby. You look like your nickname, a perfect princess." Her smile shifts, eyes lidding just enough it's no longer a warm smile, but one that heats my blood faster than anything else ever has or will.

"Thank you, Teddy. We better get this show on the road. Are we just, telling them, or are we going to hold hands and see who notices first?" Eva brushes past me, her perfume, so different from that summer we had, is dark, sultry. Floral without any sweetness. I follow her out of the room for the sake of avoiding temptation.

Her hand is held out as she puts on one of her heels and I hold her steady. I take a second before saying, "I know we decided to just go with it, between uh, re-connecting, but I don't know how to do it that won't trigger a war."

"I have the same issue," she admits, taking back her hand once her shoes are on. I slip mine on, coats are put on and we're slipping into the crisp air of the day. "I think we just be us until someone asks."

"That's as good a plan as any, princess." I take her hand, agreeing because we don't have time to plot and honestly, I don't want to waste my time with it. They'll figure it out. They can like it, or they can be shitty about it, either way, this is happening. We're happening.

By virtue of being across the lawn, Eva and I are the first to arrive at lunch. Nana steals my girl to help with getting the last pieces of food settled and I disappear into Gramps' office with him. He's got his old books of stamps out, a couple new ones laid out to be put in.

"Afternoon, Grandpa."

"Hello, Theo," he smiles over at me in greeting, and kicks out the chair nearest to him. "Come sit, Lord knows those girls of ours won't want us underfoot."

Sitting, I rub my palms on my legs before asking what's been at the back of my mind since yesterday. "Did you really think we were going to be together, Gramps? Are you really okay with it?"

Of everyone in the family, Gramps and Nana are the people I care about most. I would be more than a little upset if it turned out they were lying to make Eva feel better, or just lying to avoid conflict. They aren't the type, but I just need to be sure.

"Theodore James," Gramps sighs at me. "If I didn't approve, I wouldn't have said a damn thing but, *'get the hell away from my granddaughter,'* to you last night. You're unconventional, sure, but y'aren't blood cousins, and frankly, people have married their cousins for centuries. What am I going to do about it ultimately? Haven't got much of a leg to stand on when my parents were third cousins. I love the both of you, and I'm glad that you're not at odds. That was never natural. This…" Gramps pauses and shrugs. "This just makes sense to me. She keeps you from going overboard, even when you claimed to hate her. I remember she'd yell at you for being stupid and you'd stop. You'd focus on her, and you might take revenge later for it, but you still stopped to listen. You bring out the fight in Evanna. Clara may like to blame bullying on Eva clamming up like she did, but she started shrinking long before that," Gramps says with a frown.

"I did a lot of wrong to Evanna," I say quietly as the silence falls. "There's no way I deserve her. She's letting me into her life again. We never technically were anything, we never said goodbye. If I fuck it up—"

"Then you fuck up," Gramps cuts me off, eyes serious as he sets aside his stamps. "Theo, do you think I didn't make mistakes with your grandmother? We fought like cats and dogs in a cage when we first got married. Love is well and good, but *communication* takes time to build. If Evanna is offering you a chance to build that with her, I see no reason for you to deny yourself. Her leaving, as I understand, was not because of you."

I nod, the movement sharp. That's one of the few things I can hold onto. I didn't drive her away. Didn't have the chance and honestly, the last time we spoke before she did disappear, didn't seem like I was messing up. Did we need to talk. Yes. Would it have been awful, maybe. But, that me won't ever know.

"You're right," I say after a few minutes. Gramps has his book back in his hand, stamps carefully being placed inside. "I'm just so damn nervous about today. Clara. She's…"

"She's the kind of woman that makes you think of a harpy or one of those goddesses in old legends," Gramps grunts with a laugh. "That woman may be pretty, but her mouth and her ability to turn on a dime make her ugly. Somehow, she and Jacob fit, I'm not goin' to poke into how, tried when he brought her home. To my surprise, she clung to him harder than a barnacle on a barge. Clara will get over it. Or she won't, and you still have me, your grandmother, and father. Don't go borrowing trouble y'ain't got yet, Theodore."

"Yessir," I answer quickly, and take a couple breaths, just looking to get my head clear. He's not wrong, far from it. Clara would deal, or Evanna would turn away. Eva hasn't said as much, but there's a sharpness in that girl that wasn't there when we got together. I don't know if I should be worried about it or not, but it's there. Her turning her back and walking away has happened once—twice, hopefully, wouldn't hurt her worse than the first time.

"Teddy, Grand-Père, come out, Uncle Joe's here," Eva's voice pulls me from my seat like she's got me on a string. I don't look back, even when Gramps chortles behind me as I leave the office.

"You callin' us to foist off your duties as a hostess, or to help with somethin'," I ask in a drawl, hands slipping into my pockets.

Eva comes out of the kitchen, her blue dress covered in one of Nana's aprons. It's damn cute, the quiet dress, a simple cut, topped with a frilly, frothy apron. I bit my lip to keep from grinning to hard.

"Well, you could ignore your father if you want, I figured you'd want to say hi. We don't need you fer nothin'. No soup, so no tall cupboards, Theodore." Her eyes glint and I lift my hands up in surrender.

"Okay, damn, princess."

Dad laughs, heading toward me right as Gramps comes from around me into the room. They greet one another as they always have, the patented 'man' hug, a kiss on the forehead from Gramps, and then it's my turn.

"Dad, you're a little early." I grin as he slaps my back. His eyes shift to Evanna and back to me.

"Figured I'd come a little sooner, see if there was any news," he says it so casually if I weren't hyper aware he knows, I'd have missed it. He's askin' about us.

"Well, had an interesting phone call this morning," I say grin widening remembering Xaria's request. "Xar wants a little sister for Christmas. Had to put her off, since that's a time crunch I can't make, but she settled for a copy of my favorite book when I go see her."

Dad snorts, head shaking as he laughs. "Now I know she's yours. You asked your mother for a sibling once it was clear being the younger one wasn't as important as being older."

My brows jump up. Did I? I don't remember it at all, but I have been actively avoiding memories dealing with my mother for decades now. Still, I like the idea Xaria's got some of my personality in her. "Huh, well, her blunt desires for siblings aside, she's a smart cookie. A little shy, but direct in what she wants. Asked me if I wanted her and 'Mommy' in my life now that I knew about them."

"And?" Dad prompts, arms crossing over his chest.

"And of course I do," I reply quickly, keeping my voice low. "She just agreed to be with me, and half agreed to dropping Bishop permanently. I am not about to go pushing it to happen tomorrow. We didn't discuss if I was going to go straight to hers or go home and regroup. I think we're both more than a little nervous."

"Fair enough," Dad says with a little nod of acceptance. "So long as you two don't hurt that little girl, your lives are your own. I'm just here to be a pain and remind you that you were shattered when Eva left."

"I remember," I reply with a wince. "Anyway. Gifts. Food, it's that time of day. You got yours in yet? Oh, shit."

Remembering I hadn't brought the stuff in from my truck, I look at Eva. She's setting out plates, so it's safe enough to get her attention. "Hey, princess, you bring in your gifts yet?"

Her head snaps up, curls half covering her face. "Shit. I didn't. Can you?"

"Yeah, I got it. keys in your coat?" I'm moving as she agrees I open the door right on to the three people I'm dreading to see most.

"Ah, Jasmine, Aunt Clara, Uncle Jake. Go get comfy, I'll be right back." Over my shoulder, I say, likely needlessly. "More LeClairs on board, Dad, Gramps."

Sliding away from them as they come in, I grab keys and shoes then head down into the snow. It figures that it'd start to snow today. But it's picturesque too. Big, fat flakes just slowly raining down. The kind that don't melt on contact, so my wrapping isn't ruined. Eva's bags are in another box, so I'm juggling from her trunk all the way to the door. Nudging the inner door open with my foot, I hear her before I see her.

"Jesus, Teddy. You could have made two trips. Give me that." Her box leaves my hold and I just flash a smile.

"Now, why would I do that, princess. I had enough hands to hold on both the pile and the box." Teasing her, I toe off my shoes while she rolls her eyes. It feels... fucking great to be like this. No stiffness, no shying away from one another.

"Help Nana with the turkey while I put these in the lounge, just stick yours on top." She points with her chin at my small pile. I squint at her, but relent, balancing them on her box and watching her leave. Nana calls me, pulling me from watching her. By the time the bird is carved, the platter in the center of the table, Andi, kids, and the Aunts are all in attendance. Without seats assigned, I just grab the one between Eva and her mother. Buffers, I reason, never hurt anyone. My hand finds her leg under the table, and Christmas commences.

Evanna

Theo's hand on my leg is comforting. I don't have to be weird about it, not even in my own head, and it's really nice. In fact, I don't worry about how I speak to him, there's no second guessing, no wall between him and I. Much as I wanted to deny it, the moment Teddy started after me in the kitchen, I'd been ready to just fold.

He's that far under my skin still.

"You're looking considerably happier, Evanna," Clara's voice cuts through my conversation with Odette. The tone, the one that tells me I've chosen the wrong thing, makes me stiffen.

Licking my lips, I turn some, angling myself toward Teddy. I also mentally brace myself, because I have little faith this won't run from one thing to another, quickly. So, I cut it off at the pass. No games today. "I am, I talked to Xaria this morning, and her father will be joining us for the New Years Celebration."

Mom rolls the word around her mouth and scoffs. "Why would you give a child a name like that? It's foreign."

"Mother, my name is Evanna…it's *Welsh*. Xaria's name is Arabic in origin and means gift from love. Which is exactly what she is," I retort easily enough, grabbing the rolls when Uncle Joe asks after them to pass over.

"And her father agreed to it? This name… *Zennia*." There it is. The slight, the dig for information. My irritation bubbles up, but I won't be the one to fire the first shots here. I take a breath, eyeing Theodore carefully. I can either say yes or ask him. I open my mouth, and he shakes his head.

"I think it fits her very well, Aunt Clara. I wasn't aware you were so against names from other cultures, given you're from France," Teddy says it so damn smoothly for a second no one catches on. No one out of the know, anyway. Jasmine pauses across from me, head lifting.

I duck my head, taking a bite of stuffing. I won't say a damn word until Clara does. The war is not about to be my fault. Even if Grand-Père and Mère expect it.

"When exactly did you begin to care about anything in Evanna's life, Theodore? Especially her child?" she asks, voice like a whip in the room. Swallowing, I let my hand drop to take his. We should have planned this, but we didn't. Now, I'm about to have a full-blown panic attack.

"I care because Xaria is *mine*, and Evanna is too." Theodore doesn't even look at Clara. While I knew neither of us were going to deny it. My heart still feels like it's going to beat straight out of my chest. My lungs feel tight, too.

Joe and Grand-Père are still eating, casting cautious looks around the table. Grand-Mère, however, is staring Clara down. Jasmine is looking at me and I can't read her face. I'm not sure that I want to, actually.

"What—" Clara hisses and I brace for the impact of whatever nuclear explosion is about to take place. I don't expect Dad to say a damn thing. I don't expect him to even acknowledge he's heard anything.

"Clara." A word. Just her name, and Dad shuts Mom down. I don't know what's going to happen now. Dad being mad; it's rare. There have been two times in my life he's been angry, specifically angry enough to do something.

"Eva."

"Dad?" I don't crane my neck to see him. There's no way. I can take Clara, I know that sharp tongue, I can even counter it. Not him. Once he reduced me to desperate tears, the other time he hit me.

"Someday, I'd like to meet her, if you'll allow it."

Silence, I look at Theodore. His eyes are wide, but his shoulders are relaxed. Shock? Relief? Maybe both, because I feel wound tighter than a spring. I set my fork down and reach for my water glass. Sipping at it, I find words and remember that I'm not some little waif about to swoon.

"I'd like you to meet her, Dad."

And dinner resumes. Just like that. It takes a little while, but conversation starts back up. I eat mechanically because I was expecting war. Truly, I walked into the farmhouse ready for it; waiting for it. Scared shitless of it.

This feels like the calm before the storm, but I just eat, and answer Andi's questions about Xaria as they come.

Unfortunately, dinner ends and the family shifts toward the lounge. Gifts. This should go quickly. But I somehow doubt it will. Especially when Theodore drags me into his lap. I wasn't firing the first shots of this war, but Teddy is drawing the line in the sand.

As he settles me, a hand around my waist, my thoughts race. While I have made huge decisions here, facing and reconciling with Teddy, telling people about Xaria, I am still very much the scared girl in her mother's house. Clara's word is law. Don't fuck with the flow of things; be good. It's the rule. Always has been.

I can already hear her in my head. *You're fat, you're being slovenly, sit up straight, get off Theodore's lap. Is this how you repay everything I've done? You and your cousin, an illegitimate child together. What did I do to deserve this? Where did I go wrong? You were a good child; you did as you were told. How many people saw you fucking him, how many people in this town, our town, know you're a whore?*

"Princess?" Teddy's voice washes over me, shakes me out of my head, away from the voice in my head. Clara's voice. I don't need to double up, I suppose.

"Yeah, Teddy?" I tilt my face towards his.

"Just checking in on you, you're shaking. Breathe, don't let her get under your skin." His lips brush against my cheek, and I settle back against him.

"Have some decorum, Evanna," Clara's voice snaps against me like a whip. I freeze, Teddy's arm tightens around me as I look over at her. There's a foot between her and Dad. Dad looks...

Exhausted.

"Leave her alone, Mom," Jasmine speaks up softly and I swear my soul almost leaves my body.

Because here's the thing about our family, we leave when we can't take it anymore. It's not a fight, though that does seem to precipitate the leaving, but when Mom gets going, we just… walk away. Jasmine nearly jumped out of a plane to get the hell away from Pinehall, West and East Run, and Wercen. But she had to come back.

Oliver, however, took Charlotte and booked it. He comes home on and off, but never long enough to get past that honeymoon period of reunion. Me? I just fucking left.

I endured years of Clara's crap. I allowed her to tear me into little pieces. She reduced my worth to my looks, even though she claimed pride in my mind. The irony, of course, being she felt my looks were all of my problems, so I could never do anything right, thus reducing me to a place where I had no worth.

"Leave her alone?" Clara hisses after a stunned pause. "I do not need to sit here and be disrespected like this. She's sitting on her cousin's lap. Her *cousin*, Jasmine. You might have run off and married a Black man but—"

"That's enough, Mother." I've stood up before the decision even registered in my mind. "This is not your house, and it's a family event. There are children in this room. You want to fight with me or Jasmine? Walk outside like an adult. You don't get to traumatize Andi's children because you feel slighted."

"As if you care," she starts, and I just move. I don't know what is going on, but I'm in front of her in seconds, hauling her up the same way she'd done to me in the past. Clearly, Clara wants to have it out. Fine.

"Jasmine, outside. Now, please."

My heart thunders against my ribs and it's beating at a hummingbird's pace by the time the three of us are outside.

"What is your problem," I bark, the moment the door closes. "You couldn't wait to berate me until after this was over? Or does it have to be all about you all the time for you to be happy?"

"You've gotten bold and rude since leaving," Clara says quietly. Quiet is dangerous, and I know it. My hands ball up, eyes get wide, shoulders curl in slightly to make myself smaller. "I don't know where I went wrong, to have two whores in my family."

Something in me cracks open. I think something in Jasmine does, too. I can't be sure, because I don't give Jasmine a chance to show me. I barrel straight ahead, meeting Clara head on.

"That's *bullshit*, from top to bottom. I'm no more or less bold than I ever have been. Rude? No, I have no time for your petty drama, that's all. I am not a child who has to sit through lectures, who has to let you break me into pieces, who has to let you *abuse* me so I can live a life. Whore? Well, if I am, at least it's honest work. But funnily enough I don't get paid for my body, I am paid for my mind. Child out of wedlock? One of millions, probably billions through the arc of fucking time. Where do you get off judging me?"

"I was married at twenty, my children came after that. You have no respect for your elders, I've only ever tried to make you the best you can be," she snaps, not bothering to deal with most of what I've said.

"Well congratulations, you gave me acute anxiety order, Mother. I am the best I can be, because every day is different, but I give it my all. I was top of my classes in college, in high school, in elementary school. Do you know who gives a fuck about that? No one." I cross my arms, feeling a little chilled, and barring her away from me. The truth needs saying, no matter how hard it is.

"Clearly someone must, or you wouldn't have your job. But that's hardly important to you. No. Flaunting your daughter is more important. Your incestuous relationship with Theodore—"

"Theodore is not her cousin," Jasmine cuts in. A neat little move, a step forward, red hair tossed over her shoulder. "Theo has always made it clear he has no kinship with Evanna. Just like Granddad liked to remind you when you got to sharp … we aren't Dad's kids. His kid? A colossal prick who doesn't acknowledge any of us exist. Evanna is allowed to be happy, just like me, like Oliver. I'd say like you, but looking at Dad, I'm not so sure there's happiness to go around."

Clara slaps Jasmine. It happens so fast I'm left goggling.

"*You insolent little bitch.* I brought you into this world, Jasmine. I brought you to America with me. I could have left you, you know, with your father. You could have stayed behind in France! It wouldn't have mattered; you'd end up as you are now. Worthless because you married down, because you can't keep a man if your life depends on it. You leave and return, leave and return. If you hate it here so much, I suggest staying away. Permanently." Clara says, her voice like ice.

"I don't hate this place, I hate you," Jasmine spits the words, almost literally.

"Jas!" I take hold of her arm before I can stop myself. Logically, I am fully aware Jasmine doesn't owe Clara shit. That I don't owe her anything, either. Yet, part of me doesn't want this to be what breaks us. "Jas, don't say something like that."

"Evanna, listen to her. I owe her my life because she birthed me? I owe her my life because she brought me to the U.S.? In France, my birthfather could have at least *cared* about me. Everything else could be shit, but if I had that, it would have been enough." Jasmine's declaration makes me want to laugh and scream all at the same time. Apparently, this is going to be that unhinged, air it all out, kind of fight.

"Yes, yes. Do tell *Evanna*, how parental love would have been enough for you." Clara sounds smug and I hate it. I hate all of this.

"Don't. *You* don't get to pull that card," I snap. "Neither of you get to pull the, 'I raised you', or 'I put you in this world'. Good for fucking you. You kept me alive for eighteen years and I've kept me alive for ten, with an added human on top of that. I am not your bargaining chip, your trump card, the trophy to wave in front of all the other Moms like you're still a rich socialite."

"Your father works hard—" Clara starts, but I just cut her off.

"This isn't about Dad. Oh, he and I need to have a talk as well. But this, all of this, is me and you and Jasmine. You spent almost *two decades* pitting me against Jasmine. Telling me a number on a scale was more important than being comfortable and happy. My God, being alone is the worst fate you can think of, but when I start dating all you do is slut shame me." I'm breathing hard and Jasmine's free hand tangles with mine.

"Because you were acting like it. Kissing boys at fourteen, wearing inappropriate clothing, showing off your breasts—" Clara lists my faults like a grocery shopping list. "Theodore and your Zera are just the latest mistake. The worst mistakes. I told you to get rid of it."

"My daughter isn't an *it*, you hateful, awful woman," I shriek because I can take all the abuse in the world but no one, no one, will ever abuse Xaria. Not when I'm here to cut it off before it starts.

"Her name is Xaria. Z-are-ee-ah. She is nine years old, beautiful, and kind. She will never be a mistake, and I will never, *ever* allow you to make her feel that way. My body is a body like anyone else's. I am not responsible for what you or anyone else thinks of it. Those thoughts? Those are your fucking problems, Clara. You're obsessed with a perfect image that you don't even uphold." I shake my head, wondering at it. At all of this.

"She's right," Jasmine says softly. "You were always so obsessed with being the best. The most proper family, the most put together. No hair out of place, no awful things said behind a smile, nothing that was outside a narrow set of rules that are only in place to hurt us. I had an eating disorder because of your bullshit diets. I was never fat, you know. And if I were, would it be the end of the goddamn world?"

"No one likes fat people, you little twit. Fat people aren't held up as paragons of society. Fat people are lazy, fat people are unclean."

My mouth drops open in horror. The absolute certainty that she speaks with makes my hair stand on end. How is this the woman who raised me. How did I never, ever see this two-faced stranger?

"Your eating disorder is all in your head, like Evanna's anxiety. You buy into all the new ridiculous shit about disabilities and neuro whatever. It's all excuses. Excuse on excuse to be lazy, to be slovenly in appearance, to fuck whoever you want to on any given day. You're both shameful. Oliver—"

"Oliver would disown himself if he heard anything that had just come out of your mouth," I say as Jasmine says,

"Oliver ran from you harder and farther than any of us. Oliver is happy, really happy. Because he stays the fuck away from you. The eating disorder almost killed me. Just like Eva's anxiety almost killed her."

I flinch. Because I know what's coming now. *Ohhh, I know what's coming.*

"She needed tough love. It cleared up that ridiculousness. At the time, she valued what I gave her. She respected what her home meant. Now? I'm sure she'd run a blade—"

"Do not let that sentence finish." I shake my head, tired. So tired. "You told me when I was fourteen, after going to the ER because I was physically harmed by someone I was meant to be close to, after *years* of telling me the woman who *birthed* me didn't want me, that I was *selfish*. You stood there, you truly stood there, watching me cry, and told me I was selfish because if I had managed to cut deep enough, I would have bled all over your carpet… Your god damn carpet," I laugh, tilting my head at the sky. "I was so, *so hurt*, so tired with the life I was living, that I wanted to *die*. And your solution was to tell me your *fucking carpet* held more worth in your eyes. You didn't care that it was a sin. You didn't care that I was hurting. Fuck, I don't think you even asked why. If you'd asked, you'd have heard it all. That school was weighing down on me in ways I couldn't grasp, that the rumors were fucking with my head, that I felt worthless because I could *never* do enough for you. Because I owed it to you! All you cared about was how it would look. That's all you've ever cared about, and it's sad. But don't worry, I'm leaving again. You can tell your lies and keep face with your little friends. But I am *never* coming back here for you."

I untangle my hand from my sister's and leave them to it. My throat is raw, I'd been yelling at some point, I guess. Now, I am exhausted. The thought of the rest of my family actually fills me with dread while I stand in the mudroom. But, for the sake of a happy holiday, I start to piece myself back together. Bury the anger. Bury the resentment, the pain. Put a cloth over it for now. Deal with it later.

When I open the door, Theodore is at the kitchen table. There are presents in front of him. Confusion fills me.

"Teddy?"

"I grabbed your gifts, figured that whatever was about to be said wasn't going to be pretty. You never liked attention, and while our family loves us, they also pry." He shrugs his shoulders, watching me carefully. "You had a lot to say, princess."

"Probably more," I admit softly. "Doesn't matter anymore. I said what I needed to. I… I really want to go back to the little barn and just sleep it off."

He stands up, towering over me without trying. Instead of feeling like a rabbit about to be killed, his height makes me feel safe. Teddy makes me feel safe. His arms wrap around my shoulders, and I lean against him with a deep breath that's let out slowly.

I lost count of how many times I did that over that summer. Old patterns.

"Let's get you a nap then."

I shake my head. "No. She doesn't get to win. We stay, and I just nap on you in the lounge."

"Only if you skip cake today, to go get some real rest in the loft with me and have the cake in the morning with Gramps before you leave," Teddy counters. I smile against his shirt.

"Deal."

Epilogue

Evanna
26 December

Teddy wakes me with a kiss. It's so terribly silly, and I absolutely love it. Mornings and I don't typically get along well, no matter how I sleep. But the last two days, waking up has been far more pleasant.

"Come on, sleepyhead, let's get you some cake and coffee. Then it's on the road." His voice is still sleep rough, practically inviting me to cuddle up close and ignore the world for a few more hours.

But we have some ground to cover today, important ground. So, I sigh as I open my eyes. Nuzzling closer to Theo, I'm still reluctant to move. A little fearful of leaving our personal bubble of safety.

"We're driving straight through, right? At least if the weather cooperates. Have you checked?" I clear my throat after the first question, sounding a bit like I have a cold.

"Not yet" Theo replies, squeezing my waist gently. "I figured waking you up was a little more important."

Stalling, then. We're both stalling. When we leave the farmhouse, it's a whole different pond we're diving into. New goals, new ways to have it all blow up in our faces.

Licking my lips, I nod and pull away. "Let's get up and at least get showered, then." Anything to stave off the cold that waits for us outside of the blankets.

"Mm, good plan."

Neither of us move. For a whole two or three minutes I am perfectly happy to not move. Then I roll away from him, forcing myself to get a move on. Throwing back the covers on my side, I shiver as the cool air hits my skin. Dashing toward the bathroom, I get the shower going.

The steam comes after about thirty very long seconds. I shove myself inside under the spray with a hiss. My hair is still piled into its nightly pineapple, wrap still on for once, so I keep my head clear of the water. At least until Theodore crowds into the bath with me.

"Teddy!" His hands are already untying the silk ties and tossing it from the shower to the countertop. Cold hands settle on my hips tugging me back against him.

"Eva," he replies, and I can hear the smile in his voice. "This happens to be the warmest place in the loft now. Especially after you threw back the covers like that. Little witch."

"You said we need to get moving," I tell him tartly, half smirk pulling at my lips. "So, I got us going."

A grunt of acknowledgement sounds against my back, his hands lifting to grab my washcloth and shower gel. I lift my hands to take the items, but Teddy shifts them out of my reach, proceeding to soap the cloth. Turning slightly, I find him smiling at me, a little twist of his hand once it's free of the shower gel, telling me to turn back around.

Turning back into the spray, I feel the cloth and his hand against me. He uses a gentle touch as he washes me down in the shower. It's odd, borderline relaxing and slightly sexual when he brushes over places he knows are particularly sensitive. But all in all, it's intimate. A level that we hadn't actually achieved together.

"Relax, princess," His voice is right by my ear as the cloth works over my arms in turn once my back is washed. "Let me take care of you."

"I'm perfectly capable," I start to say, and Teddy gently cuts me off.

"I know you are. You're always taking care of yourself and then some. Let me help and prove I'm good for more than orgasms and baby making," Teddy chuckles and I feel my cheeks heat up.

"But you're *very* good at those things," I reply teasingly. His free hand splays along my hip slipping up along my side.

"Mm, you certainly seem to think so." Teddy's voice is lower now, hands lingering a little longer.

"We shouldn't start something we can't finish," I whisper, getting a hum from him in response. He finishes washing me quickly, but his touch still doesn't leave me, even as I pick up his things to return the favor.

"How is it," Teddy rumbles, "this makes me feel more exposed, and closer to you?"

"Maybe, because we're not furiously trying to bury our problems inside one another," I offer with a slight smile, looking up at him.

"True," he says in a murmur, leaning down to press his lips to mine. "Very true."

~

"Now, you're going to call us when you get there, eh?" Grand-Père says around a bite of cake. "There'll be none of this falling off the face of the planet, y'hear?"

"Oui, Grand-Père. Je ne disparaîtrai plus," I promise, and Theodore squeezes my shoulder.

"I won't let her run without running after her, Gramps. Plus, she invited you to her mini-me's birthday. You know Eva doesn't take back invitations," Theodore's lips curl into a smile as he speaks.

I blink, it takes a moment for my mind to call up what exactly he's talking about. Then I remember, my sweet sixteen. I hadn't wanted one, not by the time it crawled around, but I'd sent out invitations. I couldn't just cancel it.

"That was *years* ago," I grumble. "But he's not wrong, Grand-Père. Xaria wouldn't be happy with me if I canceled her party or told you not to come and meet her. I'm not going anywhere but a little closer to the city.

Plus, I am really looking forward to my new job, and Theodore is rather established..."

I trail off with a little shrug. Running would mean burning my job connections. Plus, my relationship with Teddy requires trust and time. I owe it to myself to give this a real go. No lies or hiding, just the pair of us living, at the very, very least.

"You're a smart cookie, petite reine. But you like to put others ahead of yourself. Don't do that this time, my girl. Be happy. That goes double for you, Theodore. You always try to break the good in your life. I will grant I haven't seen you do it recently, but the point stands. You deserve to be happy. Mm?" Grand-Père points his fork at us in turn. Grand-Mère merely hums her agreement while pouring us all some more coffee. When she catches my eye, she smiles encouragingly.

"Yes, Gramps," Teddy says in a sigh. "I won't get in my head about it or try to self-sabotage this."

"Good, good lad."

We all settle in for more coffee and the last of our cake slices. It's quiet, comfortable, and a good end, I suppose, to this visit. It doesn't feel like an ending, more of a pause. Even as Teddy and I gather dishes one more time for Grand-Mère, it doesn't feel like the door is closing.

We share hugs all around, heading out into the late morning. Both of us had chosen to pack before going to our 'breakfast'. He walks with me to my car, the same one I left the first time in, and leans against the driver's side door, his shoulders hunching.

"I'll keep you in my sights," Teddy says softly. "Feel free to call if you need to pull off for the night, or if you want to grab something to eat."

"I will," I murmur, reaching out and rubbing at his arm. "Let's get on the road. I owe my kid some See's Candy before the shops leave Annapolis, and you owe her a book, sweetheart."

His lips tilt up into a half smile. "Yeah, I do. Save driving, princess."

"Right back at'ya, Teddy."

He pushes off the car, leaning into press his lips to my forehead. It lasts just a few moments before Teddy straightens up and heads for his truck. I watch him for a few seconds before turning to get in the car. Getting on the road, I give the farmhouse a look, smiling softly.

"Right. Let's go home."

Theodore

We managed to make it to Evanna's apartment before it gets too late to justify staying on the road. I'd stopped and scoured three of the gift shop bookstands along the way and come up with two of my favorite books. *The Hobbit* and *Dune. The Hobbit* at least can be considered in the range of age appropriate. At least that's what was decided after heavy consultation from Eva.

But now, with me sitting in her complex parking lot, holding the book that's been hastily wrapped into a bag, I feel like I might vomit. I'm about to meet my daughter. My nine-year-old child is upstairs not sure if her mother is going to come home tonight or tomorrow.

"Theo? Teddy," she calls to me, pulling me from the chasm of anxiety. Eva's hand settles on my cheek, her smile soft as she looks up at me.

"Back with me?" Eva asks, thumb brushing over my cheekbone.

"Yeah, I'm with you, princess." I lean down and press a soft kiss to her lips. Gentle, a promise rather than a call to her desires. "I'm nervous as fuck, Eva."

"Breathe," she whispers against my lips. "I'm right here, and Xar isn't an alien. She's going to shriek, attack you for a hug, or hide behind me, and she'll likely ask you to read the book with her. This is going to be okay, Theodore. I promise you; Xaria wants to meet you."

Taking a breath, I let it out slowly. Another in and out before I nod seriously at her. "Okay, let's do this, little mama. Before I chicken out and hide in my truck for the rest of the night."

"*Little mama*, huh?"

I slant a smile at her. "Well, you're still small, baby. And you're a mama, specifically, my baby mama. It fits, but you'll always be my princess."

Her cheeks warm in color as she drops her hand from my face and takes my hand to lead me into the complex. I follow after her like a puppy, drowning in the surreal feeling that this generates. It's rare that I've felt like this, like I'm giddy and terrified all at once. Knowing how to express it is, honestly, a bit beyond me.

So, I just let it happen. The complex isn't what I'd have ever expected. Not knowing that Eva was working, going to college, and raising a kid. I expected something that would be called on the wrong side of the tracks. Something that screamed, 'I needed and was lucky enough to get government help'. Not necessarily Section eight but as close as it can get.

Her fob is pressed to the first sensor, her hand tugging me behind her as the door unlocks. Another set of doors requires the same fob. Inside, really inside, it smells a bit old, but also clean. Which is an interesting dichotomy to my mind.

"We've been here two years," Eva says quietly as we wait for the elevator. "Before, we'd been very strategically using a loft apartment as a three bedroom. It was an exercise in minimalism I'm not mad I had but am eternally glad is over for a while."

"Ah, I was wondering about, well, rent." My voice is sheepish as she looks over at me. Her brows raise, and my shoulders hitch in response.

"Wanted to know how badly you'd fucked up?" she asks me with a shrewd glance. "The answer is not nearly as much as you want to think you did. I made my choice, Teddy. Just like I'm making new choices now."

Her tone is so stern that I can't help the smile that curves my lips. She's fierce, always has been, but this is just another of those moments that reinforces the kitten became a lioness.

"Yes, ma'am."

Her lips pull into a bright smile. "Good boy, not fighting on that is. It'll save us a shitload of time."

I can believe that. Evanna has hills she'll die on, and so do I. This… How she lives, how she lived before, doesn't need to be a battle between us. The elevator dings, doors opening slowly, and we step inside. It's a little creaky, not as shiny as it probably was when installed. But I don't worry that I'm about to be hurtled ten floors down as soon as Eva hits the sixth-floor button.

However, the lights don't work in the elevator, somehow prompting Evanna to press her side against mine. Blinking, I vaguely recall she was afraid of the dark as a kid. Had that held over into her adulthood? It's a valid fear, but a surprise, too.

The doors open again and my heart lodges in my throat. Christ. There's not long now. Less than a thousand feet, and Eva's hand just keeps giving mine little tugs as I fall behind. Keeping me with her. No doubt she's keeping me from stopping stalk still in the hallway for a minor anxiety attack.

Her key settles into the lock, it clicks, and the handle turns. I feel like the guy in the horror movie right before he opens the door on a satanic ritual or the lair of a monster. My breath is short, chest feels sort of hollow, my hands are sweating. She guides me into the dimly lit apartment, door closing, locking it behind me.

"Xar? Keyanna? We're here," Eva doesn't yell, she just raises her voice beyond her usual volume. She clicks on a light as a squeal sounds from one room. A small person comes barreling down the hall.

"Mommy!" A cherub of a child appears, latching onto Evanna's middle. "I missed you. Auntie Key said you'd be home tomorrow, but I *knew* you'd be home tonight. I got a bunch of books and fun t-shirts for Christmas, mom. I think Santa was saying something, but I don't know what. It was nice of him to send all of that, though."

The river of words coming out of her mouth seems to have no end in sight, until her eyes meet mine. Xaria's hair is a little lighter than Evanna's natural color, a little lighter than mine, but not by much. Her eyes aren't brown, but a deep hazel tone, the barest shift to them as her eyes take me in. She has Eva's general face shape, but as her lips form a cautious smile; I see myself.

"Hello," I say, my own cautious smile on my face. "It's nice to meet you, Xaria."

"Daddy." One word. A single word makes it feel as if all of my being is anchored to this little person and her mother. "You're really here!"

"I am. I said I'd see you soon," I let go of Eva's hand, crouching so I'm down on Xaria's level. "I didn't want to wait longer than I had to, to meet you, Xaria. Is that all right?"

"Oh." She blinks, eyes round and owlish as they turn toward Evanna. Eva who looks teary, and nods toward me. As if to say don't be rude.

"I— I'm happy you're here now." Xar's voice quivers. I imagine it's as overwhelming for her as it is me, perhaps doubly so. "I've wanted a daddy for a long time."

"Aw, cherub," I shake my head, reaching out cautiously. "I'm here now, and I brought you the gift you asked for."

Her hand settles in mine, arms unwinding from around her mother. I hold my breath, not wanting to spook the kid. She's careful, like Eva had been once upon a time. Weighing everything she can set her gaze on. Right now, that's me.

"Really?" she asks, finally breaking the silent stand off we'd managed to begin.

"Really, really." Holding up the bag, I give it a little shake and her eyes shift to it for a moment before settling firmly back on my face.

"Are you leaving after?"

Xaria's question makes Eva's breath hitch. I can imagine why. Something she'd asked Jasmine. There's no doubt in my mind that Xaria's echoing one of Evanna's memories right now.

"No, not without you and your mother," I say, deciding that I won't just drive home when we wake up tomorrow. There's a little of my own worry fueling the decision. I'm not blind. Even though Eva said she wouldn't disappear on me again, even though our family knows, I'm honestly expecting her to vanish. To just be gone when I turn my head away from her for more than a few seconds.

So, I won't let it happen. Is this arrogant of me? Probably. Am I feeling any kind of shame over it? Not an ounce. Even as I look up to see Evanna watching me with a look I can't translate.

They're stuck with me until they come home.

"Would you like your gift, little bit?" Evanna asks, reaching over and running her hand over Xaria's curls. They're much looser than Evanna's are, something that must be because of my genes.

"Yes, please. May I have my gift, Daddy?" Her eyes are bright now, curiosity and eagerness plain in the little twinkles.

"Of course," I reply hoarsely, offering the bag to her.

Her tiny hands carefully unpack it, not a tear in any of the paper or bag itself. Such a switch from my childhood habits, from Eva's too, if I remember right. It's not a result of not being eager for the book, because Xaria certainly is, if the way she runs her hands over the cover is any indication at all.

She's just meticulous in how she does things. Something I wonder if I'll see displayed in other areas of her life. For now, though, I focus on her face.

"*The Hobbit, There and Back Again,*" she reads out with interest. The cover is the seventy-fifth anniversary edition. I'd been surprised to see it on the shelf, given there have to be at least a half dozen newer options in stock with the recent movie release. Xaria looks over it very intently, now reading the back cover. She's mouthing the words as she reads, and it's the cutest thing I've seen in quite some time.

"What do you think, cherub, do you want to read it with me?" I ask her too impatient to wait for her to ask me. There's an intense need in me to do this with her. Like it's a place I can start to reclaim the years I've lost with her and Evanna.

"I think it's going to be fun. Momma hasn't let me see the movies. She wants to make sure they won't scare me first." Xaria huffs, sending Evanna a little look. One that's all her mother.

Flattening my mouth, I look at Eva, who looks a bit haunted. When she sees me looking at her, Eva sighs. Her arms cross below her chest and she shrugs.

"Gollum scared me when we were younger, okay? I don't need Xar dealing with that."

"Fair enough, princess," I reassure Eva softly before giving my attention back to Xaria. "If we finish the book this year, we can watch the movies together."

Xaria grins brightly, looking back and forth between me and Evanna. She seems to be working up to something. Eva, though, can read our daughter easily.

"What's up, little bit?" She toes off her shoes finally and takes off her coat. Her hand reaches out to me, and I stand to give her my coat, removing my shoes too.

"Can— Is Daddy staying?"

I blink. Hadn't I said I was already? Eva, though. She takes it in stride, a small smile tugging her lips.

"Yes. He is. He said so, silly. Why?"

"Can... I sleep with you, then?"

It's Eva's turn to blink then before her smile turns softer. She looks over at me, head tilting in question. It's...weird, I hadn't slept with my parents after they split. But. I'm not going to say no either. So, I just nod.

"Sure, sweetie. Let's find Dad some pjs, and then you need to brush your teeth. It's late already."

Just like that, Eva shifts from the woman I know, the girl I knew, into a mother. It's a split-second transition, more pronounced than I expected it to be. But the two of them fall into routine, sweeping me up with them as they get ready for bed. I end up in a familiar hoodie, and even more familiar sweats. Both items I'd thought I lost years ago.

It's not until we're all squished into a bed too small for three, that I take it all in. Xaria dropped off like a light, burrowed against me, little hands keeping hold of fistfuls of my old sweatshirt. I look up from where Xaria is to where Evanna lays on the other side of her. She's looking back at me, her arm curled under her head, the other laying over Xaria, the same as mine. There's so much to say. I wonder if Eva sees it. Is she as off balance as I feel? Are we both just stumbling in the dark?

"Sleep, Teddy. We'll figure it out in the morning." Her voice is soft, steady in the shadows of her bedroom.

"I keep worrying this is a dream. That I'll wake up without you." The confession is easier in the dark.

Her hand finds mine, fingers lacing between my own. She squeezes once and her thumb rubs against my index finger. "We're right here, Teddy. We're not going anywhere, I promise."

Taking a breath, I make myself accept that. That this is real, she's here, Xaria's here, they'll still be around in the morning. I still uncurl my arm from under my head and reach out for her with it. My fingers slide under the edge of her bonnet up into her curls, her arm moving to adjust with the new positioning. The touch, having hold of her, calms me some. Just enough.

Eva's face turns, her lips pressing to my wrist. It's odd, this is a role I thought I would be taking. Yet here we are. Roles firmly reversed, with her comforting me at every turn. "Sleep well, Teddy. I love you. I'll be here when you wake up."

And when I wake up, it's to see her and Xaria still dead asleep. Ink-rooted blonde curls free of her bonnet, Eva looks much like the princess I call her. Xaria, with her own bonnet still on, is an angel, pressed against her mother. They're a dream. My dream, and completely real.

Want to get updates when Evanna publishes something new? Visit her website www.evannarhoswen.com to sign up for her exclusive email list - and get a free glimpse into Eva and Theo's story!

9 798986 673455